A Touch of Magic

Magic & Sorcery Chronicles

Book One

Marie Andreas

Acknowledgments

I love telling stories, but it takes a lot of help to get them into the world. I appreciate everyone who has helped get these books out there, bought my books, and told others about them.

I'd like to thank Jessa Slade for editing magic—as always, she understands my ramblings in makes sense of them. To my most awesome team of beta readers/typo hunters who plowed through the entire book and helped tighten it up: Lisa Andreas, Patti Huber, Lynne Mayfield, and Laura Shilling. And final clean up by editor/proofreader Ilana Schoonover-thank you! Any remaining errors are mine alone.

My cover artists, Joolz & Jarling (Julie Nicholls and Uwe Jarling), for creating an awesome work of art.

Other books by Marie Andreas

The Lost Ancients
Book One: The Glass Gargoyle
Book Two: The Obsidian Chimera
Book Three: The Emerald Dragon
Book Four: The Sapphire Manticore
Book Five: The Golden Basilisk
Book Six: The Diamond Sphinx
The Lost Ancients: Dragon's Blood
Book One: The Seeker's Chest
Book Two: The Finder's Crown
The Asarlaí Wars Trilogy
Book One: Warrior Wench
Book Two: Victorious Dead
Book Three: Defiant Ruin
The Code of the Keeper
Book One: Traitor's Folly
Book Two: Destroyer's Curse
The Adventures of Smith and Jones
A Curious Invasion
The Mayhem of Mermaids
An Intrigue of Pharaohs
Broken Veil
Book One: The Girl with the Iron Wing
Book Two: An Uncommon Truth of Dying
Book Three: Through a Veil Darkly
Books of the Cuari
Book One: Essence of Chaos
Book Two: Division of Chaos
Book Three: Destruction of Chaos
Magic and Sorcery Chronicles

A Touch of Magic
A Slice of Sorcery
A Dash of Devilry

Chapter One

Princess Lizeth realized her mistake the moment the spell song left her lips. Or rather, as soon as her music tutor, Boan, gave her the *look* as the song left her lips.

She hadn't meant to startle the housemaid, but coming into the magic chamber unannounced wasn't a safe idea. It wasn't Lizeth's fault that the snow beast image she'd sung into being scared the poor woman, made her fling their lunch plates into the air, and almost slam into the door on her way out.

Lizeth ran after her and sang a soothing charm. One that accidentally dropped the panicked woman into a nice slumber in the middle of the hall. She'd only meant to calm her, but in her concern took it a bit too far. Misjudging spells wasn't something Lizeth did. Ever. And it was even worse that it happened to an innocent bystander.

Boan caught her arm before she could help the woman further. "She'd be mortified if you woke her. It would be better if she thinks she simply had a case of the vapors. Let her be."

"But what if something happens to her out here? This was my fault." Not something she admitted easily, but she didn't want to leave the poor woman lying there like that.

"In a private hall in a secure palace? She'd be more horrified at you helping her up and no words you say will make her think it was your fault. Come back into the room."

Lizeth looked at the woman once more, then went inside.

Boan crossed his arms and shook his head. "Now that, all of that, is why you're going to end up dead in the woods somewhere." He was only half-joking. Lizeth knew part of him believed she wouldn't be coming out of the Challenge she faced in three days alive and intact. However, there was no way to know if the woods would be involved since no one could or would tell her anything about the Challenge details. Just the start date, that she'd face dangers, and she might or might not survive. Not at all comforting nor helpful.

"I was startled, she was startled, I over charmed her. You wouldn't let me fix it." Lizeth went back and picked up an apple off the floor. "Wouldn't that be a good thing if a bear tries to eat me? Put it to sleep?"

"You can't depend on your gifts that way. A spell cast when you're startled won't act the same against a bear compared to a spell cast when you are prepared." The older man went to his desk and sat down with a sigh. "You need to be trained and ready for calm, rational responses in any situation. Spell magic can't be your only answer for everything."

"Then why are we working on the spell songs? This whole Challenge is to see how well I use my abilities and will use them to defend the land of Astarious from all evildoers." She went to a small fountain and washed off the apple. It wasn't her fault he'd pushed her too hard. Six hours solid so far today doing spell songs. A full ten hours yesterday. She was lucky she could still sing.

Boan sighed then rang for a housemaid. "You need to know them, you need to control them, and you need to know when not to use them. Your brain is as important in this Challenge as your spells." He leaned forward. "You *have* been working on your mundane fighting skills, yes?"

Lizeth didn't really like the pleading tone in his voice. "Yes. But I am one of the strongest spell song mages ever. You even said so." She finished her apple and wiggled her fingers in the air. "Unseen potential beyond all expectations." She wasn't trying to be cocky, but it was hard to believe the concern—especially when she'd spent the past twenty years hearing how powerful she was. Her spell singing was her best weapon, and with it she really didn't need to worry about anything else. "Not to mention, the Challenge is a formality created by the oracles for their own obscure reasons. A coming-of-age ritual followed by our ancestors based on years of darkness and a tragedy that happened hundreds of years ago."

"That sounds like your sister, not you." Boan scowled. "The reason we haven't had those dark days again is because of things like the Challenge. All of the royal heirs must go through it to secure the ongoing safety of our kingdom."

Lizeth rolled her eyes. Yes, her younger sister Nevaine was more vocal about disagreeing with the traditions like the Challenge. But Lizeth could be disagreeable as well. Their kingdom was fair, lovely, and strong enough to keep itself that way—without sending all of their heirs to be tested right before their twenty-first birthday. "Are we through for today? I feel a bit of a headache coming on. Plus, I am peckish."

Boan opened his mouth, most likely to disagree. Instead, he closed the spell book he'd been training her from and shook his head. "Far be it from saving the kingdom to take precedence over lunch and an afternoon nap." That was the closest he'd gotten to sounding seriously annoyed in the ten years she'd been working with him.

"Good of you to see it that way." Lizeth shrugged and got to her feet. "I'll ask the kitchen to send you a fresh meal as well." With a flip of her blonde hair, she stomped out of his chambers. Well, princesses didn't stomp unless the situation truly called for it, and this didn't. But she put some weight on her boot heels as she left. The housemaid she'd knocked out had either recovered enough on her own to leave or more likely some other housekeepers had rescued her.

It wasn't that uncommon for household staff to scurry around the three princesses when they were younger. But the mayhem usually followed her two younger sisters, not Lizeth—the golden child.

Nevaine was two years younger than Lizeth. Not as tall or blonde as her, but powerful in her own right. Where Lizeth could charm with magic-fueled song, Nevaine used her love of research, her brains, and her uncanny ability to balance spells. She was sarcastic, stubborn, and didn't trust anyone. She was also exceedingly fond of knives.

Piallen was the baby at sixteen. Taller than both of her older sisters, she was the only one who had inherited their mother's deep blue-black hair. She was also the most athletic and would spend days in the forest—much to the concern of their parents. When she turned fourteen, they were almost ready to lock her up, but Piallen promised to stay within the secure woods around the palace.

"She'd probably make friends with the bear in the woods and then set up house together," Lizeth muttered to herself. Or she thought she was muttering to herself.

"Excuse me, your highness? Did you have a need?" The housemaid was a few years older than Lizeth and mostly stayed below the stairs. She'd been cleaning the stair railing when Lizeth startled her. The servants who worked in the palace were all well cared for, and they had doted on the princesses when they were adorable tots. Now they were becoming powerful magic users, more so than any royal in five hundred years.

It sometimes made them nervous.

"Um, no, I was going over a new speech. You know how they make us do that. All the time. Thank you though." She smiled and went on to the bottom of the stairs, then turned and headed for the kitchen. The incident in the hallway was still lurked in the back of her mind. She'd made light of it with Boan, but she'd never had a spell snap like that. Not that she would admit it to anyone. But it was something to take note of.

There were two kitchens in this part of the palace, the huge, massive, feed-half-of-the-town kitchen, and the smaller, older one toward the back of the palace. When the girls were little, their mother would always take them there—Lizeth still preferred it to dining in the great hall.

Most of the meals cooked here were for the servants and the odd royal like herself. Right now, it was only Margie manning the kitchen. The tables were cleaned and empty.

"Anything left? Boan needs a meal as well, please." Lizeth settled at a table.

"What? I sent Jalia up a half-hour ago." Margie tsked but had a platter with a sandwich and a pile of greens along with a cup of steaming tea in front of Lizeth before she finished speaking.

"It wasn't her fault; she came in while I was in mid-spell. I startled her and the food got dropped." Lizeth didn't want to go into more detail, but she also didn't want to get Jalia in trouble for something that really wasn't her fault.

Margie shoved some of her gray-streaked hair back under her cap. "Hmmm, make sure you keep control there, missy. That gift of yours is nothing to be made light of."

Lizeth nodded and worked on her sandwich and ignored the fact that Margie knew more than what she'd let on. Lizeth had a feeling she even knew more about the Challenge, but after asking a dozen times and not getting an answer, Lizeth had given up hounding her.

"Lady Margie, how are you this fine afternoon?" The rich voice came from behind Lizeth and she quickly swallowed her food and brushed away the crumbs. Or tried to. A bit of bread got stuck in her throat and she started coughing.

A pair of large hands came around her from behind and deftly pressed her stomach in a way that the offending chunk of bread flew from her mouth.

"Princess Lizeth, I didn't realize that was you." Lord Trion Hithian bowed as she turned to thank him.

Her face was exceedingly warm and while she wanted to run away, that wasn't an option. "Thank you, Lord Hithian. I'm afraid I was startled by your appearance." In truth, it was that she'd spent most of her precious free time yesterday, when she should have been studying more spell songs, traveling about the palace trying to *accidentally* stumble upon him. His saving her from an embarrassing choking incident hadn't been what she'd planned.

"I do beg your forgiveness, your highness." His second bow was even deeper than the first and when he rose, she was taken aback again by his bearing, poise, and ridiculously handsome face. Deep blue eyes and enough of a curl in his black hair to leave her fingers itching to touch it.

"Please, call me Lizeth." Formality wasn't a thing in their palace among the younger people. Plus, she wanted to hear him say her name again. Lord Trion Hithian had come from an outer province a week ago to meet with her father. Lizeth decided it was love at first sight the moment he rode in—well, more like marriage potential at first sight. Unlike some kingdoms, spouses were not chosen for the heirs of Astarious. There were guidelines, of course. Such as the spouse needed to complement the heir's magic if both parties were magic users. And one law—the chosen spouse needed to have some royal blood. But other than that, things were fairly open.

Lizeth looked Trion up in the registry the evening he arrived. It was distant, but he had royal lineage.

His mouth was moving, and she'd been lost in thought and missed whatever he said. Clearly, it was a question by the way he looked at her.

"I am so sorry, Lord Hithian, I was in music study all day and my ears are still hearing music spells. Could you repeat yourself?" She ignored Margie smirking beyond his shoulder.

"I said I would be honored to use your given name and to please call me Trion. I was looking for your sister, Princess Nevaine. She mentioned that she had a knife of lapio steel. That is an extremely unusual metal and I would like to look at its qualities."

Lizeth forced the smile to stay stuck to her face. "Oh, of course. This time of day she is most likely in the stable. Practicing throwing knives and other pointed objects. You could sit and wait if you'd like?" He was simply not the right type of man for Nevaine. His smile was completely too honest.

"Actually, I'd love to see her work. She is a legend with blades, you know." He turned to go, then swung back. "Thank you, Lizeth, and I do apologize again for startling you." He was out the back door before Lizeth could respond.

"Sorry, dove. I think he has eyes for your sister." Margie patted her arm, added some fresh cookies to her plate, and went back to cleaning the stove.

"But he's perfect for me. We even complement each other in appearance. He's well-read, smart, and handsome. Besides, I'm the oldest." She knew she whined on the last one. She'd never worried about finding someone to marry before, but the approaching Challenge marked a change in her life. She would be expected to find someone to marry within a short while of completing it. And that was an important step toward becoming an heir to the throne.

"Dove, you are lovely beyond compare, and with your spell singing, you can charm the antlers off a bull moose. But a man is drawn to what he is drawn to." She tilted her head. "Or, he could simply be extremely interested in your sister's knives."

"Knives. Bah." Lizeth polished off the cookies like a five-year-old, then got to her feet. Her intention, after finding food, at any rate, had been to hunt down Trion. She wasn't giving up—they would make a perfect match even if he didn't know it—but clearly, today wasn't going to work. What she should do at this point was work on her spell songs. The Challenge would begin in three days. No one would explain what it was, nor were there official records of past Challenges she could look at—they had them but no one could see them until after they had completed their Challenge.

Which seemed a bit pointless to her. All she knew was that it would test her magic skills, among other things. And that not every royal heir came back from it. However, she was assured that the majority came back. Some maybe not as they left, but she had faith in her spell singing to protect her and solve whatever problem she was faced with.

But she couldn't focus right now. Not to mention that she and Boan had been working for six hours solid before the interruption. That was a lot of spell magic and her head felt stuffed. So instead, she wandered outside.

The palace wasn't huge, but the grounds were extensive and designed to provide privacy for leisurely wanders. Part of that had come about when her youngest sister was born, and the king and queen realized the potential magical power the three girls possessed. And the trouble that could become of that power, both to the three girls and from them, as they aged. The large gardens kept the girls near the palace and others out. Not as important now that all three could defend themselves, but still a lovely place to walk about.

Lizeth wandered through the low gardens, full of flowers and immaculate landscaping. Her mother was often out here in the late afternoons, but right now both the king and queen were in Northalian, a neighboring kingdom and ally. At least it was presumed by most people that they were still an ally. There had been faint rumors to the contrary.

Nevaine was certain they were up to something and was annoyed when their parents didn't let her go along on the trip. Lizeth had been to the Northalian kingdom before and it was dreary and dull—she was extremely glad when it was determined she couldn't go due to training for her Challenge.

Lost in her thoughts as she roamed—mostly concerning Trion, if Lizeth were honest with herself—she didn't notice where she was until an arrow came right for her.

Boan would be proud; with a single sung note, she shattered the arrow into pieces and it fell to the ground.

"Damn it, Lizeth! I had a sign posted. This is my archery range." Sixteen-year-old Piallen stomped into view. She was wearing dark browns and greens and had a hood up over her rich blue-black hair. Her bow was almost as long as Lizeth's legs. All three sisters had blue eyes from their mother, but Piallen's always seemed the eeriest. Like she was seeing the real you. Unless she was pissed, like right now.

"Sorry! I thought your range was further out." She peered down at the arrow. She'd done an excellent job destroying it.

"It *is* further out." Piallen waved around the trees. "We're on the edge of the Hart woods. What were you thinking?"

Lizeth looked around. "I was...pondering one of Master Boan's latest spells." She tried to sound haughty as she flicked back her long blonde hair.

Piallen rolled her eyes, then started laughing. "No, that's what you *should* be doing. Who's the guy?"

Lizeth was closer to Piallen than Nevaine. There might have been more camaraderie between all three if they'd each been more than two years apart. And if Nevaine spent more time away from her books and hanging out with her sisters.

"No one." She folded her arms and sat on a log. That happened to be next to an archery target. "Fine. Trion. He's a perfect match for me, but has gone off looking at *knives*."

Piallen laughed. "He's visiting Nevaine and you're pissy." She spun and let loose an arrow without a pause for aiming. The responding 'thunk' was quite a way off.

"He's simply not thinking. I match him on all of the tests. He doesn't have much magic, but his ability to channel water isn't at odds with a spell singer. We would work well together."

Her sister sat down on another stump. "Do you even know him?" She held up her hand. "Not know *of* him. Just because someone looks compatible doesn't mean they are. You need to know them first." She pulled another arrow from her quiver, spun around off the stump and to her knees, and let the arrow loose. "And maybe he simply does like knives."

Chapter Two

Lizeth watched her sister make incredible shots for ten minutes, then said goodbye and left.

Piallen made some good points, as usual—she was always wiser than her years—more about letting feelings dictate marriage potential than anything else. But Lizeth preferred things that were in order. Planned and controlled, like music. With song magic and charm magic, which relied on songs to be carried out, one had to follow strict rules. A note that was unplanned could destroy a spell, or worse, turn it into something far different from what was intended. Fatal consequences filled the history books.

She figured that there was nothing wrong with the rest of her world working the same way. Love wasn't something to think of as a royal—she'd marry who matched her best and would be good for the kingdom. Love, if it happened, could come later. Neat and simple.

Her wandering skirted through the Hart woods, a curated but still wild-looking forest that curved around the palace grounds. It also acted as a barricade from the one nearby kingdom they were not friends with, Laiandra. That country was an example of what too much control could be like. Luckily, the woods were cut through by a massive canyon that ran past the north and south borders of Astarious. No one knew where it came from, but it had happened hundreds of years ago in the middle of an ugly war between Laiandra and Astarious. One that Laiandra might have been poised to win, according to some of the history books. The magic power to have created something like the canyon would have been massive and neither side admitted they'd done it.

One minute everyone was trying to kill each other, and the next they were divided by the canyon. As much as people from both sides tried, climbing down the canyon was impossible. Spells also wouldn't work. The trip around the canyon would take weeks, traveling through a desert on the south and a hostile kingdom to the north. It made ongoing fighting awkward, to say the least.

Lizeth wondered about that time as she drifted through the woods. Not that she wanted war, the history books had shown how brutal it was. But they also showed how alive and vibrant things were then. The world she'd been born into was safe, secure, and sometimes a bit boring.

She made it to the edge of the canyon and a chill ran up her back that had nothing to do with that sharp wind coming up out of the empty space below her. She'd been out here before with her entire family or with her two sisters when they were adventuring. But never alone.

The canyon was so wide that the empire of Laiandra on the other side was barely visible. Mostly it was filled with tall shapes that glinted in the sun. Sections of the forest were still there, but a lot of it had been destroyed and replaced by buildings. The people of Laiandra were fonder of buildings than nature.

"Be careful, the ground can be uneven near the edge." The voice was low and masculine and for a brief moment, she thought Trion had found her.

The face she turned to wasn't Trion, but a forester. He was tall, even taller than Trion, with broad shoulders but a slim build. A few years older than her, but his deep brown hair was shaggy, making him look younger at first glance. He carried a sword, bow, quiver of arrows, and a brace of knives.

He also looked dirty and in need of a shave.

"Thank you for the warning. I've been coming here since I was a girl." She used her pretty princess voice, that's what Piallen called it anyway. Polite but with a dash of snooty. Who was he to point out the dangers of *her* woods?

"I know, your highness." His grin kept flashing through even though he was trying to be somber. "I am Finnian, the woodsman. I don't believe we've met yet."

"I am pleased to meet you." Normally she would have properly introduced herself, but he obviously knew who she was. He was *quite* dirty the more she looked at him, and he'd interrupted her soulful gazing into the abyss. Or at least into the mysterious and deadly canyon.

"Were you hunting something, woodsman Finnian?" She gave his clothes a brief up and down look with enough lingering concern that her impression of them was not good.

"I do beg your pardon, Princess Lizeth. I have been hunting a foul beast for three days." His face grew somber and his rich brown eyes looked worried.

"A foul beast?" She folded her arms and watched him for a smile or grin. "Out here? Why have I not heard of it?" The Hart woods were extremely curated and controlled, not to mention the palace was in the center of the kingdom with their large populace on the other three sides. Any beasts, foul or otherwise, would have to travel through a nicely populated city to get here. Or up from the canyon. Which was impossible. Nothing lived in the canyon.

"Until we know what we're up against, the head woodsman felt we needn't disrupt you. Your parents will be home soon enough and he would rather tell them. After we've captured it." A dark shadow lurked in his eyes, but he gave a reassuring smile.

Now she was annoyed. She'd seen that look before on men who thought because she happened to be a pretty blonde princess, she couldn't handle anything of the real world. "Good of you. You wouldn't want a weak, defenseless princess staying awake at night, now, would you?" She made sure not to slump. He was still taller than her, but she was a tall woman. And presence could always make up for a few inches of height.

Before he could respond, she sang a charm, simple, but tricky in the notes used. He rose five feet into the air, bobbing about like one of the air balls given to children at the summer fairs.

"What's going on?" There was genuine panic in his voice as he kicked his feet. But he didn't drop his bow.

"How long have you lived in Astarious?" Her song would keep him there for at least ten minutes unless she released him. Right now, an annoying morning was making her not want to do that.

"I only moved to the kingdom a month ago. What is causing this?" He still kicked his legs, but it looked like he figured out he wasn't going anywhere so it was more of a token movement. "Why aren't you affected?"

She narrowed her eyes, but he truly wasn't jesting. "It's *my* spell. That song? I'm a spell singer? Sound familiar?"

"No one told me the royals were magic users. At least not this level." Finnian's face went a nice toasted shade of red. "I am sorry. How do I get down?"

"The spell will wear off in about ten minutes. But you should be safe from any foul beasts until then. Good day, woodsman." She turned and stomped off. This time, stomping was appropriate. He probably hadn't been after any creature, foul or not. Just hadn't bathed. He deserved to float around for a few minutes.

More people were roaming the gardens when she made her way back. Everyone wanted to wish her luck for the upcoming Challenge. Or find out how scared she was, while trying to make it sound like they were wishing her luck. Reminding someone of the perilous adventure they were about to have was not a good way to comfort them. She didn't feel like talking to any of them right now, but there were too many to effectively dodge without causing notice. Nevaine often avoided courtiers, cutting them aside if she felt in a mood. Sadly, Lizeth's reputation, plus the fact that, as oldest, she had to set a good example, meant she couldn't do that.

By the time she got back to the palace, she was seriously wishing she could have tossed them all in the air. Or somehow taken care of them with some other annoying but not deadly spell.

She'd entered the main hall when a ruckus came from above.

"Coming through!" The voice was high pitched and the one yelling it was small. And currently gliding through the air directly at her which would be fine except the creature couldn't fly on his own. Usually. Scruff was a grigeen, a cat-sized creature with exceptionally large ears, a prehensile tail, and prone to getting into trouble—at least Scruff was. A colony of grigeens lived behind the palace in a smaller section of the woods that surrounded the kingdom. Scruff had been her companion when she was young. All three princesses had a grigeen companion when they were children, starting after their first year, but once they grew older, the grigeens moved back to the colony. Piallen's grigeen, Tobias, had just returned to the woods two years ago. They all still visited the palace from time to time.

Lizeth caught Scruff before he could smack into her face. "Are you okay?" Grigeen's could glide down from trees, but it wasn't their normal way of travel.

Scruff chittered in his native language but it sounded more like laughter. "Sorry, had a bit of an issue with one of your guests. Had to jump." He pointed his large paw up to the balcony above them. There was no one there now.

Lizeth stepped to the side and kept him tight in her arms. Grigeens were unusual enough to make people want to stop and want to visit and she was done visiting for now. She did a quick check down a hall that had a lovely curtained alcove to verify it was empty and then she darted down it, into the alcove, and pulled the curtain shut around them.

"Someone threw you? Are you sure that you're okay?" She knew grigeens could be nuisances sometimes, but taking physical action against one, especially in the palace, would not be tolerated.

Scruff jumped onto the small cabinet at the back of the alcove and washed a large, pointed ear with his paw. "No, I threw myself. I was feeling extremely put upon. I believe he wanted to harm me." His bright green eyes went impossibly wide—what he did when he wanted to appear innocent. It only made him look guilty of something.

"Who?" She doubted that anyone would want to seriously harm Scruff or any of the grigeens, but it was better to humor him.

"A guest. One of those out there." He flicked his paw in the air and started randomly picking up the statuettes behind him on the cabinet with his tail. He'd hold each one for a bit, then set it down. All while talking to Lizeth. It was as if his tail was a separate entity.

"What was this guest's name? And I do know what you're doing. There's no gold in any of those statues." Grigeens wanted for nothing and were protected by the king and queen themselves. That didn't stop them from occasionally rifling through trinkets for gold. Scruff had assured Lizeth as a young child that it was instinct. They liked gold a lot.

"I don't know names." His tail immediately flicked back to curl around his body. "You all look the same, to be honest. It was a male. And a visitor." He gave a profound nod as if that told her exactly who it was.

"There are currently over eighty visitors registered on the palace grounds at the moment, and if we assume at least half are male, that's forty people who could have accosted you. If you want me to find him, I need more information." She adored Scruff, but he could drive her to serious annoyance.

"Male. Your age, give or take twenty years, had hair. No hair of face." He tapped his chin with a single claw. "Pretty sure it was a male."

Lizeth sighed. "I've had a long day, and figuring this out isn't what I want to do right now. What were you doing and why did you think this person was going to hurt you?"

"I came into the palace looking for you, of course. This person accosted me and asked why I was there. Then he, if he was a he, might have been a she. No facial hair, so could be either."

"Scruff? Long day? Short temper?"

"Anyway. This person followed me. They had a cape." He looked like that was another telling point.

Lizeth didn't recall him being this obtuse when she was younger. "Lots of people out there have capes. It's almost autumn. Humans can't grow a thick coat like some beings." She folded her arms and glared.

"Ah, but this one had it in their hands. They were bending down and trying to throw it on me. Cornered me on the balcony, so I jumped. Good thing you were there." His grin never looked friendly. The large canines made it hard, not to mention grigeen mouths weren't designed to smile. But he was trying to make it a nice grin.

Now she was concerned. Granted, the grigeens didn't come inside that often but none of the people of Astarious should be that shocked at seeing one—even a guest to the palace. And it did sound like the person had been trying to capture Scruff. Had the person been a newcomer and startled by the appearance of Scruff; they probably would have tried to chase the creature away, not grab it in a cape.

"But they talked to you?"

"Yes, yes." His tail flicked about in annoyance. "Said something about you. Asked me why I was there instead of guarding a tree-house...or something like that. He knew about your Challenge though." He perked up. "Ha! It *was* a he, I'm now sure of it."

"A stranger wouldn't realize you spoke. You look like an odd cat and I have it on good authority no other kingdom has anyone like your kind." She chewed the edge of her finger. Something was up here, but she couldn't guess what. "Are you sure he said 'guarding a treehouse'?" The princesses had had one years ago, out in the Hart woods, but as the girls grew older it had fallen into disrepair.

"I believe so. The words might have been different. He *was* trying to grab me after all."

"Yes. So, it was someone who wanted to grab a grigeen? Or you specifically, since they knew the connection you and I have?"

Footsteps came from down the hall. "Princess Lizeth? I know you came this way." The high-pitched voice was annoying, catty, and existed exclusively to cause headaches in anyone who heard it. Or at least the owner did.

"Oh no." Lizeth patted herself down to make sure she looked presentable. "Stay in the cabinet until I chase her off. Wait, it wasn't Lady Dalip, was it?"

"I said it was a man." Scruff chewed a paw. "Maybe a man. But not her." He slid into the cabinet and she closed the door behind him.

Lady Dalip was a courtier of the highest stature, at least in her own mind.

"Yes, Lady Dalip. I was having some quiet time." Lizeth stepped out from the alcove and flashed her best smile. "What can I do for you?"

The lady wanted to complain about some rude hooligans who had been roughhousing in the far garden. They interrupted her meditation and she wanted them locked up.

Lizeth plastered her polite and concerned smile on and listened for fifteen minutes. Then she saw the alcove curtain flick, and a tail vanish from view. She'd catch up with Scruff later.

Lady Dalip took a deep breath to launch into another volley and Lizeth jumped in. "I understand how traumatizing it must have been for you. And yes, you were right to come to me since the king and queen are out. But I do have to return to my studies. The Challenge is coming, you know." She tried to add a bit of concern but with her growing headache it might have come across as being ill.

"I will count on you to see it through." Lady Dalip bustled away.

Lizeth peered down the hall and made her escape to the back stairs. She could have used the reason of her headache. Unfortunately, faking illness in this place would probably only lead to her being dragged before fleets of healers.

The rear stairs were formerly only used by the staff back in her great-great-grandfather's time. Thanks to a period of enlightenment in her great-grandmother's early years, the staff used the main stairwells. Which left the rear ones for young royals who didn't want to get caught in whatever shenanigans they were up to.

Lizeth and her sisters used to play in the stairwells when they were younger. Now they were just handy for avoiding people.

Nevaine used them almost exclusively.

Lizeth was muttering to herself about the annoying events of the day when a body dropped from the landing above her and landed at her feet.

Chapter Three

One advantage of being a trained song mage, Lizeth could scream in multiple octaves, and with a volume the dead couldn't miss.

Bodies dropping at her feet justified disturbing the peace of the palace.

The palace guards came charging up the stairs before the final echo of her scream had vanished. Granted, it had been a long scream and her magic would have drawn them to her even faster than normal.

"Your highness! Are you hurt?" The guard captain was out of breath as he reached her. He was older and not fond of running. From the grimace on his face, the spell in the center of her scream might have pushed him too hard.

"I'm not, but I think he is." It was hard to miss the body on the landing. Focusing on the royal involved in the incident for their protection was all well and good, but missing a twisted dead man wasn't. She turned away quickly. He'd fallen far and that landing wasn't soft.

The rest of the guards came forward and the guard captain solicitously led her out of the way. She noticed he wasn't looking at the body either.

"Was he there when you arrived?" The captain was bringing her back downstairs probably for his well-being as much, or more so, than hers. The rest of his guards ran up the stairs above the landing with two staying with the body and the rest continuing to the higher floors.

"Captain, had you noticed the freshness of the body, that wouldn't be a question." Lizeth looked down at herself even though she was afraid to. The small red marks on the lower part of her dress made her look away quickly. "If you will excuse me, will go to my room now. That body dropped directly in front of me and I may be ill. Or pass out." She was rattled, but not feeling like she would do either. Not at the moment, anyway. Yet people would assume that would be her reaction. Many times it was easier to play to assumptions than against them.

The look on the guard captain's face said either action would be horrific—for him. He glanced around and yelled to two guards standing at the entrance to the stairs. "The princess has had a distressing incident. Please see that she gets to her room quickly." He looked to Lizeth with watery eyes. "Do you need your maidservants, your highness?"

"No. Thank you." Lizeth hadn't been feeling well about the poor man who had died, but the captain treating her like a five-year-old, annoyed her.

The two guards the captain had called stood waiting and it would cause more attention to make them go away than to have them escort her. And if someone was throwing dead bodies down stairwells, having an escort might be a good idea. She nodded to them and headed for her room.

She got to her suite of rooms quickly—another advantage of an escort, no one stopped her to chit-chat along the way.

"Do you need anything, your highness?" Those were the first words either guard had spoken to her.

"No, I'm fine." She started to shut the door, then opened it again. "Actually, could you ask my sisters to come here? Thank you." She shut the door as soon as the guardswoman nodded. She wasn't going to be sick, but she might have a breakdown. The tears started as soon as she got the bloody clothes off—it might have only been on the bottom of her dress, that she could see, but in her mind, the entire outfit was contaminated. Her sisters hadn't arrived yet, so she indulged in the new showering device her parents had installed. Akin to someone pouring a bucket of freshwater down on her, it had the advantage of being as hot as she wanted it. She preferred baths to relax in, but this was much better for getting her skin blistering clean.

She heard the chatter from her sisters in the front room as she dried off and got into her dressing gown. It had been a long day and if she could have her way, she wasn't going back downstairs until tomorrow.

"What's wrong?" Piallen saw her first as she came out into the front room.

"You're going down to dinner with wet hair?" Nevaine must have sensed Lizeth's upset condition; she wasn't even snarky about it.

"You've gone to formal dinners with wet hair." Lizeth curled into her favorite chair.

"Yes, but that's me. Not you. And you've been crying. Guards are roaming the halls, and the back stairway is blocked off." Nevaine flipped a small knife in the air—most likely she didn't even realize she did it.

"Did someone attack you? I thought I heard yelling out toward the canyon after you left, but it sounded like a man," Piallen said as she and Nevaine both sat on the large couch.

Lizeth didn't feel like admitting that she'd stranded a forester five feet in the air because she was vexed. Besides, he had nothing to do with the body. Probably.

"I was going up the back stairs and someone pushed a dead body down. It landed on the stoop directly in front of me."

Nevaine narrowed her eyes. "Someone *died* falling down the backstairs?"

Lizeth rolled her eyes. "No. Someone was killed and then dropped down from an upper landing onto the one I happened to be crossing. I have a feeling that he was quite dead before he hit, and I am relatively sure he started that way when he was shoved off."

Piallen was on her feet and heading for the door. "I'll go help the guards."

"They are doing fine without you; can't you tell Lizeth's upset?" Nevaine being solicitous was more annoying than her being snarky. And far more disturbing.

"I'm sorry." Piallen sat back down. "Did you see who it was?" There was the hushed tone they used to all have when they were little kids, running around the palace solving mysteries. Before they were reminded that they were future rulers of the realm and had decorum to keep in mind.

"No. But I could make a sketch." Lizeth got up and rummaged through her desk for a pad of drawing paper and her charcoals. She wasn't happy that someone had been killed, but it had been a long time since the three sisters were in on something together. She brought the pad back to her chair and started sketching. "I'm not going down to dinner tonight. Would you both like to join me here?" She didn't look up. Yes, if the king and queen were not in the palace, the three sisters were called upon to lead the palace dinner. But tonight's dinner was going to be small, and she knew the chancellor would love to take over. She was definitely not up to seeing people.

"I believe our eldest sister has had a fright and needs to be comforted." Nevaine grinned. She was always one for avoiding official events.

"Agreed. I'll contact the chancellor and ask Margie to send up some food." Piallen was gone before any minds could be changed.

Lizeth finished her sketch and held it up to Nevaine; who stood looking out the window. Her sister was many things, but pensive wasn't one of them.

"Is everything all right with you?" Lizeth wanted to ask if Trion had found her, but found herself not wanting to know at this point.

Nevaine gave a half-smile. "Just lost in thought. Let me see this closer." She reached out for the sketch. "He doesn't look in good shape, does he?" She turned the drawing around.

Lizeth knew she wasn't as talented of an artist as Nevaine, but she was accurate in her renderings. "He wasn't in good shape by the time I saw him. I only had a glance before the guards arrived, but I can assure you, that was how he looked."

"I can't tell if I recognize him or not." Nevaine handed back the sketch. "Did you notice what he was wearing? That could be important."

There were many dignitaries in the palace right now, all gathering for the ceremony that would send Lizeth off on her Challenge. And most would be wearing distinctive clothing. Or if it was someone local, that would be clear as well. She closed her eyes and tried to picture the man's body instead of the horrible mess of his face. "Linen pants, white. Dark linen shirt, blue. Sandals?" She opened her eyes and jotted the clothing she'd seen on her drawing. "He was from the Aqin region. Did they send anyone up here for the Challenge? I know Father wasn't pleased with their attempt at breaking off."

The Aqin were the most recent addition to the kingdom—if eighty years ago could be considered recent. A small region near the coast, it included a pair of valuable islands but not much else. However, joining the kingdom had saved them from a worse fate from some of the more vicious powers out there. They rarely made much of a ruckus, but five months ago there had been a group of young hotheads who were stirring things up in a misguided bid for freedom. They'd been shut down without much damage, but the region was still not on the king and queen's favorites list.

Piallen came back in. "The chancellor is taking over the dinner service for tonight and he hopes you recover from your fright. Margie is sending up a full meal for all of us to help you recuperate. I specifically said many desserts should be included." She looked around. "What did I miss?"

"Here's the drawing, but I didn't draw his clothing. He was wearing linen and sandals." Lizeth tried to see the image in her mind again. The clothing told them nothing beyond the region. Both noble and commoner dressed similarly in the warm region of Aqin. Was he a dignitary? Servant? What was he doing in the back stairwell, something that many people in the palace were unaware of let alone someone from another region? Whoever dropped him might have been local, or someone who studied the palace.

A soft knock announced Margie and two of her assistants. They brought in a table and chairs, and enough food for six people and desserts for three times that. The assistants bowed and then left.

"It is only us three, you know. You have enough for an army." Lizeth gave Margie a warm hug.

"But you have gone through trauma, and as such need sustenance to survive." Margie's face grew serious as she pulled back and peered into Lizeth's eyes. "How are you? That had to have been shocking."

"I will be fine. It was horrible though; have they released any information?" Lizeth knew there would be nothing official, not yet. But Margie often obtained unofficial information simply by paying attention around her.

"They aren't sure who he is." She nodded to all three sisters in turn then glanced down at the drawing and the notes on his clothing. "He's not a registered guest, nor is the *Aqin* ambassador indicating she knows him."

"So, he is Aqinan? That was my guess from his clothing."

"Yes, or at least he was dressed like one. You weren't the only one to notice, which could mean he wasn't actually from there." The emphasis Margie put on those words pulled all three sisters closer to her. "There is some debate as to what nationality he was. Ambassadors from many regions and countries are pointing fingers."

"Any news on whether he was alive when he fell?" Nevaine always went for the bigger questions. In this case, the more gruesome ones.

"The death takers have the body; they don't believe he was alive when he was dropped down the stairwell but need to finish their examinations. However, the priests and priestesses are in a tizzy since once the examinations are done, they don't know what service to perform to meet his spiritual needs." She shook her head. "If a life hadn't been lost, it would be comical the way they are debating the best approach. Now, no more talk of that. Eat and relax." She hugged Lizeth again. "I added a sleeping draught on the tray, blue bottle. If you need it." With hugs to the other two, she left.

"An Aqinan, or someone we were supposed to believe was one, in a secret back stairway falling to his death. Or being dropped after being murdered." Nevaine drummed her fingers on her chin as the other two started filling their plates. As kids, she had usually been the one to lead them on their mysteries and adventures.

"But who would want to murder someone *inside* the palace?" Piallen waved a roll in the air. "If I were going to kill someone, I'd do it in the Hart woods and dump the body into the canyon. Speaking of which, do you think the yelling I heard out that way earlier could have anything to do with this?"

Lizeth hadn't wanted to bring up her encounter with the woodsman, but since Piallen wasn't letting it go, she didn't have a choice. "The yelling out by the canyon was a woodsman. He annoyed me, and I *might* have sung a spell of holding on him. Floating about five feet in the air. He would have come down in ten minutes though, so you must have heard him right after I cast it."

Both of her sisters stopped eating and stared at her in shock. This was why she didn't want to tell them.

"Our pretty princess got vexed and used her magic against a subject?" Nevaine *had* initially been being far nicer than usual, but her regular dose of snark was back now.

Lizeth certainly wasn't going to mention that she'd accidentally spelled a housekeeper earlier in the day. Two in one day would be too much and the first had been an accident. "He was extremely annoying."

"Tall, dark brown hair, brown eyes, nice build, and a great smile?" Piallen nodded. "That's Finnian. He's seemed extremely nice when I've met him."

"Yes, that was the name he gave. He might have been nice to you, but he snuck up on me while I was thinking. And I believe he was laughing at me. Plus, he made up some story about hunting a wild beast in the forest. As if that would ever happen." The woodsmen had their duties to maintain the expansive woods. And yes, if a creature did become dangerous, they would take care of them. But Lizeth had never heard of that happening, in her lifetime or any of the history books after the canyon was formed.

Piallen's laughter stopped. "He said that? Something dangerous?"

"Come on, nothing has come through those woods in hundreds of years." Lizeth wasn't going along with this. Most likely Piallen had a crush on the man and would believe anything he said. "He's too old for you. You're only sixteen."

"Almost seventeen, and I'm not crushing on him. As far as I know, no one has ever dropped dead bodies down our back stairwell before either."

Nevaine was suspiciously quiet as she nibbled on a carrot.

"What? No sarcasm?" Lizeth finally leaned over and waved her hand in front of her sister's face to make her look up.

"Oh, sorry. I was focusing on our murder." She gave them both a condescending look. "Not the newest woodsman. You couldn't marry him anyway, Piallen—no royal blood."

Piallen blushed. "I didn't say anything about marriage. I observed that he was handsome, that's all."

"You only said he had a great smile, nothing about handsome." Nevaine grinned and turned toward Lizeth. "Was he handsome as our little sister says?"

"He was covered in dirt and had a few days growth of beard. No, he was not handsome." If she were to be honest, he did have nice eyes and an attractive smile. But she didn't feel like being honest right now. At least not about him.

Piallen narrowed her eyes, but then went back to eating.

Lizeth watched Nevaine, who was focused on something, but she didn't think it was the murder. "So, where do we think our dead man came from? Oh, and not sure how, if at all, this would be connected, but someone tried to grab Scruff with a cape on one of the second-floor balconies earlier."

That pulled Nevaine out of whatever she was thinking about and Piallen out of her pout.

"Who?" The two sisters echoed each other.

"You know Scruff; he *thinks* it was a man. Pretty sure it was a man with dark hair. Maybe. I was hoping to entice him to come back up here tonight to get a better answer from him." Scruff was smart, smarter than most people thought. But he was also stubborn.

"For someone to attempt to harass one of the grigeens in the palace...that isn't to be taken lightly." Piallen scowled.

Lizeth knew her little friend, like all of his kind, could defend himself. But a chill came over her. That man in the stairwell probably thought he could have protected himself as well. "That man in the stairwell had dark hair. No cape, but someone could have taken it."

"So, we think Scruff pushed him over the railing for trying to grab him? In a part of the palace that was nowhere near the front balconies?" Piallen had the best imagination of them all, but even for her, that was a bit much to believe.

"No. Scruff wasn't even that upset. He glided down to me to get away." Lizeth chewed the edge of her finger. She now wished she'd paid more attention to the people in the entrance way when Scruff had been attacked. The balconies were narrow and whoever did it had probably been looking down when Scruff glided down to her.

"Three unrelated events?" Piallen shook her head. "There's been a dangerous creature roaming the forest for a few days, someone tried to grab Scruff, and a random body gets dumped in a little used stairwell. There has to be a connection."

"If those three are related, I'd like to know how and why," Nevaine said. "But that's extremely unlikely. What if the creature in the forest is truly something we have to fear? Trion told me he'd heard odd sounds in the forest the past two mornings. He goes out there to meditate before breakfast." She distinctly didn't look in Lizeth's direction.

"Becoming close with Trion, now, are we?" Lizeth kept her voice light, but she'd told both of her sisters when he first arrived that she thought Trion would be a perfect match. For her.

"Lizeth...I didn't mean for anything to happen." Nevaine appeared genuinely distressed. "And nothing did. At least not on my end. I'm not interested in him at all. I was going to say something to you though."

All thoughts of the various mysteries vanished and Lizeth leaned back in her chair. "It wasn't only this morning and him wanting to look at your knife collection, was it?" It wasn't that Trion was perfect; she was certain he had faults, but he would have been a good match. Love wasn't something royals could aim for since any match they made had to have royal blood. She'd figured out long ago that she'd do best by finding a good match and settling for it. Trion was extremely convenient.

"No. He met me outside of the stable the first day he arrived. At first, I did think he was interested in the weapons." Nevaine paused. "Then he tried to kiss me yesterday. I didn't let him." She looked fierce as she watched both of her sisters. At eighteen going on nineteen, she still had two years before her own Challenge and her availability for marriage. But courtships had gone longer than that before.

"But you didn't say anything." The betrayal sat like a lump in Lizeth's stomach.

"I couldn't think of how to tell you. You don't even know or love him."

"How can I know? I've never had a chance." Lizeth's voice got louder as she got to her feet and started pacing. "Do you know how many men of royal blood are in this country? Of marriage age? Not a lot."

Nevaine stood up as well, ready to yell back when a knock came at the door.

Piallen jumped to her feet to answer it. "Yes?"

The guard on the other side was heavily armed, far more so than palace guards normally would be. "Your highness. I have been sent to make sure your sisters and yourself are safe. Please stay in this suite."

Piallen grabbed the door as he tried to shut it. "What's going on?" Her sisters dropped their argument and came closer.

"I'm not supposed to disturb you. Your parents will be home soon enough."

Lizeth stepped forward and looked down her nose at him even though he was taller than her and she was in her dressing gown. "I am the heir apparent. As such, I need to be able to act in our parents' stead. I can't do that without information, can I?" As she spoke, she let a soft agreeable spell song seep through her words in a hum.

"I...I guess you're correct. The chancellor won't mind that I told you. You are the princesses after all." He was muttering to himself so much that Lizeth wondered if she'd gone too heavy on the spell within the song.

"We are. And it's important for us to know." She smiled sweetly.

"Yes, well, there's been another body found. Out near the old stables. Looks like he might have been killed before the one you found. Lord Trion was most distressed at finding him. They've finished searching and removed the body to the death takers." The guard stood there for a moment, then shook his head as the spell wore off. "Yes, well. Just stay inside and be safe." He nodded and went down the corridor.

Chapter Four

"That wasn't nice, you know. Using your magic to spell him." Piallen frowned as Lizeth shut the door.

"Neither is us being kept in the dark. I am almost heir and you two are no longer children. We would have been informed if our parents had been here, so why not now?" She was still upset about Nevaine and Trion, but she believed her sister when she said she hadn't let him kiss her and had no interest.

She'd have to work on Trion later. For now, dead bodies needed to take precedence.

"She has a point. Why wouldn't the chancellor have at least included Lizeth? After the Challenge, she'll officially be heir, but even now she's supposed to be learning." Nevaine started pacing in a fast, tight circle. She was the shortest of the three sisters but could move disturbingly quickly when she wanted.

"Something is afoot beyond the surplus of bodies, although those are at the heart of it. Anyone up for some investigating?" Lizeth knew she should be studying or something in preparation for the Challenge. But her heart wasn't in it. Besides, she still had enough time.

"I'm in." Piallen turned for the door. "Just let me grab a few things."

"No swords. Or bows." Lizeth and Nevaine said at the same time.

She stuck her tongue out at both of them. "I was going to get smaller weapons. I know for a fact Nevaine has at least four on her." She left the room.

A crafty grin flashed across Nevaine's face. "Six to be exact, but who's counting?"

Lizeth shook her head. Both of her sisters were extremely skilled at weapons usage—Piallen was just more forthright about it. Along with her skill with the bow, she was also a talented swordswoman.

Nevaine was incredibly sneaky and so used to carrying concealed weapons that she did so even in the palace. Their parents had given up trying to break her of that habit when she was ten.

Lizeth had the most useful magic in terms of weaponry, so her reliance on edged and pointed weapons was less pronounced than the other two. Far less pronounced. She could use a sword somewhat, but her ability with a bow and arrow was tragic.

Lizeth added a knife to the belt that sat on her dressing table.

"You're only taking that tiny knife? Is that for if you have to fight off a mouse?" Nevaine looked at it closer. "You might still lose."

"This is a perfectly fine weapon. Besides, if we find anything dangerous, I think I can spell them." She didn't like flaunting her more aggressive magic to her sisters, but her knife wasn't that small. She did add another knife as well.

Nevaine sniffed at the second blade, but then turned her look to Lizeth herself. "You might want to change though. I know robes are in fashion, but not good for sneaking around in."

Lizeth looked down at her dressing gown. She wanted to discuss Trion before Piallen returned but it would be awkward if they got into a shouting match and Piallen came back in the middle of it.

"You're right. Let me change into something sneakier." Lizeth was trying to push aside the Trion issue and she wouldn't bring it up to Nevaine right now, but it was eating at her. Unlike her sisters, Lizeth always had a plan. Her life was to fall into predicted steps. One of those was to find a match not long after her Challenge. Being married wasn't required for an heir, but it was strongly favored. As long as all three sisters passed their Challenges, all three would be heirs and rule when their parents were gone. But any with children, or in the process of having children, would be given the first choice of what part of the kingdom they ruled. Lizeth would be High Queen as long as she was married and had a child or two. That was part of the life plan she'd drawn up at eight years old.

Lizeth sighed as she picked out and discarded three outfits. Her sisters made fun of her fashion needs, but this was not the time for them. She grabbed a dark shirt and pants, paired them with rugged boots, and put on the belt for her knives.

She came out to find both sisters dressed similarly and quietly chatting. They stopped and looked up when she came into the room

"Sorry about the delay. Shall we?"

They looked both ways in the corridor, then Nevaine took the lead and darted down an empty side corridor. The rest followed closely.

"So where are we going?" Scruff almost got flung out a hallway window as he appeared behind them and scared Lizeth into drawing a defensive spell.

"What are you doing? I could have accidentally fried you with a spell." Lizeth shook out her hands that had been curled for casting a spell. Most of her spells were driven by song magic, and being as strong as she was, they were a formidable defense. They were quite honestly the reason why she wasn't worried about preparing for the Challenge. Her spell songs would protect her. But this time they'd almost gotten Scruff. She might need to relax a bit.

Nevaine and Piallen stopped and glared at Scruff. Both had hands on partially hidden weapons.

Scruff didn't look concerned and blinked slowly at all three of them. "What would be better is for you to tell me what you three are doing. Sneaking down empty halls?"

Lizeth glared at him. "There have been some attacks, and no, not just whoever tried to grab you. We want to see what's happening, since no one will tell us."

"And that makes us sound like we're twelve years old." Nevaine put away the knife she'd partially drawn.

"It makes you sound like fun ladies. Which you haven't been as of late, I have to say. Should I call Clait and Tobias, too? Just like old times?"

Clait was Nevaine's grigeen friend and Tobias was Piallen's. Grigeens had a long and vague history with the royal family, but one was always assigned at birth to protect and guide the royal child.

The king's childhood grigeen, Maithen, still came for public visits from time to time and Lizeth was fairly sure many private ones with both the king and queen.

"No. We're investigating to see if there are any clues outside. Then we'll go back like good little princesses." Lizeth turned to her sisters. "Unless you want them to be called to join us?" She adored Scruff, and the other grigeens, but right now having him along could be a liability. Having two more would compound the issue.

"Not until we know there is something of import." Nevaine kept her face sober. "We don't want to waste their time."

Scruff shrugged and started down the way they'd been going. "I'm still sticking with you, so that's enough." He got a bit ahead of them but they hadn't moved. "Well? Coming?"

Lizeth shrugged and motioned for Nevaine to continue. Once Scruff decided he was involved in something—he stayed that way. At least until something else distracted him. As a child, Lizeth had never been able to distract him long enough to get away with much, so the easiest thing was to bring him into her confidence on her adventures. Good to know that still held true.

They made it undetected down a lesser-used stairwell. Not as unused as the one in the back, but it was free of nosy guards and dead bodies. And it led to a short corridor and the outside.

"Shouldn't there be a guard out here?" Scruff sniffed around as they came out. "You are having an alarming number of bodies around and I would think guards might help."

"I don't know if that would make a difference. Everything is open because of the Challenge." But Lizeth did wonder about the lack of a guard though. This wasn't a well-known entrance or exit, but if there was enough concern to request that the princesses remain in their rooms, then there should have been guards on all outer doors. She'd make a note to ask the chancellor when she got back.

"What are you expecting to find? I am fairly certain the body was already removed." Scruff didn't seem concerned; he acted more like he was out for a stroll.

"There could be things they missed." Nevaine held up her hand. "Yes, it's dark, but some of us see fine in the dark." Part of their shared bright blue eyes was a talent for night vision.

Scruff looked ready to continue his discussion but Lizeth looked at him over her sister's shoulder and shook her head.

They made their way in silence through to the stables. There were still no guards and no other people.

Nevaine not only had excellent night vision, but part of her magic was a light rod she could create with her magic. Not large nor powerful, but a stick about a foot long that glowed for a few hours. She called one up now.

Lizeth sang softly and a lightly glowing ball appeared. Boan had been having her work on the spell recently and she was pleased with the results.

"You know that means people can see you all more easily." Scruff wasn't impressed, nor did he need their light magic.

"And this will block anyone from seeing it." Piallen put up a magic shield around the stables. It wouldn't hold against weapons, although once she became more proficient in magic it could be quite efficient. Piallen was trying to convince her parents she should follow battle mage training and this was one of their spells. But right now, it took care of the light generated by Lizeth and Nevaine so it wouldn't go beyond what they wanted it for. "I'll check the horses."

"I'll go look at my knife training area; they weren't clear where the body was found." Nevaine walked around to an outlying building, that while technically part of the stables, had been taken over for her knife practice once it became apparent that she was gifted and stubborn. She'd been about five at the time. Most likely she wanted to make sure her weapons were safe before she looked into any dead body mysteries.

Scruff shrugged and waddled into the main storage building. Lizeth followed him—he still had the best nose of them all.

"Do you smell anything?" Lizeth smelled faint lavender that told her which mages were involved in the removal of the body and any evidence. Certain types of magic carried scents, not all, but in the case of cleaning magic, all users left a light scent. There were two who used lavender, Flot and Zilth. She didn't know either well, but they were both young and new to the palace, so perhaps they missed something. The body might not have been here, but something that needed cleaning up had been.

"Not sure." Scruff bounded ahead of her and into the rest of the building.

The entrance looked normal, at least from what Lizeth could tell. This building was used to store equipment for the horses and anything else deemed too outdoorsy by the queen to be stored in the palace.

Straw was spread around the floor, but although it was fresh, that wasn't unusual. The extreme cleanliness of everything, including the floor, was. Things that would normally be clumped together in baskets were neatly spread out on benches. Bits, bridles, other odds and ends that would be used by the royal army. "But why out like this?" She was talking to herself but Scruff jumped down from the loft he'd been investigating.

The fur on the back of his neck rose as he got closer. "Stiklins." He hissed out the word and froze before he slowly approached the bench. "These items are cursed. Stiklin magic. Things up in the loft too, but the scent is stronger here. They were trying to leave behind spells that would injure or kill any who used these." He sniffed again. "Someone found them before they finished."

Lizeth took a step back. Stiklins were magic-wielding savages from far on the other side of the canyon. Beyond even the empire of the Laiandra. They had been a menace during her great-great-grand-parents' time, but not since the canyon had appeared.

"But how could they be here? They'd have to destroy the Laian-dra on the other side, cross through the canyon, then find a way back up here. Nothing crosses the canyon." Lizeth almost picked up one of the pieces but pulled her hand back. There was a lingering feeling of wrongness coming from them. Scruff might have said they didn't finish their spells on them, but they still gave her a bad feeling.

"Unless they had another way to cross here." Scruff stalked around the area, the fur on the back of his neck continued rising.

"These have a lavender smell, don't they? Besides the Stiklin mag-ic you sense. I smell it, but you do as well." It wasn't a question; if she had fur on the back of her neck it would be rising too. "If those pieces were cleaned, then the cleaners sensed the Stiklins." That was far worse than those creatures possibly having been here. That two of the royal mages realized it and did nothing. The entire palace should be locked up solid and guards on full patrol if there was even a chance that something as deadly as Stiklins were somehow here.

He looked up and nodded. "They had to have sensed it. But there's more." He scrambled up the ladder to the loft, motioning for her to follow.

Lizeth wasn't as nimble as he was, but she made it up there. The cleaners hadn't been up here, or at least if they had been it had only been a quick look and leave. No lavender scent came from the area. Scruff's head popped up from behind a straw bale. "Back here."

Lizeth had to duck to go anywhere in the loft, but it wasn't large. "What did you...is that a cape?"

A dark russet cape bundled around a large lump. There wasn't a scent but Lizeth suddenly didn't want to move forward. "What is it?"

"It's bad. You probably shouldn't have eaten as much as you did. But since you did, you really don't want to see this. It's a head. I'm not sure, but I think it might be the man who tried to grab me in the palace."

Lizeth's stomach turned and she backed away. "Thank you for not making me look, but how are we not smelling anything? No blood?"

"It's sealed in a protection spell. My guess is whoever did it was planning on coming back for it and didn't want it found before then." He lashed his tail a few times. "That body that dropped on you earlier had its head, right?"

"Yes, he did."

"The one Trion found did as well. I listened to the guards dealing with that before I came to find you three. This is a third dead body."

"And a third that's missing a lot. Where is the rest of him?" Lizeth would have to anonymously report the head to the guards, but she wasn't going to disturb it.

She followed Scruff to the ground level, covered her hand with part of her cloak to keep her skin from touching anything, and grabbed one of the spelled horse bits.

"Lizeth, you need to see this," Piallen whispered from the entrance. Then she noticed Lizeth's face. "What's wrong?"

"A lot that I want to wait until we're back in my rooms to discuss. What did you find? We shouldn't stay here." Lizeth but the spelled horse bit back with a shudder. Even not touching it directly was nasty.

"Something that's not good, but judging from your face, not as bad as what's in here. Is Scruff poofed up?"

Scruff shook himself and his fur settled down.

Piallen watched him as she led them to the main stable. The horses nickered lightly as they came in, but there were fewer than there should be. These stables held the majority of horses for the royal family, important hangers-on, and the palace guards. There was a second stable compound a mile away that held the thousands for the army.

But this one should have still held at least a hundred plus. There were about twenty. The royal family's horses were in a separate section and aside from the ones belonging to their parents, were all there.

"Could the guards be out on them?" Lizeth knew the answer as she said it, but the question came out anyway.

"They wouldn't go out at night unless things were dire. Not enough magic users to keep them safe in the dark woods." Nevaine came out from one of the stalls and answered before Piallen, but Piallen nodded in agreement.

"And their gates were busted. Someone chased them out. There are even signs of a struggle in one of the back stalls," Piallen said.

"Someone set the palace horses free? For what purpose?" Lizeth slowly walked around the empty stalls; one hand held out as she sang a song of revealing. Most of the stall doors glowed a soft yellow. Not good. There had been magic used to open them and yellow tracing meant it was neither good nor bad. Or someone having to cast the spells under duress.

"These were spelled. Even the ones that look broken. Yellow magic mostly." Both of her sisters had magic but not as flexible as Lizeth's. They wouldn't see the colors but they would understand what they meant.

Nevaine narrowed her eyes. "Why break them if they opened them with magic?"

Piallen walked toward the largest stall, the one the king and queen's horses would be kept in had they been home. She quickly backed out. "And why are there two headless bodies in our parents' stall?"

Chapter Five

"What?" Lizeth didn't yell, but it was close as she and Nevaine ran over. Scruff beat them there and was sniffing, hissing, and lashing his tail at the entrance to the stall but wouldn't go in further.

Lizeth took a deep breath and stepped around Piallen. Like the head Scruff had found, there was no smell, nor any blood, but her throat kept closing up when she tried to call up her spell again.

The bodies were both male and dressed like average citizens of Astarious. She forced herself to step closer. Her magic might not be accessible at the moment, but plain observation could do something. She peered at the clothing. It was of higher quality, if simple. Lower nobility perhaps.

Piallen and Nevaine came closer as well.

"Scruff, can you keep watch? I don't think we want to be caught out here." Lizeth nodded as Scruff darted back to the front doorway of the stable.

Nevaine used a stick to lift one of the men's hands. "No calluses and no defensive injuries."

Piallen had been looking at both sets of booted feet. "Neither have any debris on their boots. Nothing at all." She glanced pointedly at the mud and dirt right outside the stall. "They killed them elsewhere, brought them here, and then washed off their boots?"

Nevaine scowled. "There is a spell that can be used to track where someone has been. Hisu recently began teaching it to me. It's tricky, but someone didn't want anyone using it on these two and seeing where they came from."

Lizeth nodded. She'd wanted to wait to tell them this news, but waiting was over. "Scruff found a head in the loft of the storage building. It was magically sealed like these two are, and I bet we'll find the other head somewhere around here."

Neither sister looked shocked—the headless bodies already did that.

Scruff had been outside but darted back in. "I believe the head might have belonged to the man who tried to grab me. I did not do that to him though." He ran back to his watch post outside the stable.

Nevaine stood up. Her magic wasn't driven by song like Lizeth's but by carefully balancing spells on top of each other. She chanted and held out her hands. Her spells always sounded like gibberish, but as long as the layering was correct, they worked.

The bodies slowly rose off the ground.

"Was that what you meant to do?" Lizeth asked as she and Piallen backed out of the stall. The bodies weren't rising at the same rate, arms and legs went higher than the torso. It was as if a bad puppeteer was pulling at them.

Beads of sweat built on Nevaine's upper lip. "Check. Under. Neath." The words came out through gritted teeth as she focused on keeping the bodies waist-high.

Piallen ducked down first, Lizeth followed. Neither went under the bodies.

Focusing on the ground and not the bodies hanging above it, Lizeth was finally able to sing a spell of searching. Words appeared in the straw; they'd been done when the straw was there so nothing obscured them.

"The unbelievers will die." She'd just spoken when the bodies crashed down.

"You need to get out of here." Scruff came back in but kept glancing out the main stable door.

Nevaine dropped to her knees in a stupor from the draining of her spell, but Lizeth and Piallen each grabbed an arm and pulled her up.

"Good thing she's the smallest." Piallen looked down but Nevaine was a limp rag doll and her eyes were shut. "She's out of it. We'll have to carry her."

"Are you leaving now? Right now?" Scruff was getting frantic. "Go back to the palace. We'll hide you." In the darkness behind him, dozens of small furry shapes appeared. Aside from the few assigned to the royals, grigeens didn't socialize with humans. They were out in force this evening however.

"But aren't the people we're trying to avoid coming from the palace?" Lizeth would deal with the grigeen assistance later, but there was only so much they could distract from. Lizeth dropped her magic spell light. Nevaine's had extinguished when she collapsed. They wouldn't be able to see as well, but them being harder to see would be more important and Piallen couldn't move her shield well at this point. She'd have to drop it once they left the stable.

"Not coming from the palace, coming from the forest. You need to *run*." Scruff ran to join the rest of the furry shadows.

"Head or legs?" Piallen asked.

"You're taller, take her head." Lizeth grabbed Nevaine's feet.

They could hear people running toward them but were hopefully close enough to the palace that they wouldn't be noticed. It sounded like the grigeens were leading whoever had been coming toward them behind the stables and into the back woods.

There was still no guard at the door, which was both good and bad. Had a guard been there he or she might delay them with questions, or help defend them if the attackers turned toward them instead of doing loops around the stable.

"Hold her." Lizeth opened the door with a few magic passes over the handle. This door wasn't locked, but did have a way of opening that was only known to a few. They got inside when the yelling started from inside the palace.

"We have to get back to your rooms." Piallen was carrying Nevaine on her own and finally threw her over her shoulder.

The yelling was stronger now, but still not at their end. Lizeth led the way up the stairs to her suite of rooms.

They'd shut the door behind them when a loud knock came. Piallen hung on to Nevaine and kept running into Lizeth's bedroom. Lizeth grabbed her dressing gown, threw it on, and opened the door.

"Yes?" Lizeth stilled her breathing as she opened the door. Another benefit of being a spell singer—great lung control. She kept the door only partially open and leaned on it as if she'd just woken up.

"I am sorry to disturb you, your highness. But we are under attack. I've been assigned to stand watch on your door. Are your sisters there as well? Their chambers were empty."

"Yes, after my earlier trauma they are both staying the night. Who is attacking us?"

He paused.

"Need I remind you that until my parents return, I *am* the ranking royal?" It was odd, she'd never noticed being so discounted before. Something was definitely up.

"The chancellor—"

She stood up taller and glared at him. "Is *nobility*, but not a royal. I would know what we are facing or my sisters and I will go down and find out." She doubted that he knew much more than they did, but the hairs on the back of her neck were standing up.

He looked around, then dropped his voice. "Yes, your highness. It's unclear, but the captain of the guard believes they are Stiklins. They are being pushed back, but a few did get inside the palace."

Lizeth felt the color drain from her face and the guard reached for her in case she was going to pass out. Under normal circumstances, hearing of a threat from such beings as Stiklins would be cause for fear. When it came after finding evidence of those same beings in their own stable, it became full terror.

Of course, she couldn't tell the guard that. There was no way that the mages who went to investigate the body Trion found could have missed the Stiklin scent. Therefore, there was no way to tell who was a friend and who was a foe. She waved off his hand. "I'll be fine. Thank you for telling me. My sisters and I will wait here until whatever the menace is has been contained." With a bow from him and a nod from her, she shut the door.

Piallen came out from the bedroom. "Nevaine is still out, I think that spell hit her harder than she expected. What did the guard want?"

"They know who is attacking, and it *is* the Stiklins." She moved further into the room. It was doubtful that the guard could hear through the door, but always better to be safe. She filled Piallen in on what Scruff had sensed and what the guard said.

"That's ridiculous. Not that I don't believe Scruff; I trust him more than the chancellor. But those things haven't been seen here in hundreds of years. There's no way for them to cross the canyon, and the lands around it are too populated for them to pass through."

Lizeth took off her dressing robe and paced. "I know. But whatever was out there...wasn't normal. We need to wake up Nevaine. Now." She ran into her room. Her sister was still unconscious but was rolling about on Lizeth's bed like she was trying to fight something off.

"Let her rest. Sometimes her spells are too much for her to process."

"No. If those are Stiklins out there, they could be why she's unconscious." When Piallen didn't look like she got it, Lizeth rolled her eyes. "They steal magic. At least according to myth, they can pull a spell out of a mage. She was spell casting as Scruff said they were approaching." She shook Nevaine. "You have to wake up."

Nevaine responded by reaching for her knife with her eyes closed. Lizeth caught her hand. "No. You're safe, but you need to wake up." She looked back to Piallen. "I have to use a spell song." Once the three had become stronger magic users, they'd sworn to never use their abilities against each other. This had to be done though.

Piallen gave a tight nod but stayed across the room with her arms tightly crossed.

Lizeth sang a soothing song first; one you might use on a child who has overslept. Nevaine stopped twitching, but she didn't wake up. Lizeth switched to a harsher song. One with awkward discordant notes. It was called the song of the dead and while she doubted it would raise the dead, it was annoying enough that even if the spell didn't work, the song itself should wake a person up. She was grateful Boan made her learn it—even though she hadn't been happy at the time.

Nevaine's eyes stayed closed, but she was muttering something and kept trying for her knife. Lizeth held both of her hands down and kept singing.

"Stop. No spells. Sister." Nevaine opened her eyes slowly but squinted around the room like she'd been in the pub the entire night before. "Where am I?"

"My room. You were casting a spell so we could see under those two headless bodies. Then you collapsed. We believe Stiklins are attacking the palace and might have gone after your magic."

Piallen darted out and came back with a glass of water. "You look horrible." She handed it over as Nevaine pushed herself into a sitting position.

"That spell they cast...whoever left those bodies, wanted someone to find it. But why wouldn't the mages who'd checked the other body have seen it? They had to have gone out there."

"There was something odd about the missing horses and the bodies. I believe that the mages sensed the Stiklins in the storage room, which points to at least some of the palace mages not being who they seem—or they are traitors to the crown." Lizeth wished she'd had time to cast more spells before they'd had to run—there was too much they didn't know.

"And the horses, how could they miss that many horses disappearing?" Piallen gave Nevaine another glass of water and glared at her until she drank it.

"And who is behind it?" Lizeth started pacing. There were too many things going on, and all when the king and queen had been delayed on their return. "The chancellor."

"Come on, Lizeth. I know you don't like him, but high treason? That's more my line of thinking, and I don't even believe that." Nevaine stayed on the bed at a glance from Piallen. "I don't even know if he's bright enough for that."

"I've never trusted him." Lizeth folded her arms. She hadn't since her magic came into full bloom at puberty. He'd always seemed to be sneaking about, giving false smiles when she caught him. Of course, no one believed her. Even Boan said that she didn't have the type of magic to sense evil. She strongly disagreed. Magic wasn't the only way to tell a bad character. "And he would have been the one to send people to investigate the stables."

Piallen helped Nevaine drag her legs to the edge of the bed. "Maybe someone is using him. Or he's been spelled."

Nevaine shook her head. "Or, if Lizeth is right, he was waiting. Lots of strangers moving through, king and queen not here, Lizeth about to take her Challenge—which causes all sorts of magic weirdness according to my tutor. This would be the time to make a move." She got to her feet and stretched a bit. "If I was trying to take over the kingdom."

"You think that's what's happening? Maybe I should ride to Northalian and check on our parents. They need to be back now." Piallen looked ready to charge through the palace, jump on her horse, and take off in the dark. She'd do it too.

"You wouldn't get far if we are under attack, and I don't think you'd help their situation. Whatever the delay is." Lizeth shook her head. She'd been shoving her status down the guards' throats to get them to do what she wanted. But, with her parents still being delayed, she *was* the one who needed to take charge. She just had no clue what to do. The fact that some of the palace mages might not be who they thought made her question their options—at least for now.

"I think we need to assume there is a coup of some sort and behave accordingly." Nevaine was still moving slower than normal, but anger was helping her recovery.

"It's the middle of the night, and we're still not sure what exactly is going on. Our choices are minimal right now." Lizeth wanted her sisters to stay with her. For their safety more so than hers; there was too much weirdness going on.

A rattling came from the window in the front room. A wet and annoyed Scruff sat on the ledge lashing his tail. Lizeth quickly opened the window and hid her smile. "What happened?"

He went to the center of the room and shook. "They threw water on us. The Stiklins, if that was even who was out there, took off not long after you three went inside. But we were ambushed by a group of the housekeeping staff. They were too distant to see us clearly but somehow felt freezing water would chase off whoever was attacking. Didn't see a single guard though. The rest of my people went back to the woods. I'm staying with you three."

"There's no real attack?" Lizeth had heard the yells as they came in. And the guard seemed nervous enough to imply there was something afoot.

"Oh, there was one. Stiklins were strongly mentioned. But now the official statement is that it was some upset peasants. They are also blaming the stolen guard horses on these same mysterious peasants." He curled his upper lip at what he thought of that theory.

Lizeth turned. "We don't have upset peasants. We don't have peasants at all." Yes, not everyone in the kingdom lived a life of luxury, but they had free people, not peasants under the yoke of a tyrant. "Who used that term?"

Scruff sighed. "The chancellor."

Lizeth turned to her sisters. "I told you! He's up to something and is trying to take over the kingdom." She didn't like being right about this, but there was no way the chancellor wasn't up to something. "Anything new? Did they find the bodies and the head?"

"Yes, but not through their own searching. A nosy forester had been trailing whatever we led astray when you three escaped to the palace. He found the bodies and pointed them out. The chancellor didn't look pleased."

"Wait, the woodsman, was it Finnian?" Lizeth was beginning to wonder if she shouldn't have done something more drastic to him earlier.

"Aye. He was going to call in the others to search for the attackers, but the chancellor kept saying it was only peasants."

"Which we don't have." Lizeth retracted her thoughts about Finnian. He might have annoyed her but he, in turn, annoyed the chancellor, so that was a tick in his favor.

Nevaine scowled. "And who were originally claimed to be Stiklins."

"Just tell me if there is someone I can fight?" Piallen was the only one still standing as the other two sat when Scruff joined them. She had her hand on her dagger. "I should get more weapons." More than the other two, Piallen was action-driven. Sitting here with her sisters while there might be mayhem afoot wasn't her way. She left the suite after a quick check down the corridor.

Lizeth thought about stopping her but didn't bother getting up. Who knew what was happening and if Piallen felt that having her sword was useful, so be it. She doubted a bow and arrow would be a good idea inside the palace, regardless of what was going on.

"You're certain that the chancellor didn't believe Finnian?" He might have annoyed her, but Lizeth figured earnestness and honesty weren't Finnian's problems.

"The chancellor shut him down and threatened to call in the head woodsman to deal with him." Scruff stalked in a circle on the footstool and settled in.

"Who was it that initially claimed there to be Stiklins inside the palace?" Nevaine was still a bit groggy but she clearly saw the strangeness of what was being reported.

"The original claimant was a guard, one who has gone missing." Scruff snarled.

Chapter Six

"Wait, so the yelling we heard when we came in was based on one guard? Were they fighting anything?" With all the yelling they'd heard, Lizeth was surprised that there hadn't been a true attack.

Scruff licked some damp furs down, then turned to her. "That is a good question. The guards are now saying it was a mob of townsfolk. The captain wouldn't say peasant, but he did glance at the chancellor before he spoke." It wouldn't be that difficult for the chancellor to quiet the rest of the guards.

Nevaine shook her head and got to her feet. "I have more weapons on me than Piallen, but I'd like to increase that. Not to mention, if we are staying here, I'd like some better clothes." She slipped out the door.

Now that the immediate bout of adrenaline-inducing information had been shared, Lizeth found fatigue settling in. "Any word on Trion?" That wasn't what she'd intended to say at all, but better to ask when Nevaine wasn't around.

"As far as I've heard, he went to his chambers after the shock of finding the body in the stables and collapsed." Scruff licked another damp section of fur, yawned, and then blinked at her. "You still want that one? He has the personality of a rock. A dull one. Not one of the pretty sparkly ones." Like most grigeens, Scruff loved sparkly stones—precious and semi-precious preferred.

"He does not. He's smart, interesting, and...very neat." Lizeth tried defending him but she was too tired. There had to be more to him than being convenient to her plans.

"Sounds like a bore. You can find someone better," Scruff said around a huge yawn and dropped off to sleep.

Lizeth watched him but found that being alone was making her less sleepy. The immediate threat might be gone, but whatever had happened needed to be resolved. She went to her closet and dug out a formal white suit of leather. Vaguely military-looking with brass buttons in a double row up the fitted vest and a thick embroidered line down the outside of both of the narrow legs. Add her knee-high black riding boots, a severe hairstyle, and she'd look the part. She'd commissioned it when she had her official viewing of the troops when she turned eighteen. Hadn't thought of it since then, but it was perfect now. She was going to have to remind the chancellor that he had to face her if he planned on doing anything against the kingdom.

"That's nice. Haven't seen that one in a while. You planning on stomping down there tonight and taking on the chancellor?" Although she'd only been gone for a short while, Nevaine was back with a bag full of clothing and weapons. She started sorting things as she claimed the larger of the two sofas. They both could be adjusted into beds.

"Tonight would be pointless. Tomorrow. First thing. I'll call the chancellor to the throne room and find out what is going on. You and Piallen can stand there looking intimidating too." Honestly, she'd rather do it now, but this evening had been too hectic. To pull this off she needed to make an impact. And it was known the chancellor didn't like early morning meetings. Their mother was an excellent strategist and while Lizeth found it boring when she was young, she did pick up a few things.

Nevaine looked the outfit over. "Didn't it have a cape?"

"Scruff said capes were dangerous, so I gave it to him for a nest." Lizeth knew he'd taken advantage of her, but the outfit didn't need the cape and it made him happy to think he tricked her.

Piallen came in, her collection of weapons more impressive looking than Nevaine's as they were all larger and weren't intended to be hidden. She dropped everything on the second couch. "There's still something going on out there." She got up and shoved a chair from the writing desk under the door handle. "Need more locks in these rooms," she muttered to herself.

"Isn't that excessive? Scruff said things were cleared up."

"Then why are there guards coming down the corridors slowly searching for something? Or someone? There's something wrong that we're not being told, and Scruff missed it because he came back here."

Scruff was on the overstuffed footstool and sound asleep. Or so he looked. "They had it taken care of when I left." He yawned. "What did you see now?"

"As I said, guards doing a slow search of the corridors. I wasn't going to ask them what they were doing."

Lizeth hung tomorrow's outfit back up and smiled. "Maybe I should. Just guards, correct?"

"Yes, no one but guards." Piallen stood by the door. "But if there really were Stiklins, and they did get inside, that could be what they're looking for."

"Or they could be looking for anything." Lizeth's current outfit wasn't as impressive as the white suit, but she wanted to save that for tomorrow. "Just a moment. If anyone knocks, ignore them." She darted back into her bedroom and changed into an outfit far more fitting for a woodswoman. Dark leather pants and a black vest over a dark green shirt. "There." She came back out and both of her sisters shook their heads.

"And what is that for?" Scruff jumped off his footstool and stalked around her legs.

"I look a bit more fighter-like. Now you three stay here and I'll go on recon." She went for the door, but Scruff was at her heels. "Seriously?"

"I've looked over you since before you could walk, not going to stop now. Particularly since I might have ended my surveillance too soon." His tail twitched at that admission.

Lizeth was going to order him to stay. It was difficult enough to be taken seriously, and having a fluffy grigeen with her wasn't going to help. But she knew it would be pointless. "You can come along. But don't say anything. Stand behind me looking fierce." He puffed up and flashed a grimace. "Or simply stand there. We'll be back in a bit." She nodded to her sisters and she and Scruff went down the corridor.

"So, how are you feeling about your Challenge?" Scruff kept pace with her and refused to drop back.

"What? There might be dangerous invaders inside our palace waiting to kill us in our sleep and you're worried about that? Besides, they may have to delay it if we are actually under attack." They'd only gone a short way, but she hadn't seen or heard anything. There was an open balcony area up ahead that overlooked the large inner courtyard of the palace. It would be easier to see from there what was going on.

"They can't delay or stop the Challenge. It will happen at the appointed time, regardless of anything else." Scruff stopped walking so Lizeth did as well. "You did realize that? The time of the Challenge is set by the oracles. If *they* change the time, the Challenge is changed. Otherwise, it will happen when they say."

"Wait, so I don't have a say? We could be in the middle of an attempted coup, and I can't postpone it? I can't leave everyone here if we're under attack."

"The Challenge has a lot of ceremony around it, but it is to disguise the reality. The challenger pops out of existence and reappears when the Challenge is done. The smoke and mirrors are only for show."

Lizeth slid against the wall. "And no one told me of this? Isn't that sort of something I should know?" They'd been keeping their voices to a whisper but Lizeth found it was getting harder to keep her voice down. She'd been training for the past six months, and been hearing about the Challenge since she was a child—yet no one mentioned this part?

"Because of your current response. Normally the challenger is not told of the situation to keep their reactions true. However, I think your parents would agree this is not a normal situation." His face scrunched up a bit.

"You're worried for them, aren't you?" No one had taken the delay of the return of the king and queen as too much of a concern, even this close to their eldest's Challenge. But there was no way them being missing wasn't related to the current situation. "People are being killed, attacks are going on, and my parents are missing in a questionable country. I can't go on the Challenge." She slid to the floor and found Scruff peering at her closely.

"I wish I knew where they were. My people's territories once reached past the far lands, but now we are only here. It's the only place we are safe." A flash of sadness crossed his face. "Regardless, you will be taken when the oracles claim you."

Lizeth put her head down on her knees. "At least we still have tomorrow. Things might change by then." She looked up at his silence. "Right?"

Scruff was frozen, looking down the hallway ahead of them. He put a paw over her mouth and shook his head. "There is something here. I sense it. We need to go back to your room. Slowly."

Lizeth didn't see or hear anything, but an odd feeling struck her. Keeping her voice barely above the sound of a breath, she sang a spell of revealing.

Three shapes shimmered into view at the end of the hall, across from the balcony. Scruff hissed and she looked back to see two more shapes flicker into being just past the doors to her room. Tall, almost impossibly thin, with long white arms, pale hair, and silver uniforms. Stiklins.

Chapter Seven

It took the intruders a few moments to realize they were visible, as Lizeth's magic had broken through their spell of hiding. Lizeth scrambled to her feet and broke into a run with Scruff bounding behind her. The Stiklins were at both ends of the hall, but the main stairway was closer to Lizeth and Scruff so they ran that way. Lizeth threw a lock spell at the ones behind them. At the least, it would slow them down if they intended to get into her room.

Hopefully they would keep following her and Scruff away from her sisters. They ran down the stairs, Scruff keeping pace even though he could have outrun her. There should be guards on the ground floor, but they would probably be scattered and easy for the Stiklins to attack. The best bet would be to lead these monsters out of the palace, then hopefully spell them with one of her heavier immobilization songs, and then retreat for reinforcements. They drained magic for spell users, but not already cast spells. She just needed to not let them catch up to her until they were out of the palace.

Scruff had far better night vision than she did, even though hers was enhanced. He cut ahead of her as they fled the palace. The sounds of the Stiklins pounding behind them did wonders for her speed and she kept up with Scruff easily.

"This way." Scruff darted to the right, across a patio, and into the forest.

Lizeth dodged around a large clump of trees and slammed into a body. One that had been upright and running in her direction until they hit each other.

Scruff skidded to a stop and ran back with his teeth bared.

"Princess Lizeth?" Finnian carefully tried to get out from underneath her without putting hands on her royal person. Not easy and he was making things worse by the way he was moving against her.

Lizeth got to her feet and brushed herself off. "Woodsman Finn-ian, we are being chased by Stiklins. Run with us or move aside." Her plan to lead them off and spell them wouldn't work until they got to a large clearing. Her magic was strong, but she couldn't cast the biggest spells while running. She stepped around Finnian and she and Scruff continued running.

With his long legs and knowledge of the woods, Finnian easily caught up to them. "Shouldn't you be running toward the palace? Let the guards take care of them."

"Those things were inside the palace and the guards didn't see them. I thought it best to draw them out here where I could spell them, *then* get guard assistance." She sped up but he didn't have a problem staying near her.

"Hang them up in the air?"

She glanced over to see his smirk and laughed. "Maybe. I was thinking something that would more permanently disable them." She didn't want to admit that as confident as she was about her spells, she'd been afraid to try to spell the Stiklins in the palace—especial-ly on the same floor as where her sisters were. If she couldn't contain them, the amount of damage they could do inside the palace was too brutal to think about.

"Lizeth?" Scruff had been dodging around the trees but suddenly appeared next to her. "We have a problem."

"I've noticed. They aren't that far behind." Lizeth gathered her spell songs in her head. She might not have much time to sing them.

"No, well, yeah, they are an issue, but up ahead—bigger prob-lem."

Up ahead should be the meadow she was aiming for. "What is it? Focusing on magic here." She could see trees and a vague area ahead. She'd assumed it was a fog in the meadow.

"The meadow is gone." Scruff darted to the side but Lizeth and Finnian were still running at full speed. All three ran into the void that had once been a meadow.

And tumbled through to *something else*.

As she fell through seeming nothingness, a chime rang in Lizeth's head. Then an ethereal voice. "*You have begun your Challenge. Be fleet of mind, gentle of foot, and strong of heart. Blessings of the oracles are upon you.*" Then another chime and she slammed into the ground.

She rolled as she heard Scruff yelling and Finnian swearing. They landed near her but more shapes were coming through after them.

Lizeth grabbed Scruff and Finnian's arm. "The Stiklins." She ran to a thick wood nearby. The land was rougher than the forest around the palace and she wished she had more than just a dagger with her.

Scruff scrambled down from her arms but shook his head like something was in his ear. Finnian had allowed her to pull him along but looked stunned.

"I don't think we're supposed to be here," Scruff whispered.

"Where is here?" Lizeth kept her voice low and tried to keep the fear she felt out of it.

Before her question could be answered, six Stiklins came through the woods toward them. They started as six, but as they moved forward, they began to fade, then vanish, until only one remained. He lunged forward but Finnian ran him through with his sword.

Lizeth had a spell song ready, but dropped it as the dead Stiklin vanished. "That can't be normal, nor good. Where are we, Scruff?" For the moment she ignored the words that had been in her head. She'd deal with them, but not now.

Scruff looked even more agitated and his tail lashed back and forth as he stalked off. "Not here. Let's go find a cave or something. I smell rocks in this direction."

Finnian looked to Lizeth but she shrugged and followed Scruff. "What are you talking about? If those things are gone, dead, whatever happened to them, we need to go back to the palace."

"Can't." Scruff started jogging.

"Why are we following the tiny furry being?" Finnian asked as they ran. "I'm with you, let's go back to the palace. I can bring back more of the foresters to find out what happened." He hadn't sheathed his sword yet.

"Scruff knows more about things than we do, even about forests. But I don't like these trees, why are they so tight together?" Lizeth rubbed her arms as she ran. It was colder here.

"They shouldn't be. The forest around the palace is curated and the trees have room." Finnian moved closer to her as she got closer to Scruff. "These don't look right at all." He still had his sword out but was scowling at the trees and looked like he wanted to stop and take a longer look.

"To be fair, you're not a native. You've lived here, what, a few weeks?" Not that Lizeth disagreed with him, but she felt like disagreeing with someone. There was a serious wrongness here. And as much as she wanted to ignore them, the words that had come into her mind wouldn't leave her alone. *This* was her Challenge? One problem—rather two—no one could go with the challenger. Unless she was imagining Scruff and Finnian, they were here with her. Wherever here was.

"And I've explored every part of the woods around the palace—these aren't the same." He slowed down as Scruff approached a hillside made of massive rocks. "And this shouldn't be here."

Scruff circled one direction, then vanished. Finnian motioned for her to follow.

Scruff found a cave. The entrance was small, like crawl-into small, but it opened up to an area the size of her front room.

Lizeth sent forth a pair of magic light spheres to illuminate the space. "How did you know this was here?" She was impressed. If more Stiklins than the six they'd seen came after them, they would be hard-pressed to find this place. Or if the five that vanished right in front of her reappeared. A chill hit her as she realized in her soul that the rocks that created this cave weren't anywhere in the palace forest.

"I'm not sure. I just felt it." Scruff didn't sound confident or forthcoming as he stalked around the area. "This should work until we sort things out. How did you do this, by the way?" He was looking directly at her.

"Me? I didn't do anything. We were running, then fell into some hole."

"And? I heard the words of the oracles." He sat back on his hind legs and stared at her.

"What words? How could she have pulled us anywhere? Unless you spelled us?" Finnian sheathed his sword but still stayed near the entrance.

"They couldn't be true. This isn't my Challenge. It's too early." Lizeth stomped over to a semi-flat boulder and sat. "And I didn't *do* anything."

Scruff snorted then looked to Finnian. "The oracles spoke as we hit what should have been the meadow. They called this Lizeth's Challenge. The ritual words were all there."

"I thought it was tomorrow? Or the day after?" Finnian shrugged. "Sorry, we don't keep track of the palace events out in the woods."

"The day of Challenge is dependent upon the oracles. They give an expected date but can sometimes be off by a bit." Scruff chewed on a claw. "Mark my words, this is her Challenge. And somehow, we were included. The oracles could have kept us out, but didn't."

"I thought I have to do it by myself?" In one way, Lizeth was glad that there hadn't been the lead-up to the Challenge. The level of pomp that had been set up was almost annoying—and she normally loved pomp. At the same time, this wasn't how she wanted to begin the first steps of her life as a queen of Astarious. A little pageantry might have been nice. Not to mention, if she was going to have help, it wouldn't have been from Finnian.

"You do, and that's what is worrying me. But the oracles themselves were involved in sending the two of us with you, so they must know what they are doing." He chewed on his tail in annoyance.

"Or the arrival of the Stiklins caused a mishap." The oracles were a group of ageless and non-gendered beings, made of power and magic. But what if some magic-stealing Stiklins interfered with their plans?

"Then where are we and how do we get back? We don't have supplies, nor much in the way of weapons. I can scout the area when the sun rises, but we can't stay here." Finnian sat on a boulder near the entrance. "Wherever here is."

"I won't know where we are until we go out. And Lizeth would have had a pack of supplies given to her at the start of her Challenge. The oracles might have still found a way to send something along, but again, we should wait until daybreak," Scruff said

Finnian got up and walked around the cave. "There's a long tunnel in the back. Let me gather what branches I can, and see about a fire closer to it. The tunnel should point the smoke away from the entrance." He tilted his head as they both watched him. "Unless you two want to sleep in a cold, dark cave?"

Lizeth forced a smile. "No, things are already bad enough. Thank you." She stopped short of giving him a royal nod, but she felt herself slipping into that mode. Nevaine used to mock her for going 'royal' on people, but it was easier to fall back on a persona than deal with reality right now. Her only hope was that in the morning they'd find out this had been a mistake, they'd resolve this entire thing, and she'd go back to the palace and have her real Challenge. Finding out that the Stiklins and the dead bodies had been some sort of mass hallucination would be handy as well, but she wouldn't push things.

Finnian came back after a short while with an armload of thin branches. He set them up and was pulling out a flint when Lizeth stood.

"I can at least do that." Lizeth sang a small fire song, a basic one taught to her when it was determined that she was old enough not to burn down the palace. At first she felt resistance, as if the flames didn't wish to come when she called. It took three times for the small flames to arrive. She'd seen Finnian out of the corner of her eye readying his flint after the second try, but studiously ignored him. The fire started slowly but eventually caught.

Finnian handed her a water pouch. "It's not much, but it should get us through the night. I found a rock that might hold some water for Scruff."

Lizeth wanted to decline, but she was thirsty, and creating food or water from nothing was beyond her abilities.

After she handed the bag back to him, he dusted off a small curved rock, sat it near Scruff, and poured some water into it. "Sorry, didn't know if the pouch would work for you."

"It wouldn't. I can hold it, but it's much easier for me to lap water. Thank you." Scruff's people were cat-like even though they weren't cats. Right now, his delicate lapping was very feline.

Chapter Eight

Finnian refused to move away from the main entrance, so he stayed furthest from their little fire. Lizeth hoped that Scruff was right about some sort of support pack for this adventure. Things were going to get difficult without supplies. Of course, there was still a chance that this was a dream, nightmare, or hallucination. She could hope.

For something that she, like all royal born, had trained for for so long, there were far more things she hadn't been told about the Challenge than things she had. If the situation remained the same in the morning, the first thing she needed to do was find out where they were. Clearly, Finnian was simply confused and didn't recognize this part of the forest. With a nod to herself, she curled up tighter and fell asleep.

Waking up what felt like ten minutes later to the bellowing of two bull moose was not what she'd expected.

She rolled over slowly. There were a lot of rocks in this cave and she'd managed to sleep on a collection of them. Nope, Finnian and Scruff only sounded like moose because of their failed attempts to keep their voices down and the echoing of the cave. For some reason, males often felt speaking softly meant lower register but still kept their volume up.

Finnian and Scruff were near the main entrance to the cave and animatedly carrying on.

"If you were trying not to wake me, you failed. Horribly. I was hoping to get more than a few minutes of sleep."

"You've been snoring for a few hours," Scruff said as he stalked away from Finnian. "This one thought he should go do recon while you slept. I pointed out that this is your Challenge and we're along for the trip."

Lizeth pushed herself up and shoved her hair into place. A few hours? She'd doubt him, but Scruff looked both serious and annoyed. If she were honest, she'd rather they had taken care of things. Not that she intended to shirk her duties, but there was an order to the Challenge. One that was not being followed. If this *was* her Challenge and not something else entirely.

"So, what is this recon you were planning? Is there any more water? And anywhere private?" She was not going to the bathroom in a cave, at least not one they were staying in and with those two about.

"I can show you to a sheltered spot, and I have fresh water when you come back." Finnian led her around the back of the cave.

Bushes and shrubbery weren't her thing, but you made what you had work. Or so Boan had kept drilling into her head. A small pack was at the edge of the shrubs when she came out, soap, and other necessaries. She had no idea where it came from, but brought it back into the cave with her.

"You found one too? This was outside the front, by a tree." Scruff had been pawing through a pack larger than him. He moved aside as Lizeth started taking things out. Food, nothing exotic, and most of it dried. Water bottles. A small healer kit, a few basic changes of clothes for her—all similar to what she was wearing, but not ones she recognized. And the knives she'd left on her nightstand. She picked them up and frowned at them.

"What's wrong?" Finnian didn't come closer but watched as the items came out.

"I had these in my room. Last night. I only brought the one dagger with me. How did whoever made this bag get them? My sisters were in my room, and they would have noticed." Another thought hit her. "What if this is part of whatever the chancellor is doing? What if they got me out of the way and have taken my sisters?" Having a creative mind helped with creating song magic but wasn't always great in real life.

Scruff had been chewing on a bit of dried apple but stopped to look up. "Do you even know your sisters? I mean, you grew up with them, yes, but do you *know* them? Neither would be taken easily. We probably should have led the Stiklin to them instead of out of the palace." He went back to his apple. Another non-catlike item for the grigeens—they were extreme omnivores and leaned toward fruits, vegetables, and nuts.

"Yes, they can fight, but this is all too weird. They wouldn't have let anyone take my things. And I still don't know why you two are along if this is my Challenge. And where are we?" She felt the hysteria building so she grabbed one of the extra sets of clothes and went behind a rock abutment to change.

"I've walked an hour out and back, didn't want to go too far away in case you had trouble. But I don't recognize this forest. We're not in your kingdom." Finnian was clearly disturbed.

Which made Lizeth disturbed. He might be new to the kingdom, but if anyone should know where they were in the palace woods it should be a forester. "Scruff? Any ideas?" She came out after changing and took some food.

"Not really. My people do know a bit more about the Challenge than your people. We're closer to the oracles than you. But this has never happened in any tales I've heard of. I think figuring out why this is a different Challenge is a part of the Challenge."

Finnian laughed. "Spoken like a true oracle, my friend. My people don't have Challenges, so I'm useless as to what is going on. But I'll help where I can."

"Where *are* your people?" Lizeth didn't mean to sound rude, but if she was stuck with him wherever this was, she should know a bit about him.

Finnian paused long enough for Lizeth to get concerned at what his answer would be. "From Rashia. Small kingdom a month's ride west of here."

"I do know our neighboring kingdoms." Lizeth let some snark come out in her words. "That's a far way to travel for a job as a woodsman, don't you think?"

He shrugged. "I left home years ago and have been traveling and working as I went. Staying in one place for long doesn't appeal to me."

Scruff tilted his head and leaned closer. "You don't look Rashian. They are mostly shorter and stockier."

"My father wasn't from there. When my parents were killed a few years ago, it felt odd to stay." There was something he was holding back.

"Where was your father from?"

"He never said. Neither did my mother. My deep family secret was that my father might have been a criminal from some other land, hiding in Rashia." He rolled his eyes. "No offense to my birth country, but if that had been the case, I'd like to think he would have picked a better country to hide in. Rashia is fairly boring, unless you like farms." He got up and adjusted his sword, bow, and arrows. "If you have no more questions, Princess, I will go search south of us now."

Lizeth stuffed her items into her pack. "And we're going with you." She flashed him a smile. "First, can you show me where you found this pack? And please call me Lizeth while we're on this adventure." She had no idea what was going on, nor why someone like Finnian had been included. But having him be in dealing-with-royalty mode was going to be exhausting for her.

Finnian opened his mouth to argue about some part of what she'd said, then shook his head and shrugged. "Then let's go." He gestured for her and Scruff to crawl out of the cave first then moved to walk ahead of them. "I found the pack here. After Scruff's comment, I was looking for something, but I honestly wasn't expecting it to be this blatant. It might have even been in place last night, but I didn't notice." The doubt at that being the case was clear in his voice.

Lizeth looked around the tree he pointed at. No magic portal that she could tell. Perhaps they were being watched, and since there hadn't been time to get her a pack beforehand, the oracles did so this way. "What's this?" Another pack, a well-used one, sat in a nearby bush. There was no way Finnian could have missed it when he found hers.

"What's...my pack?" Finnian spun around looking for someone who might have left it. "How did my pack get there?" His hand dropped to the hilt of his sword.

Lizeth watched him as he refused to step closer to it. He was willing to accept a pack appearing for her, along with weapons she knew she left in her room—but one of his own upset him. "Are you certain that's yours? Maybe, at least, pick it up?"

His dark brown eyes were wide and he looked a bit paler than before. "How can that be mine?"

Scruff shook his head. "He's a Rashian all right. I'm surprised you even came to our magic-filled land." He gave a rude snort.

"Your people don't believe in magic?" Rashia was far enough away, and not influential enough for her to have spent much time studying them. "You do realize that I held you in the air with nothing but magic, right?" She was surprised he hadn't been more upset about it at the time.

Finnian stalked around the pack, or rather the bush it was sitting in. "We...don't. Okay, I know logically it exists. Wherever my father was from believed in it, but he never used any that I knew about. No one in Rashia does. So, someone went into my cottage, loaded my pack, and brought it here? With magic?"

"Halt! Who goes there? Stop in the name of the empress!" The shout came from some distance away, but from the sound, armored knights on foot were clanking toward them.

"Grab the pack and get us out of here. We don't want to join them," Scruff growled toward the direction the sounds and shouts were coming from.

"Do you know who they are? No adjacent kingdoms have an empress." Lizeth adjusted her pack to be able to run through the forest.

"No idea. But we need to run." Scruff's voice sounded like he might have an idea but wasn't sharing it right now.

Finnian looked between his pack and the knights. He finally grabbed the pack and threw it over his shoulder. "Come this way. We can lose them." He ran, but made sure both Scruff and Lizeth were close behind him.

The knights kept yelling and were getting noticeably closer. But from her quick glance, their armor was bulky and not good for running through thick clumps of trees.

Scruff bounded ahead of both of them as they reached a meadow with heavy forest beyond. "This way." For someone who didn't know where they were, he had a definite idea of where to go. He ran into the dense forest and down a side trail—then he turned through a grove of thin, white-barked trees that grew so close together it was as if they were a single plant. Trees that Lizeth knew she'd never seen in the kingdom before.

Running through these was worse than the rest of the forest and the knights didn't even seem to be trying to catch them at this point. They'd slowed as they approached, then stopped before entering the white trees. Scruff stopped, ran up one of the slender trees, chortled, then dropped to the ground and kept running.

"They stopped chasing us. And I've never seen this kind of tree before." Finnian sounded personally affronted by the latter.

"I will explain. But we need better shelter. One those clanking brutes can't reach." Scruff was looking for something, but it was all delicate white trees as far as the eye could see.

Lizeth was ready to demand Scruff halt and explain himself when he darted to the right.

She hurried to follow, with Finnian close behind. Scruff stopped suddenly, making her stop, which caused the woodsman to skid into her, and both went down in a pile of twisted limbs. Scruff, far faster than the humans, avoided the collision.

Finnian tried to scramble to his feet, but the ends of the leather ties for his wrist bracer got tangled in her hair.

Lizeth started laughing. "No one is going to hang you for mishandling the princess. As long as you don't rip off my hair, I'm not mad at you." She tilted her head around so she could see Scruff. "You, not so much." She tried twisting a bit, her pack wasn't the best thing to be lying on. After a few moments, Finnian freed his bracer tie and got up.

"It's not my fault you humans run on two legs. Four is far more stable." Scruff sat there grinning like he'd gotten into some wine while she got to her feet, dusted herself off, and fixed her hair.

"Why did you stop like that? Where are we?" Lizeth was glad Scruff had gotten them away from the knights, but the idea that this was a Challenge for her, not Scruff or Finnian, kept kicking around in her head. It was hopefully a good sign that Finnian's pack appeared as well, but she knew she needed to be the one facing the Challenge. Whatever that was.

"I am not sure." Scruff held up a clawed paw. "But I have an idea where a safe refuge is. Don't ask. Just follow closely." He gave a smug smile. "I promise not to make you stop suddenly." He didn't wait for her to agree but took off at a jog between the trees. Soon he stopped and looked far too pleased with himself. "Here it is. I knew it had to be here, just look at the trees. Of course, this would be where they'd put it."

Finnian kept looking around for pursuit but focused on the area Scruff was watching. "Put what? There's nothing there, Scruff."

"Oh, ye of little faith." Scruff turned to Lizeth. "Sing, my child. Something of faith, love, and beauty, things lacking right now."

"A spell song?"

"No, not now. Just a song of beauty."

Lizeth shrugged and sang. As she did so the trees before them changed and a delicate cottage appeared out of what looked like thin air. Lizeth kept singing until the vision of the place looked solid, then stopped.

"What is that? Did I make that?" She didn't think any magic crept into her song, but who knew how things worked here.

"It's your safe house. Not all Challenges have them, but when I saw the trees, I felt yours might. You didn't create it, but without your music, we never would have seen it. Now say thank you to the trees and let's get inside."

Chapter Nine

Lizeth led the way to the door. It was odd that even though she'd never seen a house with this design—the roof was extremely peaked and the eaves ended in delicate curls—it felt familiar. She frowned. Like something out of a story her father had read to her when she was a child. "Are you sure my magic didn't create this? This is exactly what the maiden's cottage looked like in the fox with the seven tails story." She stayed on the porch but didn't reach for the door handle.

"Isn't that a child's book?" Scruff was behaving far too innocently. Or rather he was trying to appear innocent. She wasn't sure what he knew that he couldn't tell her. But there was something behind those wide, cat-like, green eyes.

"Yes, as well you know since you used to sit at the foot of the bed while he read it to me. The description was exactly like this. Down to the color of mint green on the shutters." She folded her arms. "Why? And how? Is this all really in my head?"

Finnian followed them up on the porch but turned back to watch the direction where the knights vanished. He kept his hand on his sword and was looking far more like a guardsman than a woodsman. He glanced back at the house. "This is a fairytale house? Where are we?" Considering that he'd been dragged along against his will on a random adventure that he hadn't a clue about, he'd been holding up fairly well. From his voice, that patience and willingness to go along might be coming to an end.

Lizeth might not know him, but she had a feeling that stubborn jaw he had was justified. She didn't need to be fighting with him, trying to figure out Scruff, and sorting out this Challenge all at the same time.

"I can't speak to why this house looks like something from an obscure fairy tale. But it is what it is. Can we please go inside?" Scruff winced and glared at the nearest trees. "The trees are glad you're here, but they can't hold off the people looking for you forever." He tilted his head at the trees. "Unless you want to become part of them. They can do that."

Lizeth looked at the trees and gave them what she hoped was a soothing smile. Aside from the closeness of them they hadn't looked threatening. Until Scruff's words. "Thank you for what you're doing. We'll work this out inside." She reached for the door handle, hoping it wasn't locked, and jumped as a shock ran through her hand and up her elbow. "What in the...it shocked me!" She waved her hand around and the stinging vanished.

She'd barely touched it when it shocked her, but the door popped open and Scruff walked through.

Finnian came up the steps. "After you, Princess. Unless you would prefer to have me guard the trees to make sure they don't attack?" He gave a warm smile but his eyes were laughing.

"No, I believe they are right where they need to be." She flounced as best she could; flouncing in boots and leggings simply didn't have much impact, and went inside. The cottage from the story of the fox with the seven tails only had a description of the outside, but the inside matched it perfectly. Everything was new, but at the same time comfortable and familiar. And if she had been designing an out-of-the-way secret cottage, she would have done it exactly like this. Part of her didn't like that whoever was behind the Challenge was in her head, the other part was glad for the comfort. Not to mention, the chance to not spend another night in a cave.

"Still doubt this was for you?" Scruff had wandered through the entire place—not difficult as it wasn't large—and settled on one of two chairs near a small fireplace. There was also a couch and in the small kitchen, a dining table for four.

"But how? And why? You said it was a Challenge cottage, do all challengers get them? How do you know about prior Challenges anyway since no one is allowed to talk about them when they get back except to others who have already completed them?" Almost against her will, Lizeth drifted down onto the couch. It might have been because they'd spent the night in a cave but this felt like the most comfortable couch she'd ever sat upon. "And please tell me there are beds and a bathroom?" The beds were optional, she might simply fall asleep here. The bathroom was non-negotiable. If there wasn't one, she might have to see if she could spell sing one into existence.

"I found one bedroom, a bathroom, and a storage area. I think our woodsman and I will be sleeping out here. Our appearance might have been a bit unplanned initially." Scruff wandered around the front room, sniffing the furniture. "As for Challenge cottages being for all? No. Some don't need them, some have to spend most of their time in them. The oracles must have felt you needed a boost after your rough start."

Finnian had remained near the window next to the door but finally came away from it. "If these Challenges are all predetermined, set up, etc., how can they have suddenly added the two of us—which, from what you've said, isn't a good thing—and not have planned for it? Your oracle is odd."

"Oracles. Plural. They watch over your country as well. But, being as they are magic, your people probably ignore their existence."

"Just because my people don't rely on magical abilities to get through life, doesn't make us worse. And you still didn't provide a valid argument for the oracles messing up this event." He folded his arms. He was still armed and had only removed his pack.

He also had a familiar stance.

One of Lizeth's jobs as impending first heir was to view the troops. She hadn't noticed it before, but his current stance was military parade rest. She narrowed her eyes. "You can come in and get comfortable. You're not about to be called up for inspection."

Finnian gave a start. "I'm not sure what you mean?" He removed his sword, bow, and quiver, but kept on the large knife.

"You act more like military." Lizeth saw him wince slightly. "*Former* military, then, rather than woodsman. Where did you serve? According to my limited knowledge, Rashia doesn't have a standing army." She stayed on the couch but was ready to sing a spell of holding if he wasn't who he'd claimed to be. Scruff rose to balance on his back feet in his chair and also watched Finnian closely.

"As I said before, I left Rashia years ago. I did serve time in the free army of the Tholian duchy, but I realized that wasn't a life for me, so I resigned and moved on. I would have told you, but I didn't think it was pertinent to our situation." He didn't sit but made an effort to relax his stance. "The training was thorough and, in some situations, automatic."

Lizeth watched him, then smiled. "Such as being thrown into some odd land, on a quest that's not yours, and being chased by knights in heavy armor? Justifiable. But Scruff and I grew up together, so we know each other quite well. If there is anything else in your past that could be important, you need to tell us. Even if you might not think it is. It might save your life, or ours." As she released it, she noticed that the spell of holding she'd called up was more powerful than she'd expected. Which brought up another issue. What if her magic behaved differently here than back home? Boan had tried to make her prepared for any contingency, but he couldn't have predicted all of them. As the spell released, she realized it might have held Finnian all right, about fifteen feet in the air regardless of the number of trees in that same space. She could have hurt him badly. Or worse.

"And that face isn't good. What's wrong?" Scruff decided that Finnian was okay again and settled back into his chair by the fire.

"Nothing." Then she glanced to Finnian. Not fair to demand the truth from him while she kept secrets. "Fine. I had been holding a spell song in reserve right now and as I released it, I realized it was more powerful than I intended." She shrugged. She knew how big of an issue that could be, but hopefully Scruff wouldn't mention it. Advantage of Finnian being from a non-magic country—he'd have little background on magic issues. Had she not been looking at him closely, she would have missed the brief widening of his eyes. Not a look of fear though. Something else that vanished quickly.

"I'll take your word for it being an issue, I don't know much about magic." Finnian turned to Scruff. "Now, we're here; where are we, and what do we have to do?"

Lizeth watched him. There was something he wasn't saying. Coming right after an open plea to share things, that meant it was something serious and not something he would give up easily. She'd need to watch him carefully about magic issues.

"That is a darn good question." Lizeth also looked toward Scruff. "Why me?"

"Because you've already indicated more knowledge than I have about these things. More than anyone who hasn't been through one of these things should have, I might add. Not to mention, you said you'd tell us what you knew once we were inside." She shook her head. "I realize that this Challenge might have been changed from the norm. It's certainly not remotely like I was expecting. There's never been a history of a challenger going off without a formal ceremony and preparation, for one thing. For some reason, my timeline was expedited." She got up to pace, it helped her think sometimes. "Maybe since the fact that something changed my timing, it meant the oracles couldn't give me the preparation I would need, so they included you two. Finnian as a protector and Scruff as a teacher." She folded her arms and tilted her head at Scruff. "So, teach."

Scruff curled his tail about him, lowered his ears, and looked guilty of a variety of things. And annoyed at being caught.

"I made the same conclusion when we were all pulled through whatever it was we went through to get here. As far as I knew, according to the oracles, you should have gone through normal Challenge procedures and then been sent off—alone—at the appointed time. I was as surprised as you two to be pulled through here. I'm operating on instinct about all of this."

Finnian sat on the other chair. "Who would have been taken along to help protect if I hadn't run into you? Or would it have been me no matter where I was? I don't like any of this. Not to mention those knights chasing us follow an empress? No nearby country has an emperor or empress."

"There is a massive empire across the ocean. Could we have been sent there?" Lizeth racked her brain for what she knew about that land—it was next to nothing. She promised to pay more attention to Boan if they got back. *When* they got back, she corrected herself.

"The Offialian empire?" Scruff's face wasn't designed for scowls but that didn't stop him. "I don't see why. The point of the Challenge is to test the new heir, to make sure they can successfully adapt to challenges and control their abilities. These Challenges have always been small and unique in design. Sending you to an empire that no one from Astarious has had contact with in centuries would be a first."

Lizbeth spun on her heel. "Which brings us back to where are we? How did you recognize the forest and those odd white trees? How can I resolve anything if we're hiding here? And as nice as it is here, how long are we expected to stay?" She paced her way to the kitchen. The nicely well-stocked kitchen. There were enough supplies to last the three of them for months. Not good, in her opinion, for a Challenge that shouldn't last more than a week.

"That's supposed to be made clear during the introduction event. If the oracles thought Finnian and I could take the place of your preparation, they were extremely wrong." Scruff wandered into the kitchen, pulled out a fresh apple from a bowl, and happily chewed away. "As for recognizing the area, it was instinct. There was an odd familiarity to the cave and the forest we landed in—but I couldn't tell you where it came from."

"Concerned that the three of us are stuck somewhere unknown with no way out and you eat?" Lizeth shook her head but did pick up a wrapped loaf of bread, some honey, and jam. "Actually, we might as well join him. Our breakfast wasn't great and we were running. Let's take advantage of this while we can."

All three settled in to eat and Lizeth studied the thin white trees through the window. They weren't menacing really, but there was something odd about them. She felt like she should know them, but it wasn't anything she could grasp.

They stayed lost in their thoughts as they finished eating. Scruff still out ate her and Finnian, but Finnian held his own. Lizeth watched him for a while. She knew little about him, yet he was here to protect her? There was a charm there, a quirk to his smile. Now that he wasn't so grubby looking, she admitted she could see why some women might find him attractive. Thick dark brown hair that fell into his eyes enough to lend a boyish charm. His brown eyes were warm and gentle. His features were pleasing and he was in excellent shape if the way his shirt pulled when he moved was any indication.

And she needed to stop thinking of him that way. Even in a purely scientific manner. Maybe he was trying to make her be attracted to him for some nefarious reason.

She narrowed her eyes.

"Do I have food on my chin?" Finnian took a napkin and wiped it. "Or were you staring through me in royal thought?" He didn't sound upset, but he was mocking her.

Lizeth was embarrassed at being caught but drew herself up. "A princess never stares through anyone; they are peering into the distance and surveying their domain." Her laugh at the end ruined the effect. "I never could get haughty down right."

"I wouldn't say that." Finnian shook his head. "You were pretty haughty when you hung me up in the air."

"That was for startling me. I'd been trying to think deep thoughts about the canyon, and the meaning of it all, when you approached." She shrugged. "I was vexed. What was the creature you said you'd been after?"

Finnian's face darkened. "I wish I knew. Something had been attacking deer on the edge of the forest near the canyon. Usually at night, and they took most of the ones they killed. But they were ripped apart and some parts were left behind. Parts that a normal predator wouldn't have wasted."

Scruff had been toying with more food, but looked up at that. "An animal like that in our forest? That couldn't have happened. My people would have known."

"I thought the grigeens stayed in your woods behind the castle? My people said you were more like royal pets." The look on Finnian's face said he regretted the words the moment he said them. "That's what they said anyway. Obviously, they were wrong."

Scruff lifted one corner of his lip to show his canine teeth. "We have not been, nor ever will be, pets. To anyone. We have lived in agreement with the royal family of Astarious after we joined in battle a long time ago. Most of my people were lost and they offered us a partnership and a place to live." He savagely chomped a bunch of grapes.

"I'm sorry that your people were killed."

"We don't know they were killed. It is believed so, but there had been great magic in this battle and they vanished. That was a few hundred years ago, when the kingdom was new, but they have never been seen again."

That silenced all of them. Lizeth finally picked up her pack and went to the bedroom. "I need a bath. Then I think all of us should take an early rest. Tomorrow I want to explore the forest and beyond—we have to find out where we are. And what it is I'm supposed to do."

"But those knights. Empress or not, those knights were extremely well armed." Finnian wasn't a coward, at least from what Lizeth could tell so far. He was a pragmatist.

"On one level, I agree with you. However, this Challenge can't be finished if I can't start it. To start it we have to figure out where we are. And leave this cottage." She turned to Scruff and folded her arms. "Am I correct that in other Challenges, the challenger finds clues as they progress?"

"Yes, but we have no idea how much changed in this one. Nor why. I won't lie, it's not good that something caught the oracles off guard like this." Scruff chewed on his tail, a certain sign he was upset.

That was unsettling. Lizeth made a mental note of it, then set it aside. This Challenge would be met with grace and planning—like everything else in her life. Whether the Challenge wanted it or not. "As I said, I will be retiring. Please make yourselves comfortable, you may use the bathroom when I have finished for your evening ablutions." She gave a royal nod. "Good evening, gentlemen."

She went in to the bathroom, took a quick bath, then went into the bedroom and flung herself on the bed. Her tears weren't out of fear, but frustration. This wasn't the Challenge she'd imagined, and while she was grateful for Scruff being trapped in it with her, she wasn't sure about Finnian. She was also worried about her sisters and her parents. Hopefully all of the Stiklins had followed them through whatever they fell through and died when they vanished. But what if there were more? How had they even gotten there?

Chapter Ten

Lizeth slept fitfully as her dreams were invaded by Stiklin hordes attacking her family and tearing apart the kingdom, all while she watched from a throne, unable to help. Her mother had always said to think happy thoughts before going to bed so she'd have happy dreams.

As Lizeth woke up from the latest nightmare, she wished she'd listened more to her mother. Thinking about everything that had gone wrong in the past two days as she fell asleep wasn't a good idea.

She got dressed and crept out of the bedroom. She had no idea what time it was but if the other two were sleeping she would try to let them remain so. She wasn't selfish enough to ignore the fact that while this situation was upsetting to her, it *was* her Challenge. Neither Scruff nor Finnian should have been involved. If she got a chance to speak to the oracles, she was going to give them an earful.

Her silence was unnecessary, as both were in the kitchen, sitting at the small table talking softly. Scruff said something to make Finnian laugh and the change in his features at a full, unguarded laugh was terrifying. He went from attractive to stunning. She might have to forbid laughing during the Challenge—it was nice to have a former soldier to help protect her and Scruff, but she didn't need a distraction like him.

When the Challenge was over, she would find a suitable husband of the required royal lineage. She did not need a scruffy woodsman meddling with that. When she was younger, flirting and casual dating was fine and harmless, but she was of age now, and that playtime was over. She gave a cough in case they were discussing anything they wouldn't want her to hear.

"Good morning, Princess." Finnian gave a half bow from where he sat. "I rescued breakfast for you from the voracious Scruff."

He started to get to his feet, but she shook him off. "Thank you, I can seat myself. I think we probably should make no reference to who I really am when we go out. We've no idea what the people in this land are like." Nor, for that matter, where they were.

Finnian frowned and waved a piece of bread toward the window. "They have an active militia; of that, I know. I woke early so I went out past the white trees. There are patrols going through the forest, but they are still staying clear of the white trees. I don't get it though; they are still armored knights on foot. I could see you wouldn't want to run a bunch of horses through that forest, but for that same reason you wouldn't want to be wearing armor. Not to mention, they are not successful at moving silently."

Lizeth took the plate of food he'd saved for her and sat. He'd also made tea and she gratefully took a few sips to clear her head of her nightmares. "Can we avoid them completely? No offense, but I would be much happier if I knew what my Challenge was and got it over with without interacting with those knights. We need to get back home as soon as possible."

"I think we can avoid them." Scruff responded as Finnian opened his mouth to answer. "However, our woodsman wants us to be careful, map out where the knights are marching, and wait days until we know where their patrol breaks are." He actually smiled at Finnian. Grigeens' smiles were disturbing to most people not familiar with them as they had a lot of teeth. But Finnian laughed. Obviously, the two had done some bonding.

"Sorry, Finnian, I agree with caution in most things." Lizeth ignored Scruff's laughter. "But I'm with Scruff on this. We're in a foreign land, one none of us recognize, and I have some sort of mystical Challenge to solve. Plus, we've no idea what's happening at home. Time is crucial."

"I don't like how many unknowns we're dealing with." Finnian frowned.

She smiled. "You were a strategist in the military, weren't you? My mother is one and she's said variations of those words since the day I was born. Normally, I'd agree. In theory, at any rate. Having things planned out does make things neater. But we don't have time for it."

Scruff moved closer and put his paw on her hand. "Your family is probably safer than we are right now. The king and queen should be back and they do have an entire army at their disposal."

"But the bodies...you're right. We should worry about us at this point. So, what is your grand plan, Scruff?"

"We go out the back door." He nodded and tapped the side of his head as if he was brilliant.

She looked to Finnian. "Is there ale in this cottage? Did he drink it? Grigeens can't hold their liquor."

"I haven't been drinking. Although, I might have if they had stocked any—those oracles can be sanctimonious." He held his insulted look for a few seconds, then shook it off. "The back door of this place leads to a river. Most societies build their towns near rivers. Therefore, if we float downstream a bit we can find out where we are and what you need to do." He looked far too smug with himself.

"Float on what? And what if the knights have archers? That river would have to be exceptionally wide for them not to shoot at us as we floated by." Lizeth finished her food and went for more bread and tea.

"Well, we have a woodsman." Scruff pointed to Finnian, who rolled his eyes. "And as we are in the middle of a large wood, he could probably build us a small boat. Actually, there is one started on the side of this place; he only needs to finish it. And as you so often point out, you do have some magic skills. I believe Boan was coaching you on an invisibility spell a few weeks ago."

Lizeth put down her toast. That spell was possibly one of the most complicated known in the world of magic. After a week of lessons, and failures, she told him she simply couldn't learn it. That wasn't completely right. She understood the spell and could sing the soft lullaby that created it. But it always felt like she was being pulled from this world when she gave it power. Plus, it gave her a horrible headache. "No. I can't. That's too complicated. And what happens if the invisibility spell drops in the middle of the river? Or worse, the middle of town? And how far is town? Do you realize how hard it is to sing a spell for any length of time? Let alone something like that one?"

Scruff rolled his eyes and turned to Finnian. "And this is how she gets when she is afraid of something but doesn't want people to know she is."

"Yes, I'm afraid I'll be the death of us all. That would be a bit unfortunate." She wasn't denying she was afraid. They needed to do something, she agreed with Scruff about that. But sailing down into possibly hostile lands protected only by a spell she'd never mastered wasn't her idea of something. It was idiocy. "There must be a third option."

The debate went through two more pots of tea before Scruff finally won. Sort of. The partial boat he'd found had been a small two-person fishing boat once upon a time but was now falling apart. Finnian looked it over and suggested making it flatter with a low rim. The river wasn't that deep and he could make a few poles to move the boat down the river. If they stayed near shore, it should work fine.

"It'll take me a few hours to build it. And when we're on the water, Scruff stays in the middle." He wasn't happy, but he was already working on taking the boat apart. Finnian waved a piece of wood at Scruff. "You get distracted a lot. And that river is fast. If you fall off, we won't be able to go back for you. And Lizeth will need to pole as well as sing. Can you do that?"

She smiled. "The poling is the least of my worries, so yes, I can. As the afternoon is already starting to age, and I'd rather spend the night here, I am going into my room and practice making the bed invisible." She started to turn back toward the door, but spun around. "A word of warning, once we are on the water and I'm singing, neither of you can disturb me at all. The poling will be fine, it's an automatic function. But my mind will be focusing on the spell—any disruption could prove disastrous for us all."

Scruff solemnly nodded, and although he looked confused, Finnian did as well.

Lizeth left them to their boat making and went inside. The invisible spell had an official magical name, but like most of those long-winded and dusty sounding names, she'd forgotten it. She just knew she hated it. It always seemed to tickle the back of her mind—like there was something she should know about it, but the knowledge stayed out of reach. Extremely annoying.

After clearing her throat, running a few scales, and some simple singing exercises, she admitted to herself she was stalling. With a steady breath, she started singing the invisibility spell. It was a light melody, Boan said, because it worked on the people who heard it as much as actually changing the visible spectrum the spell-enclosed item could be seen in. Although soft and light, the spell was powerful enough that it could only be consciously heard by someone standing right next to the spell caster. Which was handy as it meant no one would hear you and ruin the effect of not seeing you.

She'd gotten her bed to flicker at the edges, looking like it was starting to shrink, when the walls shook. Her focus was on the spell so she was off balance and fell. Scrambling to her feet, and swearing under her breath if Scruff or Finnian had anything to do with what happened, she ran out the bedroom door.

There was nothing wrong in the front room, so she kept running.

Finnian and Scruff were under attack by a pair of nathrachas—at least five feet long, deadly snakes. She'd only seen them in books growing up as they had been eradicated in her kingdom hundreds of years ago—obviously that didn't happen here. All of Finnian's weapons were still inside the cottage, but he was holding his own, fighting to keep the vicious jaws of one of them from biting him. One of the monsters was against the wall and looked dead—that must have been what caused the shaking. It was large enough to have taken some plaster down with it when it was flung there.

Scruff was using tooth, claw, and speed to keep his opponent at bay. She debated running back in and grabbing Finnian's sword, but then two more of the monsters came out of the forest and joined in the attack against Finnian.

This was it; she'd trained defensive and offensive spell songs for this moment.

And she froze.

Lizeth opened her mouth to sing a spell song and nothing came out. Terror flooded her. There was nothing in her mind. Those things were going to kill her friends and she could do nothing. Finnian yelled as one of the snakes bit him in the thigh. Scruff had finished off the one he fought and dove to help, but Finnian was already collapsing from the poison.

Lizeth ran forward. She'd pull them off by hand if she had to.

No. Better to send them flying. That spell came to mind and she sang it loud and as powerfully as she could. She wanted those things gone. Preferably up past the level of air to breathe.

The nathrachas all turned toward her, hissing, but she kept singing. The massive snakes were pulled into the air and kept going until even in the clear area away from the trees, she couldn't see them. She waited a few more minutes, then stopped singing.

She let out a sigh of relief at sending them away, but then saw that Finnian was curled in a ball and twitching. She ran over. "I'm sorry! I froze. I couldn't do it."

Scruff grabbed the sleeve of her arm. "Right now, that's neither here nor there. I need to get some herbs to stop this, but you need to sing him to rest. It will slow the poison."

Doubt grabbed her. "But I can't..." She bit her lip at the look Scruff gave her and started singing. The pain in Finnian's face faded. This wouldn't heal him, but it should slow his body down. There were some practitioners who could drop a person into a deep coma with a few lines of song. She needed to keep him alive until Scruff got back. She'd deal with the magnitude of her failure after they saved him.

Chapter Eleven

Finnian's twitching slowed and his body unclenched from the tight ball he'd curled into. His eyes stayed closed, and she doubted he was aware of her or anything around him. Nathracha poison acted to subdue the victim and destroy them from the inside. It also sped up the victim's heart rate until their heart exploded. Then the snakes would feed.

Lizeth pushed all of that information aside as she kept singing out the spell song of peace. There was a song of healing as well, but she didn't want to try it and make things worse for whatever Scruff was bringing back. If the plants he was hunting for were magical, they could react poorly with the magic she'd use in a healing song. Not to mention, she wasn't as sure of it as she should be. She'd been cocky about having the spell singing abilities to face anything the Challenge threw at her—but she'd figured on only having to worry about herself, not others.

The spell song for peace seemed to be keeping him calm and she added to it with a light sleep spell. Those could be dangerous, but she needed the reinforcement to keep his heart rate down as the poison fought her to raise it.

A scrabbling in the tall grass behind her split her focus as she raised her hand to throw a fire spell. She froze before, that wouldn't happen again.

Scruff removed the large clump of plant life he carried in his mouth. "Easy, it's me." He ran forward and started putting the plants on the wound in Finnian's leg. He also brought over a small rock and sat it next to Finnian. "Good job, you kept him calm and slowed the poison. Now we have to get it out." He looked at her expectantly.

"Isn't that what the plants are for?"

"The plants will work like your peace spell, slow things down. Now, you simply have to get the poison into the rock and he should be on the road to recovery." He gave a reassuring smile and nod.

"Is that all?" Lizeth held up her hands. "Of course, that's all I have to do. Easy peasy. Just zap all the poison into a rock. Learned that spell as a kid." She folded her arms. "Oh wait, I didn't, because *there is no such spell*." She was doing good at keeping her complete breakdown at bay, but that wasn't going to be true much longer.

"There isn't because it hasn't been invented yet. All spells start somewhere, you know." Again, the reassuring smile and nod that were actually neither.

"Scruff, creating a new spell takes months, if not years, of focus, testing, and more testing. I've never done it."

He gave a long exhale through his nose. "Have you ever been on a Challenge before? We don't know where we are, how we got here, or why Finnian and I are here with you. This is new territory for all of us." He pointed to Finnian, no longer twitching but growing paler. "He doesn't deserve to die because you are afraid."

Lizeth blinked to keep the tears from going past her eyes. He was right. She thought she could be a queen and now she was too scared to think beyond her training to save someone? She didn't deserve to be queen. She drew herself up and pretended this was a test from Boan. Not life or death—only a test. "I'll need the essence of the poison." The nathracha that Scruff had killed lay on the ground, so she went to it and bent down. A hummed summoning spell brought the poison's essential elements to her. She couldn't describe them, but they built an image in her mind. Then she walked to Finnian and touched his bare arm. What elements made up Finnian also made an image.

She sat cross-legged near Finnian and the rock and wove her spell song. She called out to anything that was not Finnian, focusing specifically on the parts that were the poison. She used a will-o-wisp spell song to lead those into the rock. It felt like it took days and the poison was slow to move. Then she noticed the rock glowed a deep red. With a sigh she fell over, not unconscious, just too tired to move.

Staying on the nice grass felt good. She felt like she'd run ten miles, but she was okay. Her mind was already storing the spell to share with Boan and the rest of the magic community when she got back.

Finnian sat up, blinking and bleary-eyed, but no longer pale. "What happened? Princess?" He scrambled over to her side along with Scruff. "Are you injured?"

"She saved your life. Made up a brand-new spell and everything." Scruff peered closely at her. "You planning on staying there long? There might be a seriously bad kickback from creating something new magically, might be best to be inside if it hits."

Lizeth really wanted to stay on the cool grass. But he was right; while she'd never created a spell before, she'd read of the consequences. New spells meant a new form of magic had entered the world—and often the creator was quite ill as their spell found its way in the magical world. She started to get up, but the world went sideways.

Finnian grabbed her and lifted her up.

"You're still weak, I can walk." She didn't actually believe that; her legs were overcooked noodles at the moment. However, Finnian was recently pulled back from death—that had to be worse.

He adjusted his hold and started walking to the cottage. There wasn't a waver in his step or the arms that carried her. "Unlike you, I'm fine now. I'm not sure what you did, but I do know I was dying. You saved me. The least I can do is get you to the couch."

Scruff nudged open the door and Finnian got her inside and gently put her down. "What else might she need?" He looked to Scruff.

"An herbal tea; roxlina root, bright purple leaves, I saw the container of it in the cabinets. Handy that it happened to be here." The look on his face indicated he didn't think the placement was coincidental at all. "And she needs to stay down." He added the last bit as Lizeth started to sit up. "Seriously. I'll sit on you if I have to."

"Aside from some exhaustion and a bit of dizziness, I feel fine." Lizeth stopped trying to get up however. Scruff was too heavy to comfortably sit on anyone.

"Uh huh. Because you've created so many new spells in your young life, you know exactly what's going on." Scruff peered at her closely and snorted. "Putting a new spell into the world is not something to be taken lightly."

Finnian came over to the couch and set down a teapot and one cup on the small table next to it.

Scruff sniffed the tea, then nodded. "She needs to drink as much as we can get into her. Then rest. We weren't going to be able to leave today anyway."

Lizeth took a sip of the tea and tried to put the cup back down without tossing it. "That tastes like dirt, ash from a fire, and some weird sour plant. It's nasty."

Scruff blocked her move to set the cup down. "Tough. Not everything is honey and roses, you have to drink it—as is."

Lizeth frowned. When he'd mentioned honey, she thought that might help. He'd caught her reaction and shook his head. "This stuff is probably why no one creates new spells." She held her breath and forced some more down. "Could I at least get something to eat? Might cut the taste a bit." It was truly vile. She promised to never again create a new spell if this would just go away.

Finnian headed for the kitchen but Scruff verbally cut him off. "Nothing more than plain bread." He looked down at her with a wince. "Trust me. You're not going to like having anything in your stomach."

Finnian brought out the bread. "If nothing else is needed, I'm going to finish our boat."

"But there could be more nathrachas out there." Lizeth didn't try to get up but she noticed Scruff moving closer in case she was going to.

"I can get some more glotbane, that plant Scruff found. It works to keep them away as well as having other properties. I'll spread a layer of it around this cabin and where I'm working." He gave a grimace. "They have those things in Rashia, only in the wild northern forest, but my people do know them."

Scruff nodded. "Be careful. And if you could come back in a bit to help carry her into bed, that would be good."

Lizeth sipped some more of the vile brew, then started crying once Finnian had shut the door behind him. Saving his life was one thing, letting him see her breakdown was another entirely.

Scruff jumped on the couch next to her legs. "Are you okay?"

"I froze. Scruff, at the time I needed to be strong and protect the two of you, *I froze.*" She hiccupped as the sobs grew worse. "You both could have died...and *I stood there*! I can't be queen; I shouldn't even be in the royal family." She knew there would have been no way either of her sisters would have frozen. Of course, neither depended as much on magic as she did, but she did nothing. She didn't even throw rocks at the things. "Can we end the Challenge? I'm not worthy." She finished the rest of the nasty tea in her cup—fitting punishment for a coward.

Scruff watched her expressionlessly for a few moments, then licked his paw. "Are you done? Any more failings you want to admit? That you are not perfect will come as such a shock to the oracles and your family." The sarcasm was thick.

"What? I failed, Scruff. Trained my entire life and I failed. You could have died. Finnian could have died."

"Yes, you did. And you will again, I assure you. It doesn't mean you are a failure, nor that you're not worthy. It means you need to learn who you really are and to trust her. You're far more than who you present yourself to be. But you don't believe in her. Too much palace song mage and not enough real Lizeth."

Lizeth poured herself another cup. Her mouth was mostly numb now, so the taste wasn't so bad. "But my parents—"

"Both of them messed up hugely in their youth. And your sisters will as well. Being royal doesn't mean you're perfect. It means that the needs of others come first, and nothing, even yourself, can stand in the way of that."

Lizeth nodded, then noticed Scruff seemed further away. "And I did make a spell, a new one." Her words sounded slurred even in her head.

"You did. But don't get cocky about it. Accept your losses and your wins, but don't let either define you." He grabbed her tea cup as it tilted.

"Smart Scruff." She sighed. "I'm so sleepy." The world slid sideways and then went dark.

Chapter Twelve

Lizeth woke in the bedroom, stumbled to the bathroom, got violently ill, and crawled back to bed. Her dreams were almost worse than the being sick part. Vague, disjointed, and generally off balance. They left her feeling groggy and confused, but there was nothing she could pin it on. Aside from having a pretty awful few days.

If she were back in the palace and something threw her off this badly, she'd order her favorite foods to be sent to her room, and simply read novels all day.

Sadly, that wasn't even an option to consider. This place had felt like a shelter, and it was, but something inside her knew they needed to get moving.

She swung to get out of bed and the world twisted the opposite direction. She lurched to the bathroom to be ill again and gave herself a strong talking to in the mirror. She was a princess—being sick right now wasn't going to work. Then she bathed, and her hands only shook a little as she dressed.

The other two were talking softly in the front room. She'd tell them they needed to leave today. This cottage might have been made from a favorite childhood memory, but she couldn't help but feel it was evil. Or at least a threat.

Finnian was packing food supplies and putting back things Scruff kept trying to sneak in. "I told you, we need to keep things light. Go for food that will travel well, has high nutritional value, and is compact."

"Taste is important too. How long will we be out there? You might live on dried goods, I can't." Scruff sat on his well-fed back haunches and glared.

"You need to adapt, Scruff." Lizeth came out and took a fresh apple out of his hands. Seeing the two of them chased away the vestiges of her odd and vague dreams. "Finnian is right. Unless you're planning on carrying the packs?"

"Well, no way I can really do that, is there?" He snatched another fresh apple and took a bite before she could grab it. "I can eat this before we leave, you know."

Finnian finished stuffing the smaller pack and handed it to her. "I left room for your things on top." He adjusted the second, much larger pack, for himself.

Wanting to get out of that cottage as quickly as possible motivated Lizeth into the fastest packing time ever—not that she had much to pack. "Do we ride with packs on or off?" The hair at the back of her neck was rising with the need to leave. At this point she would swim to get out of here. It might not be the cottage's fault at all, but something was wrong in this place.

"I think I can balance everyone better with the packs off and stacked in the center of the boat. And I found some netting to wrap around them. If we take a spill, grabbing one giant bundle will be easier." He opened the door and bowed. "After you, Princess."

"I told you, call me Lizeth." She wasn't certain why he was reverting to the princess bit, but there had been something odd lurking in his eyes since she saved him. Something had definitely changed.

"As you wish." He smiled and waited for her to leave. Scruff shrugged and went through, so she followed.

He came up behind them as they stood gawking at their boat.

"You did that in a few hours? After almost being killed?" The simple flat boat was larger than she thought it would be, but didn't look like the size would cause a problem in the river. The sides were higher than expected, coming to right above Lizeth's knee, and had multiple brace areas for the people poling to get leverage. But what got to Lizeth was how well-crafted it was. "It's cute." It was far more than that, but that was the first thing out of her mouth.

"Cute?" He turned to her and laughed. "Not what I was going for, but any job worth doing is worth doing right."

"And he didn't stop until almost midnight." Scruff approached the boat and sniffed it. "I gave him some lights to keep working. Then I went to sleep."

"That was above and beyond. Thank you." Lizeth smiled and was surprised when he blushed and turned away quickly.

When he faced her again, he had recovered. "The least I can do for a royal princess who saved my life. Now, let's push it into the water, solve this Challenge of yours, and get back home."

Lizeth joined him in getting the netting-covered packs anchored to the center of the boat. He secured the knots on the netting, then Scruff jumped on as well and they pushed it into the river. But she watched Finnian. He'd not seemed to be concerned about her royal status before, so why now? When he took up a poling stance as far away from her as possible, she narrowed her eyes, but said nothing.

If need be, she'd get Scruff to find out what his issue was. It wasn't that she was concerned on a personal level, it was the principle. He was part of this group, and like it or not, she feared they'd need to work together to get out of this mess.

The river was quiet, and Lizeth didn't feel like breaking that with talking. She would wait until they were underway before casting the invisibility spell. She wasn't certain how long she could hold it, so waiting until it was needed was the best option.

Besides, she needed to work on memorizing the spell she'd made to remove the poison from Finnian. She thought she had committed it to memory when she first cast it, but it already felt as if it were spiraling away. As if her memory wasn't enough to hold it. Writing wouldn't work as supposedly nothing could come back with the challenger. So she fought to make each aspect part of its own song, and that made it easier to remember. She was proud of her new spell, but still horrified at her freezing when she was needed. No matter what Scruff said, she wasn't going to forget what happened for a long time.

The white trees around the cottage gave way to a dense forest of pine. An old forest. The woods around the palace back home were carefully maintained to give the illusion of wilderness but were in fact carefully curated by people such as Finnian. Lizeth would have been hard pressed to tell the difference before, but she wouldn't be anymore. These trees held a power she could almost taste.

It wasn't that the forest felt evil, just exceptionally old. The trees felt like they had more spirit in them than the ones back home.

"They are different, aren't they? The woods back home used to be like this. Strong and fierce." Scruff's face fell. "Then they were cleared in a battle long ago. They never came back the same."

"It feels like they're watching us." Lizeth poled from the back and opposite side as Finnian. She'd never done anything like this before, but she was a quick mimic.

"They are." Finnian kept looking ahead. "This forest is old and powerful, with a strength lost to time. I've heard of places like these, even those of us without magic can feel them."

Lizeth reached out to the trees, a soft song of greeting. At first there was no response, then a wave of curiosity flowed over her. It was like having her soul licked by a dozen puppies. She laughed and almost dropped her pole.

"Easy there, tree whisperer." Scruff brought her back to the job at hand. "Might be time for your hiding spell if you feel comfortable enough to reach out to the local plant life."

Finnian glanced back. "Good idea. Judging by the increase in distant homesteads, we're getting closer to a town."

Lizeth couldn't see anything down the way beyond the river and more trees. She'd take his word for it. "I'll need you two to keep as still and quiet as possible." She took a deep breath, there was no way this would be easy. But she did make up a spell on the spot, right? Sadly that thought wasn't as comforting as it could be.

Focusing on the spell, on the stillness of being invisible, helped chase away the last bits of guilt she had about freezing. Oh, it was still there—but it was locked away until she could face it head on. Preferably when she was safe back home in her chambers surrounded by masses of baked goods and chocolate.

She kept her poling movements automatic, a repetition her body would continue on its own once she turned inward to her spell. Then she closed her eyes and sang the song, opening them when she felt it was in place. There was no way to verify success with her eyes, or those of her companions. They would still see each other since they were in the spell bubble. But she felt it snap into place. Boan would be proud as they came into view of a small fishing village and the children gathering small stones near the water's edge didn't even look up as they passed.

She realized she'd been holding her breath and released it quietly. Finnian nodded and they kept going.

Scruff stayed in the center near the netted packs, but his tail lashed at something off to the right side of the river. The same side their cottage had been on. Lizeth kept softly singing her spell, but watched where he looked. A flash of metal in between the trees almost made her drop her spell song.

Knights.

They were marching along the river, but not near the bank, they also didn't seem to be trying to hide in the forest. Speaking would be problematic since she needed to keep a low level of the spell song going. But Scruff looked over to her with a frown. She shook her head—she didn't think the knights knew where they were.

Could dealing with the knights be her Challenge? Perhaps her Challenge was more about diplomacy and dealing with them, and the empress behind them. That would definitely be perfect with her training in mediation and dealing with other kingdoms. Running, hiding, and fighting off nathrachas was definitely not.

She kept singing but a soft sigh escaped. Diplomacy was normally one of her best skills. Which meant it probably wouldn't be what was being tested in a Challenge. Then again, she should never have people with her on the Challenge either, so who knew what was going to happen. She was ready to face whatever was coming—but she hated waiting.

The knights veered off deeper into the forest. Finnian had been watching the village as they passed and the scowl on his face wasn't good. She made a mental note to ask him once they could stop again.

The river continued past two more villages, both surrounded by farms. No one noticed them and there were no more signs of the knights.

Lizeth found a soothing pattern between the poling and the spell singing. Part of her felt like she could keep it up forever, but a tiny voice—sounding a lot like Boan—pointed out that fatigue had been the death of many spell casters. Once she thought about it, she realized they'd been on the water for a few hours. Scruff was sound asleep on the packs, and Finnian looked to be locked in a daze. That wasn't good. She could only see his face in profile, but he really wasn't moving beyond breathing and poling. His eyes were locked open and staring directly ahead.

She could check for outside spells, but it would mean dropping her own and exposing them. Now that she was paying attention, she felt a vague spell slipping around them. Had she not been focusing on the invisibility spell she'd probably be struck like Finnian.

Who now seemed to be poling faster.

If there was a spell, and whoever was behind it wanted them to get to wherever this river was taking them faster, they needed to go ashore. Immediately.

There were no villages or people around that she could see, but she didn't have a choice. She took a breath, dropped her invisibility spell, and stuck her pole hard into the river bottom.

The spell that had felt vague while under her own one of invisibility, was now painfully clear. A compulsion spell. That Scruff was sound asleep could have been a reaction to it, or just sleeping. Grigeens reacted differently to most human magic. The spell was a command to continue down to a swamp a mile ahead.

She dug in even harder with her pole as Finnian unconsciously fought to keep moving. She had a spell to break the compulsion one, but exhaustion was already hitting her and she didn't trust her ability to cast it. She pulled up her pole, ran to Finnian, and tackled him. Both poles stayed in the boat but hers landed on Scruff.

A second later arrows started flying over their heads.

Chapter Thirteen

"What did you do that for?" Scruff leapt to his feet and shook out his fur. An arrow missed him by inches, so he flattened out against the bottom of the boat.

Finnian blinked repeatedly, rolled out from under her, and crept to the rim of their boat. "I don't see them, but there's thick cover over there. I meant to stop at the first bend after we launched...how did we pass it?" That he didn't question her tackling him was both good and bad. Could be residual from the compulsion spell.

"We were spelled and have been traveling for a few hours. We have to get off the river." She grabbed both poles, but there would be no way to stand up to use them. Whoever was firing at them might be well hidden, but they had a lot of archers and arrows.

"I can't get us to the other side without poling." Finnian kept blinking and shaking his head. The compulsion spell was obviously lingering.

Lizeth felt spell exhaustion in her bones, but she really didn't think they wanted to be caught, or killed, by whoever was shooting at them. "Both of you stay down, and hang on. I'll get us out of here, but I might pass out after." She didn't give them a chance to respond, or in Scruff's case, protest—he would be able to sense her magic exhaustion and from the look on his face he was going to object.

She let loose a guidance song to send them to the other side of the river. She kept her voice low, but like most spell songs it had to be vocalized. The boat took off as if a giant was pushing it. Steering wasn't good since she stayed on the floor of the boat, so she really couldn't see much, but she was able to get it away from the archers and to the other side.

Finnian looked pale when they crashed ashore and Scruff's eyes were wide. She might have had less control over the speed than she thought.

"We need to get out of here." Which would be easier if her legs would work. She tried pushing herself up—nope, arms weren't working either. On the plus side she hadn't passed out.

Finnian grabbed the net with their packs and flung it ashore. Scruff peered into her eyes and scowled.

"She's overdrawn her magic and is exhausted. You'll have to carry her." He looked too annoyed for her to point out that she didn't have much of a choice.

Finnian kept watching the way they'd come as he quickly scooped her up and got off the boat. "We need to destroy this so it doesn't point out where we left the river. We came a good distance down from where they ambushed us, but if those archers have horses, it won't take them long to follow." He sat her down on a rock, then took out a small axe and started hacking the boat apart.

"Let me try a small spell—"

"No." Both Scruff and Finnian kept their voices low as they cut her off.

Finnian hacked a few more times in the center of the boat, then kicked it toward the center of the river. It wasn't sinking fast, but it was sinking, and moving downstream. He put away his axe but held on to an arrow he'd taken from the side of the boat. It looked like a normal arrow to Lizeth, but he looked upset about it as he shoved it in his pack.

"Scruff, can you scout ahead and find us a safe place to hide? How long will she be like this?" Finnian picked up both packs, shredding the netting as he did so. He scattered the pieces around then went to Lizeth.

"I *can* speak for myself, you know." Lizeth felt like one of the packs as he awkwardly picked her up again. "I simply can't move at the moment. Probably quite temporary." She was fighting hard to keep the terror out of her voice. She'd heard the tales of magic users who overdrew—they weren't pretty. She had ignored them for the most part because she never thought it could happen to her.

"How long will you be like this?" Finnian sounded like he was fighting down his own worries.

"I'd say, maybe an hour." She wasn't sure, but it sounded like Scruff snorted from ahead of them.

They were quickly in a forest and Finnian kept following Scruff. At least Lizeth assumed so. He was moving with intention but he'd had to carry her in such a way she couldn't see ahead. She did have a nice, albeit distracting, view of his behind though.

A tree branch skimmed her head as Finnian ducked down. The trees were thicker here and it looked like there was an actual path under the needles. Old worn stone peeked out in random sections.

"Has anyone been here recently?" Finnian was speaking to Scruff, but as he hadn't turned around, she couldn't tell where *here* was.

"I don't smell anything, and trust me, my people have an exceptional sense of smell. It looks like it was a crofter's cottage and long abandoned. We need to get her resting and warm quickly. Her exhaustion is going to get worse before it gets better." He'd dropped his voice on the last bit but Lizeth still heard him.

"I'm going to get worse?" Her voice sounded ragged even to her own ears.

"Yes." Scruff came around to her as Finnian entered the small building. The concern in his eyes was more worrying than her rough sounding voice. Almost. "I won't lie, you're in bad shape."

Finnian put her down as he dug through the packs and came up with their bedrolls and extra blankets. He put down one of the bedrolls in a clear spot, moved her to it, and covered her with more blankets.

"You both look like I'm dying." Her voice sounded like she needed to clear it—but it felt fine.

"You could be." Scruff stomped over to the packs and started pulling supplies out. "I know our choices were slim out there, and you probably saved the three of us. But you never should have gotten that overdrawn, even before we were ambushed." He turned to Finnian. "I know it's risky, but we'll need a small fire and fresh water."

Finnian nodded then left.

"I will be okay, won't I?" Lizeth couldn't even move her hands and wipe the tears that rolled down her face. Embarrassing; princesses didn't cry in public.

"I don't know." Scruff shook his head. "I won't lie, I really don't. But it won't be for a lack of trying."

Finnian came back and built a small fire, then he handed over three full water skins to Scruff.

Scruff quickly made a horrible smelling drink in a small cup from one of the packs and made Finnian hold her up, still wrapped in her pile of blankets. "You have to drink it all. It's going to be nasty."

If she could have pushed it away, she would have. On a plus side, the vile smell stopped her crying. They got about half the glass into her in tiny sips before she started sputtering. "I can't. I'm going to throw up."

Scruff and the cup retreated a few feet. Finnian was behind her and stayed holding her up.

After a few moments, Scruff snorted and came back, shoving the cup at her. "All of it."

"I really feel ill. Can't we wait a bit?" The feeling of wanting to throw up was passing but she swore that the nasty sludge she'd swallowed was crawling around inside her stomach. Combined with the taste of nasty boiled shoe leather and rotting apples, she really didn't want any more of it. It made the tea in the cottage seem like a honey wine. When she got home, she was going to find a way to make magic restorative drinks that actually tasted good.

"Do you want to die?" Scruff wasn't holding back. "I have no idea what would happen to Finnian and me if you die when we're here. But I do know that if you die during a Challenge, you are dead. This isn't a dream world—it's our reality right now. I'm not trying to scare you...well, yes, I am. But this is deadly serious. You. Could. Die."

Lizeth waited for her tears to start, but they didn't. "I did what I needed to do to save us. All of us. This hasn't turned out at all like I thought. I—" Her words were cut off as Scruff darted forward and dumped the rest of the contents of the cup in her mouth. Luckily, there wasn't much left, but even so, she was surprised she didn't choke. That sludge had a mind of its own and crawled its way in. She sputtered, but it was down.

"That was sneaky."

Scruff dabbed the corner of her mouth. "It worked. Desperate times and all. Let's get some more blankets on you and let that drink do its work." He nodded to Finnian who gently leaned her back in the bedroll.

"I'm not cold." The moment the words left her mouth a chill like she'd never felt before slammed into her. She still couldn't move but wanted to curl into a ball. Finnian came and tucked more blankets around her.

"Wh...where did these come from?" Not only was her voice sounding like it was being dragged out through a rusty tube, she was shaking so hard it took everything to get the words out. They'd only had three blankets and their bedrolls with them from their mysteriously delivered packs and from what she could see these didn't look old or bug-eaten enough to have belonged to this cottage.

"A new pack appeared outside of this cottage. Wasn't there when we came up, by the way." Finnian shook his head. "Whoever is watching us didn't see fit to keep you from overusing your magic or stop those people from shooting at us, but they dropped off a new pack. Mostly filled with blankets and herbs." He glanced to Scruff. "Lots of herbs."

"Good, we might need them." Scruff looked up at her. "You won't sleep, sorry, but try to rest. Speaking will become impossible soon."

Lizeth opened her mouth, but nothing came out. Finnian dug out a final blanket and tucked it around her.

"Rest." His smile was sincere, but his dark eyes were worried.

She smiled back and went back to shivering.

"Can we talk, or will it disturb her?" Finnian stepped away from her mountain of blankets.

"We can talk. She's going to be going in and out of consciousness for a while and it's best if we're nearby."

She couldn't see Finnian or Scruff, but their voices were soothing as she drifted through a pain-filled fog. Every nerve ending was on fire and frozen solid at the same time.

"I found this arrow." Even half out of it, Finnian's voice sounded extremely upset to her.

"We were being shot at by a large group, I'd think you found more than one."

"Look at it. Closely."

"It's an arrow," Scruff's long-suffering sigh brought a smile to Lizeth. Or would have if she could move her face at this point. "It's a...is that a Laiandran arrow? How did they get here?"

"It is," Finnian said. "See these symbols drawn along the side? That's an old Laiandran symbol on a seemingly new Laiandran arrow. Like a few hundred years old. Don't ask for details, they're boring and not essential now, but I've studied ancient weapons, and trust me—this design is old."

"It looks new?" The sniffing sound told Lizeth that Scruff was using his powerful nose to find the truth. "It *is* new. Yet I believe you on the age of the symbols on it. This isn't good."

"You shouldn't be here." The voice that spoke in her head was the same one that told her she was on her Challenge. *"This is not as planned. But sometimes that's what is. I can't save you, none of us can as we are limited right now. But I can show you things that might help if you survive. Things have gone wrong along the timeline and your entire world is now in danger, not only you."*

The sounds of her companions faded and even though she knew she was still on the floor of the cottage, she found herself being pulled through the forest. She couldn't speak, nor control where she was going—even when she passed through solid trees. A village appeared ahead of her. It was crude and surrounded by knights. During their trip down the river, she hadn't gotten a good look at the villagers as they passed. She did now.

Their clothing was so old fashioned she wondered where they'd been for the last few hundred years. She was a bit of a clotheshorse herself and aware of fashions—the clothing she saw now was only found in dusty history books.

"Yes, you are in the past. A past that should be different, but is not. Your Challenge is like no other, but perhaps a sign of things to come. The oracles are under attack and we won't be able to help guide you—if you live—trust your companions." As the last word fell, Lizeth found herself slammed back into her body on the floor in the cottage. *"We can't help you more."* That bit was a whisper.

"I need to scout the land. You've said it yourself; this isn't normal for a Challenge. We need to know where we are and why they're using these weapons." Whatever she'd missed while she was out, Finnian was pissed.

"The past." She thought she'd said it in her head, but she felt both of them come next to her. With some effort she forced open her eyes. "How long?"

Scruff climbed up next to her and looked down. "Only a few hours. You should be still recovering."

"Might have had help." Her voice was rough, but she felt better. "Water?"

Finnian vanished, then reappeared with the water bag and held her upright. She drank half of it, then wiped the water from her lips.

"You moved!"

Lizeth looked at her hand, then lifted the other one. She felt like a newborn kitten, but she could move.

"Who helped you?" Scruff asked as his tail twitched.

"The oracles, I think. We're in the past. I don't think it's where we were supposed to be, but something has gone wrong. They can't help us anymore."

Chapter Fourteen

"How do you know this?" Scruff's furry brows were low over his eyes and his head tilted in a familiar way. One that usually indicated he'd caught someone trying to trick him.

"The oracles came to me and showed me a nearby village. I might not know weapons, but I know clothing. Those fashions are a few hundred years behind the times, yet the clothing looked well worn, but in good shape. More of those archaic knights, too. Their armor was the same as in the back hall of champions at home—the fallen enemy's chamber." That they looked newer than the ones in the back of the palace gave her a shiver unrelated to the cold that was slowly leaving her body.

Neither of them looked surprised, they must have reached some of the same impossible conclusions while she was out traveling with the oracles. It didn't feel like she'd been with the oracles for more than a few minutes, but clearly time behaved differently with them.

Scruff jumped off her blankets and started pacing. His tail was now in full flapping mode and could probably knock over a small building. "This is not good at all. My people do know a bit more about the Challenge than we let on, and I have never heard of such a situation." He spun back to her. "What exactly did these oracles say? We need the precise words if we're to sort this out."

Lizeth sighed. She had a headache the size of the palace, had hopefully survived a massive magical overdraw, and he wanted her to recall exact words. That oddly came immediately to mind. The oracles said they couldn't do more, but maybe they wanted to make sure she told her companions what was said.

Scruff had her repeat it twice.

"That's not good. The packs are one thing, the challengers face the Challenge not the elements. But for them to have taken you out of body, then said they themselves are in danger?" Scruff stopped talking, but his tail moved almost too fast to see.

Finnian ran his fingers through his hair. "I don't understand any of this. So, we're in the past, and not even in your kingdom, but in Laiandra? Just what is your Challenge?"

"Whatever it was supposed to be, I have a feeling that's changed now," Scruff said. "It might have been messed up when it first started and you and me were pulled in to try and balance it."

Lizeth adjusted herself into a sitting position. Still massively weak, but that was a start. "I'd say right now we need to figure out what's messed up the timeline, why this past isn't what it is supposed to be, and not get killed." She was uncommonly pleased at how steady her voice was. It still sounded gravelly and awful, but at least she sounded confident.

"That sounds easy." Finnian shook his head and brought out food from the packs. Jerky and travel bread were going to get old fast.

Her mother's lessons started trickling in. "I think we need to look at what was happening back home right before we were taken. How did those Stiklins get there? Who killed that man in the stairway, and the others we found in the stable?" She shook her head. "We can't only look at what is happening here. There's something more than that, there has to be a connection between the two." Her mother had spent most of Lizeth's youth trying to get her to notice connections in the world around her. She was mildly annoyed then, but grateful for it now.

Since Finnian hadn't been involved for the incidents in the palace or the stables, Lizeth and Scruff filled him in while they ate. Accented by a few fresh apples that Scruff had hidden.

Finnian might not have wanted him to pack them, but it didn't stop him from eating one as he pondered what they told him. "That's interesting, and it ties in with what I saw in the forest. A group of

Stiklins raced through. No idea where they came from, but they were heading away from the canyon."

"No one can cross that," Lizeth said. "I spent an entire not-so-exciting month with my tutor debating that. It's not passable."

"But any other way to our kingdom would have made them go through heavily populated lands. Not to mention all of Astarious." Scruff said. "Yes, they can mask themselves, but only for short periods, and it uses a lot of their magic."

"Why is the canyon not crossable?" Finnian held up a hand. "I know, it's not. I was told that repeatedly when I arrived. But humor me. I've traveled a fair amount and I've gone into canyons that look far worse than that one. And I've climbed back out. Is it a spell? Could the Stiklins have broken it? Even though the chancellor didn't believe me, I know what I followed to the palace."

Lizeth looked to Scruff, but his brows were furrowed and he scratched his ear. "I...I think it's magic? That's odd. A few days ago, I could have given you a dozen examples of it not being crossable, but none of them make sense now."

"The timeline is broken." Lizeth didn't like where her thoughts were going, but she needed to share them in case she was right. "The oracles said that. Could what's going on here in the past have messed things up enough to allow the Stiklins to cross the canyon? Especially if that canyon should be crossable without magical interference?" She flashed Finnian a grim smile—he'd guessed it. "The magic on it might have fallen." If it had been a spell that had kept the canyon impassible for the past few hundred years, and she had to admit it looked like that had been the case, the amount of power needed to break something that strong was enough to make her run away screaming. If she could actually run at this point. She felt stronger, but she doubted she could do more than a slow walk. Maybe.

"Stiklins drain magic, right?" Finnian asked. "Could enough of them have joined together and torn down the spell on the canyon?

The bit about us being here, impacting the present time *before* we came here hurts my head. That might be the truth of it, but I need to think about other options."

"My question would be, how did they get through Laiandra? That kingdom is directly across the canyon and I doubt even they would make a deal with Stiklins." Lizeth had been perversely interested in the Laiandrans. They'd fought her people for decades, only finally to be stopped by the canyon. "And that's whose land we're now in." She shook her head. "Why did the oracles drop us here?"

"To fix something. Something they can't." Scruff had polished off his second apple and was looking for another. Annoyance made him hungry, and his tail hadn't stopped twitching once.

"But if us being here caused the Stiklins to invade the palace, before we came here?" She shook her head. "I'm with Finnian, it's too complicated. And what if we do the wrong thing? What if we already *did* the wrong thing and the future is changed horribly already?" None of her tutors had ever taught her anything about time travel—aside from it not being possible. Which was now looking to be extremely incorrect.

"Second guessing isn't going to help. Not even my people have any record of time travel." Scruff started putting small items back into the nearest pack. "We're going to have to condense things down, but I think we can get everything inside."

"I'm still not certain I can walk, and you want to get back on the road? We don't even know what we can or can't do." There was a fear in her gut now. Had her actions caused the invasion? Were her sisters and parents now in peril because she messed something up? She'd always been sure and confident of what she was doing. That was all crashing around her now.

"It's almost night. I'd recommend we wait until morning." If Finnian was upset about them planning on taking off without resolving the time issue, he gave no indication.

"But we don't know—"

"What to do." Scruff cut her off and finished her sentence. "Agreed. But we have to believe the oracles think we can do something. They need us to do something."

Finnian nodded. "And they most likely didn't take you to that village just to show you the clothing."

Lizeth sighed. She might have been happier when Finnian was simply annoying. And not making sense. "Fine. But, as pointed out, our clothing doesn't fit the times. And do they even have grigeens in Laiandra?"

Scruff stopped packing. "They did. Many of my people were lost during a series of battles across many lands. We're still not certain if they survived and started new colonies somewhere far away or were killed. But we were here before that loss."

"I can get us some clothes from the village you mentioned in the early morning. At least a few nondescript pieces that will help us blend in but not make us look like clothing thieves," Finnian said.

"I might be able to cast a glamour on us too."

"No." Scruff responded before she even finished speaking. "Sorry, but your recovery might have been assisted by the oracles, yet you still sound awful. Casting a spell now could send you right back to where you were."

Lizeth thought there was more to it than that—he wouldn't look her in the eye. But her voice still sounded like she was speaking down a gravel-filled tube, so she dropped it. Spell songs relied on specific notes and there was a chance she couldn't hit those. "For now, I'll agree. Just make sure you take simple pieces of clothing. And we'll need to make a harness for Scruff out of something." She might not know what happened to them, or how to fix it, but she recalled enough history books to know grigeens were considered pets long ago.

"A harness? Never."

Lizeth folded her arms and tilted her head. "Do you want someone else to grab you? You said yourself that you've no idea what would happen to you or Finnian if I died while we were here. I think the same concern has to be made for getting separated. We need to stick together. According to my history studies, unharnessed grigeens were considered free game—in any country."

"Such an uncivilized time." Scruff shuddered. "Finnian, see what you can find to make me a harness."

Finnian kept from laughing as he nodded, but his smile lingered. Scruff was extremely put out.

"Now, let's settle in and sleep. You can take some of these blankets back, I think I'll be—"

Lizeth's words were cut off as the walls and ceiling of their borrowed cottage started shaking. First Finnian, then Scruff, vanished.

Chapter Fifteen

Lizeth screamed as the cottage also vanished.

That her scream was echoed by distant yells didn't calm her down. The fact that they sounded like her sisters made her jump to her feet—surprisingly she didn't feel exhausted any more. The forest looked like the one back home, only some trees were shattered and a fire burned where the palace should be.

A moment later everything was back to normal. Beyond Finnian and Scruff both giving her alarmingly concerned looks.

"What happened?" Finnian was looking paler than before as he dropped to sit on the ground next to her. "The world shook, then you vanished. Right in front of my eyes. Did you cast a glamour spell?"

"She wasn't hidden, she was gone." Scruff tapped his twitching nose. "I know of no spell to do that. I have no idea what caused the shaking, but I feel dizzy as well."

"Not to mention glamour spells are extremely difficult to pull off." Lizeth was trying to stay calm, but that failed a second later. "And I did vanish. I think I was back home, but there was fire, the palace...I heard screaming. We have to go back now and save them. We have to." If she thought she could stay upright long enough to run out of here she would be gone. But the brief flash of normal strength wherever she'd gone had vanished. She had no idea how to get back, but those images and sounds terrified her.

Scruff came closer and rubbed her hand with his cheek. She calmed down immediately.

"Thank you. I'm sorry, but that was far too real. We have to get back." As a child, Scruff had always been able to calm her. Good to know he still could, unfortunate that he needed to.

"Do you know how to do that?" Finnian's voice was low and soothing. Most likely what he used with wild animals. "And what if what you saw was the future if we *don't* fix whatever we're supposed to remedy here and now? If the timeline is more fluid than we thought, you might have seen the reason we need to see this through." He shrugged as both of them stared at him. "I took a number of university courses in the philosophy department. And I just realized that the way of thinking of the philosophy greats might be better at explaining the oddness of time travel than anything else." He actually looked embarrassed and slightly turned away.

"I didn't take more philosophy than needed—that was more Nevaine's area. But I suppose that could make sense?" Lizeth wasn't sure, but she needed to hang onto something to keep those yells out of her head. And from a twisted logic it could be true. Philosophy was murky enough, at least in her head, to have implications for time travel theory. If such a thing existed.

"I think our woodsman is far more than he seems." Scruff narrowed his eyes. "What university did you follow philosophy at, again?" He didn't look angry, but wary.

Lizeth watched them both carefully. They'd appeared to have been becoming friends of a sort, but Finnian's look was now also guarded.

"The University of Sonesberg. Dropped out before I got a degree. Found that being in classrooms wasn't my style." He didn't look happy about Scruff's questioning but was trying to play it off as not bothering him.

Lizeth continued to watch them and finally shook her head. "Oh, come on you two. Scruff, Finnian got dragged along with us on this against his will and he's not even really one of my subjects. Stop harassing him." Lizeth wasn't sure why philosophy classes set Scruff off, but she was back to feeling exhausted and she didn't need these two bickering like cranky old men. "If you expect me to be able to walk and possibly run or cast spells tomorrow, I need sleep."

Scruff continued staring at Finnian for a few more moments, then shook his fur and settled back on his haunches. "Agreed on sleep. We will discuss this later, I'm sure." He gave Finnian a smile, but since grigeens had long canines, his smile looked less than friendly. Then he turned to her. "But I wouldn't try any spells just yet. You took a serious blow by draining yourself so badly. Rest and recover your magic—use your weapons training for once. If you must use spells, stick to the non-augmented magic ones—no spell singing."

Lizeth nodded but wasn't happy. Like her weapons training, she'd let her non-augmented magic training slide a bit. Augmented magic, such as her spell singing, was far stronger than the lower-level spells, the non-augmented magic, so she'd never focused on them.

"Good point on weapons," Finnian said as he readied bedrolls for he and Scruff. "I'll see what else I can find when I look for clothing in the morning. Aside from a harness, is there anything else you need?" The emphasis on the word *harness* as he glanced back to Scruff said he wasn't surrendering to Scruff yet.

Scruff kept his non-friendly smile up. "Thank you, but no. My people don't need weapons beyond what we were born with." Grigeens' claws, like those of cats, were hidden inside their large paws. He extended the ones on his front feet and bared his fangs even more.

"Seriously. No posturing, taunting, or anything else that doesn't help us fix whatever we need to fix and get back home. Or I will smack both of you." Lizeth settled into her blankets.

Scruff retracted his claws and laughed. "That sounded more like your sister Nevaine. But you have a point." He nodded to Finnian. "Truce. At least until we're back home."

Finnian nodded. "I'll keep first watch. I'll wake you in a few hours." He went to the doorway and sat right outside of it.

"Do we really need...what am I saying, we're in Laiandra. I could take a watch too." Lizeth needed a little sleep, then she'd be fine.

"Nope. Woodsman and I will take care of it. You'll be no good to anyone if you have to be carried tomorrow." Scruff dug up the bedding Finnian carefully put down for him, bundled it into a pile, and curled up. "Sleep."

Lizeth wanted to disobey, but her body betrayed her and she dozed off immediately.

No dreams this time, at first.

Then the same yells, fire, and terror from before flooded her mind. They were closer to her this time, but she couldn't see anyone. Just the forest on fire around her. But she felt the heat from the flames—everything was more real than the last vision.

When she couldn't see anything else, she forced herself to wake up. She must not have screamed in her sleep this time as Scruff was sitting guard by the open doorway. The sun wasn't up yet, but a gray predawn was starting.

Scruff moved out of the way as Finnian came into the cottage with a huge lumpy bundle. He was wearing dark clothing and had something that looked like lampblack on his face and hands.

Scruff sniffed the air outside. "Were you followed?"

"Do I look stupid? Is that the issue?" Finnian dropped his bundle and started untying it. "No, I was not. My formal education aside, I am well trained in woodlore." He looked to her. "Shouldn't you still be asleep?"

Scruff spun—he obviously hadn't noticed that she was sitting up. "Why are you awake?" He sounded like she'd deliberately broke his commands.

Lizeth rubbed the side of her head. "Another vision. I don't think they're nightmares, maybe they are? But they feel too real. And I was able to get out of it faster than a nightmare. Before you ask, same as before. The palace, the forest, my sisters—only more terrifying if that was possible." She shuddered. "I could smell the smoke."

Scruff came over and sniffed her. "It's fading, but I smell it too. That's not good."

"No, it's not." Finnian dropped his bundle and came closer. "I can as well, and it's not from our fire. Different type of trees." His scowl grew deeper. "The ones around your palace. I've heard of these kinds of visions, never believed in them, but I didn't think traveling in time could happen either." He kept watching her, caught himself, then looked away.

"And what are they called? How do I stop them?" Lizeth wasn't happy about the visions, but his reaction was making things worse.

"Darlantes. Visions that affected some people throughout their lives. But they weren't real." He looked away quickly as he added the last part.

"A Laiandran word." Scruff kept emotion out of his voice, but his tail twitched as he spoke.

"That doesn't mean anything. There are many such words in our history and I assume in the history books in most universities." Lizeth responded before Finnian could. As a royal she never went to university, although she'd wanted to. Her education matched that of the best schools, but it had been lonely. Maybe when they got back, she'd rally for her sisters to be able to go. That thought brought a smile. The small feeling that not all hope was lost was welcome. Whatever that vision thing was, it wasn't going to be her reality.

She noticed that Finnian was still shooting concerned glances her way. "And? I don't want you and Scruff arguing, but I also think that anything pertinent needs to be mentioned. We've no idea what might make a difference and if that hop I made was an alternative future, there is no way I'm letting that happen." She folded her arms. It would be more impressive if she got to her feet, but while she did feel better, she didn't want to blow the image by stumbling to her feet, then falling over.

He gave a tight shrug. "And the people who see them were considered cursed."

Chapter Sixteen

Finnian held up his hand before she or Scruff could speak. "Or blessed. The definition went either way. The myth was that it is something that starts when one is reaching a major crossroads in life." He looked ready to say more, then shut his mouth and smiled.

A smile that wasn't reflected by his eyes.

"What else? I'm not going to be happy if we have to draw everything out of you bit by bit." She put enough 'annoyed royal' into her tone that hopefully he'd stop stalling.

"It was said—and again, this is an old tale—that those chosen to see these visions lead a life of seeing what others don't. But they lose their greatest gift in exchange for the visions." He shook his head. "It was a folk tale, nothing more. There is a rational explanation of what's going on, I'm sure. Perhaps your oracles are influencing events even though they can't directly interfere." He held up his hands and pointed to his face before she could respond. "This stuff will set if I don't wash it off. I'll be down at the stream." He was out the door before she or Scruff could comment.

"Do we believe him?" She pushed back her blankets and tested standing up. Getting up from the floor took more effort than it should and she was glad Finnian wasn't here to watch. Even though his help might have made it easier. But once up she didn't shake and her balance was solid. Her voice still sounded awful, at least to her trained ears, but being able to move was a good start.

"On some things, yes, others, I'm not sure. We have no idea what is going on and whether your Challenge is in this muddle somewhere. I've never heard of this vision tale he speaks of, but something is obviously changing with you." He peered up at her carefully, as if he could see the source of the troubles on her face.

"You don't think it could take away my singing, right? That's my greatest gift—I can't be without it." Her voice went up a few levels as she cut herself off—panic and terror tended to do that. There was no way losing her ability to sing spells would be offset by being haunted by images and visions of a deranged future.

"I doubt anything can take that away." He smiled, but his tail still moved. "You'll be fine. How are you feeling now?"

Lizeth wanted him to lie better, but the truth was, he probably didn't know any better than she did. She looked down and smoothed out her wrinkled clothing. "I need a bath, a change of clothing, and something to eat. But aside from my voice, I feel fine." The sun had risen and if they were going back on the road today, she needed to get ready.

"Your voice sounds fine today. You were a bit raspy yesterday, but you sound perfectly normal today." He tilted his head. "Does it sound wrong to you?"

"Of course, or I wouldn't have mentioned it." She shook her head as the words came out sharper than she intended. "I'm sorry, I shouldn't have snapped. Piallen always gives me grief for not adjusting to changes quickly. I guess she's right. This has been a few days of massive changes. But my voice sounds awful to me. I wonder why you can't hear it?" Yes, as a trained song mage, she could pick up extreme subtleties in pitch, but this was more than that. She sounded like a fishmonger who'd been yelling for a week. So why couldn't Scruff hear that?

"You truly sound your usual dulcet self. We will add that to our ongoing list of things to look into. You might as well go take advantage of the stream. Finnian might not be who we think he is, but he does have honor—he won't watch you bathe and change. I'd rather someone was there to guard you."

Lizeth almost pointed out she was perfectly capable of protecting herself, then stopped. With her song magic off the table, she wasn't left with a lot. It looked like there were at least two swords in the lump of things Finnian brought back. She'd have to freshen up her sword fighting. Like all royals she was trained with sword, knife, and staff—but she didn't keep up with it as much as she should have.

She went through the bundle. By combining the rustic skirt and blouse Finnian brought back with some of her own clothing from the pack, she found something that should work. Of course, she'd be wearing her boots and leggings under her skirt, but better to be prepared.

She didn't grab one of the swords, but did take two knives. "I'll be back, don't eat all of the food." The way to the stream wasn't hard to find, but her thoughts were on her voice. Why was it so wrong to her? She'd ask Finnian, but if it didn't sound off to Scruff, with his far superior hearing, she doubted Finnian would pick it up.

"Ah, feeling better?" Finnian was heading toward her from the stream, the staining on his face and hands was gone and his hair was damp.

"I am, thank you for asking. I do however, apparently need a guard while I take a brief bath. Scruff assures me that you are a man of honor and would never peek at a woman bathing."

Finnian laughed. "He did, did he? And I thought he didn't like me." He bowed low. "It would be my honor to guard the princess royal. I will stay only feet away but keep my back turned unless you scream."

Lizeth gave him a royal nod and made her way to the edge of the stream. A rock outcropping would provide some coverage if there was anyone with less honorable intentions drifting through the forest.

The stream was barely above freezing so she took the fastest bath ever. Her teeth were still chattering as she joined Finnian.

"Sorry, should have warned you the water's cold. I'm used to it, but I'm thinking your water is heated in the palace." There was only the tiniest bit of smirk in his tone.

"Yes, we have specially heated water brought up by flocks of birds with golden tassels." She gave her haughtiest look, but laughed at the end. "Okay, maybe not that far. Do you truly prefer living in the wilds?"

"I do. I can think better out here. Not as many distractions." He gave an open grin. Now that she'd seen it, she could tell that most of his other smiles had been guarded and practiced. Good to know, if she were to figure him out. Like his open laugh in the cottage, this was really him.

A small voice in her head pointed out that she didn't need to figure Finnian out. Nor find his smile enticing. Work with him to repair whatever needed to be fixed for the timeline, get back home, and go their separate ways. Yes, he worked near the palace, but she rarely saw any of the woodsmen or woodswomen who worked in the forest.

She'd make sure that trend continued with Finnian. There was something unsettling about him that she didn't need in her life.

The silence made the trip back to the cottage longer. She was about to ask some inane, yet silence-filling, question, when Finnian raised his arm to block her. He moved his finger to his lips, looked around, and led her to duck behind a massive boulder.

She wanted to ask what he thought he was doing, but he looked far too serious. A moment later she heard what caused his reaction. A small group of people, men and women from the sound of it, were talking as they crossed the path she and Finnian had been on. Their voices were low, but not enough to hide their passage, so they must not think anyone was around. Or they were going about their day. It said much that her current thoughts automatically went to people sneaking around and doing evil things.

From the intense look on Finnian's face as he grasped the hilt of his sword, he'd gone down the same mental path she had. She hadn't seen much of his fighting, but that sword looked well used. Nevaine always said know the blade, know the man. His blade said he was a far more experienced fighter than a normal woodsman. Yes, he'd said he'd been briefly in the military—this seemed to be more than that.

The voices dropped and the sound of footsteps stopped.

Lizeth looked to Finnian and pulled out both of her knives. Now she wished she'd taken one of the swords. She wasn't great with them, but if they were facing a real fight, knives weren't the best weapons. But, while she wasn't nearly as accurate as Nevaine about throwing knives, she could if needed. Then she'd have no weapons at all. Speaking with Finnian had pointed out her voice was still out of sorts. Whether or not Scruff or Finnian heard it—she did. There was no way she could cast a spell song with it, she wasn't even sure she trusted a lesser, non-augmented spell right now.

"Who's there? Show yourselves." The voice was gruff and male. "We have you surrounded."

Lizeth looked to Finnian. There was no way anyone could have gotten behind them. The stream wasn't that far back and the way had been covered in small stones—ones that were noisy to walk on. He gave a tight shake of his head and motioned for her to stay put.

"We know you hear us." This voice was female, and almost as low and gruff as the male. "Come out and fight instead of lurking in the shrubbery."

Finnian relaxed a bit, but didn't release his grip on his sword. Lizeth heard another noise, a group of people coming from the other direction. Just how many people were out here? Were they looking for them? Had Finnian stolen from the wrong people in the village? This didn't seem like a big gathering spot.

The new arrivals came closer. "It's us, you daft idiots. We were waiting for you. Crof and Jonel got nabbed by the knights. Now we're short for the big job." This new voice was less gruff than the other two but just as annoyed.

"Crof was an idiot and Jonel couldn't find her ass with both hands." The original speaker said. "This wasn't where you were supposed to meet us."

"Eh, the pub you mentioned to meet at got burned down two months ago. And there are knights all over the village. Lots of knights—looking for someone. Or looking for anyone. Seemed better to meet you here."

Finnian still didn't put away his sword, but he sat down and took a deep breath.

"I have some people coming in. Highly recommended mage and swordsman and they can help us on this job. Larking and Groun—yeah, *that* Groun. Supposed to be the best swordsperson in the empire. Would have been better with Crof and Jonel too, but I think we can pull off the job."

Lizeth adjusted to sit down as well but misjudged the number of small stones she was crouching on and they made a slight grating noise.

"What's that? Do you have anyone else coming? Did the knights follow you?" The woman again, and sounding closer than before.

Finnian leapt to his feet, raised his sword, and waved it toward the path. "You were looking for us, I believe?" His grin was almost feral and his demeanor completely changed. If Lizeth had seen him on the road like this, she would have blasted him with a spell song without a second thought. And it wouldn't have been to only hang him in the air.

Chapter Seventeen

Lizeth slowly rose next to Finnian. And tried very hard to not look like a displaced princess. She still held out her knives, then put the right-handed one in its sheath and cupped her hand as if holding a spell. If Finnian was planning on what it looked like he was planning, she was going to have to work on her non-augmented magic. This was not a good idea and she had no logical hint as to why he thought it was. Maybe she'd wildly misjudged him and he was one of those risk-taking adventurers. It would explain him moving around a lot. He probably skirted away from being arrested many times.

"Groun? You're a hell of a lot younger than I expected. And Larking? Princess, are you sure you're not going to break a nail out here with us? Not to mention, there's no way you are in your forties." The man in front of her was the first speaker they'd heard and his looks didn't match his voice at all. The voice called forth images of a massive bear-like man—this guy was shorter than her and extremely thin.

The hulking blonde woman fighter behind him fit her voice well though. She looked like she could have picked up the boulder Finnian and Lizeth had been hiding behind and toss it into the stream. "They aren't what I've heard of, that's for certain." Her grin was definitely not friendly.

There was a total of six fighters: the short man, the hulking woman, and two more average-looking thugs right behind them. Facing them was a slender blond man who kept his face completely neutral, and another woman. The woman had a bow and had drawn an arrow before Finnian even finished getting to his feet.

None of them looked happy to see Lizeth or Finnian. While she wasn't happy about Finnian's choice to pretend to be whoever these people were meeting, she knew first impressions were critical.

Without saying a thing, she threw her dagger at the leader, sent a non-augmented spell after it, and waited. The spell caused the dagger to stop in front of the man and flick off a button from his shirt. Then drop to the ground. The spell seemed impressive but it was little more than a child's play spell. A lot of the non-augmented spells, were more show and less substance. But there were far more magic users with access to non-augmented magic than the augmented types such as spell singing.

Finnian froze for a split second, then laughed. "Larking doesn't like being called a princess, and her age is a touchy subject. Let's leave it at mages don't age like the rest of us. Same sometimes for their partners." He sheathed his sword and stepped forward with his hand extended. "As you guessed, I'm Groun. The village was too dangerous to stay in, so we've been hiding out here."

Lizeth followed forward as the leader picked up her knife.

"I'm Tomas. Good to meet you." He looked at the knife before handing it back to Lizeth. "Wouldn't it be better to have the blade magically return to you?"

She watched him as she sheathed the knife. Finnian better have a damn good idea what he was doing pretending to be others. "It's an issue of trust. I demonstrated that I could have killed you without a problem, but I didn't. You returned my blade to show me I was correct in that decision." She let a small smile out, one not unlike Nevaine's when she was being sneaky. "Had you not returned it, we would not be having this discussion."

The woman behind Tomas nodded and stepped forward and stuck out her hand. "Maurial. Nice to meet you, Larking." She looked up to give Finnian a favorable glance. "And you, Groun." She gave an appreciative whistle. "Definitely not what I would have expected."

The change to Finnian was still going strong. He gave Maurial a lecherous smile and kissed her extended hand instead of shaking it. "I am honored to meet you."

Lizeth refrained from rolling her eyes externally, but she did in her head. Yes, Finnian was attractive in a rugged, woodsman sort of way. But the flirting bit between them was going to get old fast. Not to mention depending on where and when they were, Maurial could be his great-great-great-great-grandmother. She gave a shiver. That wouldn't be good.

"Are you all right, Larking?" Tomas stepped forward. He was looking at her a bit too much like Finnian and Maurial were still looking at each other. Lizeth channeled Nevaine again and scowled. He took a step back.

"Sorry, just had a terrifying thought." She needed to find out why Finnian was now aligning them with a bunch of rogues. And how they were going to get away.

Tomas finished introducing the rest of his gang. Finnian, for all of his changing into a thug, politely greeted each by name and warmly shook their hands. Lizeth struggled trying to catch all of the names. As a royal, people were constantly presented to her, but slowly and with decorum. Not with names grunted out quickly.

Finnian turned back to Tomas after the introductions. "Before we get on the road, Larking and I have to pick up our things. We've been hiding out in an abandoned cottage with a grigeen."

Maurial's eyes lit up. "You can get good money for those."

"He's mine." Lizeth stepped forward with a snarl. "No one is selling him or hurting him. Understood?" She knew Scruff could fend for himself for the most part, but she didn't want to have to worry about what these people might be thinking. Clearly, Finnian was planning on traveling with them for at least a while and she needed to keep their risks down. Not to mention, they still needed to figure out her Challenge.

"I didn't know the great Groun and Larking traveled with a grigeen," Arcadia, the archer, said as she put her bow over her shoulder. She was extremely tall so at first it was hard to see how long her bow was. It was close to five feet if Lizeth had to guess. Bows in her time were short compact things for the most part, but the army had some longbow archers with them. They were deadly but hard to master.

"He's a new addition." Lizeth folded her arms and glared. "Is there a problem?" Advantage of royal training—haughty attitudes were ingrained.

"Not at all. We wouldn't want to interfere with whatever method you two have." Tomas grinned. "We have a major job, and your expertise will come in even more handy since we lost two of our own." He glanced around as if he'd suddenly realized they were in the middle of the forest. "You have a cottage nearby? Let's finish this discussion there."

Lizeth really wished there was a way to warn Scruff about what happened and to ask Finnian what he was planning. But they were already moving as Finnian took the lead. Lizeth jogged to catch up as an idea hit her.

"It might be best if I go ahead, unless all of you wish to see how serious my trap spells are." She hadn't put up any, but had she actually been this rogue mage, she would have. Going in ahead would give her enough time to fill Scruff in.

Finnian laughed. "Trust me, folks, our Larking might look sweet, but her spells have a nasty bite."

Tomas nodded. "We'll give you five minutes lead?"

"Aye, that should do it. Just don't arrive early. I'm not responsible if any of you get fried." With a look to Finnian, one she wished would show what was in his head, she jogged down the path.

"Took you two long enough, I was wondering if you'd drowned each other." Scruff had made a massive mound of all of the bedrolls and blankets and blinked a few times as he rose to his feet. He'd been sound asleep. "Where's Finnian?"

Lizeth quickly gathered their things as she filled Scruff in on Finnian's rash decision.

"What is he doing? We had a plan, a nice safe plan. Well, as safe as anything could be, given our current situation. What is he thinking?"

"That is a good question and as soon as we can get him free of our new friends we will find out, be assured of that." She put her hands on her hips and looked over the cottage. She was certain that a bunch of thugs wouldn't care if the place was messy or not, but their packs could have items that would give them away as not being who they were claiming to be, so better to have them all packed to go. She also took the smaller of the two extra swords and buckled the belt and scabbard on. Yes, her persona was a mage, but she could make up a reason if needed for also being armed. And better to have it with her.

Scruff started to ask another question but froze as the sound of people approaching was heard. He came next to her. "I still don't want to wear a harness," he said quietly.

"You might not have a choice," she whispered back as Finnian and Tomas came into view. They were making conversation but the tone was casual so probably not about whatever this job was.

"Nice pet." Maurial came to her and nodded to Scruff. "I meant nothing by appreciating your man, by the way. There were rumors, but I didn't know you two were a couple." She smiled. "He's a fine one though. Ya ever get tired of him, send him my way, right?" She cuffed Lizeth on the shoulder hard enough to almost knock her off her feet.

Lizeth nodded, unsure what to say. Finnian needed to fill her in quickly, or she was going to screw something up out of ignorance.

Maurial dropped her voice. "He told me on the way here about you two. Don't worry, Tomas doesn't care who sleeps with who in his gang, as long as they get the job done." She turned back to Scruff. "What's the wee beastie's name?"

Before Lizeth could answer, Scruff spoke. "Sorlin." Lizeth had no idea why Scruff wasn't a good enough name, but since she and Finnian weren't using their real names, maybe Scruff wanted to play along.

"They do talk! I've never met one before. Only see the dead ones at the traders." Maurial winced. "Sorry about that. I never traded in your people—alive or dead—none of us here have."

The fur on the back of Scruff's neck rose and he showed his long canines. "That's a good policy. I defend my own, human and grigeen."

The sound of running came their way and Lizeth noticed that the archer and the blond taciturn man, Arcadia and Janus if she remembered correctly, were missing. The archer came in first with the man on her heels.

"The knights found us. I swear we didn't lead them here, but they're only a few minutes behind."

Chapter Eighteen

Tomas started swearing as he and the rest of his people filed out the door. Finnian grabbed his pack, Lizeth grabbed hers, and they followed. She was now extremely glad she'd packed their things up as soon as she got there.

"You'd better ride on my pack, Sorlin." Lizeth knew Scruff could run faster than any bunch of humans, but she didn't want them to get separated.

He jumped to the top of her pack, dug his claws in, and stayed silent.

"This way!" Tomas and Maurial took the lead and raced through the forest. The sound of armored people following echoed in a now otherwise silent forest.

Lizeth ran alongside Finnian and caught a glimpse of his face; he was worried. Very worried. Those knights could be after the gang they were now running with or them. Which was something she would not be bringing up to Tomas or Maurial.

"I think they might be chasing us into a trap." Finnian kept his voice low so probably only Tomas, Maurial, and Lizeth heard it. "We need to break north."

Tomas glanced around him. "Are you sure? Janus usually can tell these things."

"It might not be in what you've heard, but I'm an expert in the forest. We *are* being herded."

Lizeth felt Scruff dig deeper into her pack. She didn't blame him. In this, she trusted Finnian. A quick glance told her Janus wasn't even looking around but had dropped further behind the rest.

"One way is as good as another. Lead." Tomas held up his hand and motioned for the rest to follow Finnian. Finnian took off and the rest of the group followed.

Lizeth moved in closer to him. "*Are* we being herded?"

"Yes. And those knights came up fast. Unless they followed the group that came from the village, they were already out looking for someone." He kept the 'for us' silent as he changed direction. "To be honest, I'm surprised that those knights can run as well as they can."

"Ah, it's the magic armor." Maurial said as she easily pulled up alongside them. "New invention from the empress's folks. Light, but still able to do the job of protecting what's inside it. Since we're so close to the capital, we're the first to see it. Lucky us." She scowled. "It's been out for a few months and that armor has brought down more good people than any weapon."

Lizeth schooled her face to look suitably impressed, but that was a terrifying concept. Not for the same reasons Maurial thought though. There was no such thing in her time. The armor in the palace from the Laiandran empire was extremely heavy. She and her sisters had tested it with painful repercussions when they were kids.

The other, almost more frightening, thought—the amount of magic needed to do something like change the properties of metal plate to such a degree—was beyond contemplation. It was not only unheard of, but according to her history studies, it had never even been seriously contemplated.

"Aye, that's the look. It scares the pants off of me too. But Groun seems to know how to avoid them." Maurial might have given up trying to woo Finnian for now, but the expression on her face said the admiration was still there.

Lizeth nodded. She needed to save her breath for running. She wasn't out of shape, but there was a vast difference between her normal day in the palace and what she'd been doing the past few days. She really hoped they didn't have to run too much further.

Finnian picked up speed. Lizeth swore in an extremely un-princess-like manner in her head and dug in deeper to keep up. She couldn't even blame the much longer legs of both Finnian and Maurial; Tomas was shorter than her and he was having no problem keeping up.

"I see running shapes to the left," Scruff called down from his perch. Lizeth would take his word for it; he didn't have to keep his eyes on the ground to avoid tree roots and rocks.

"I see them. They're blocking our choices of where we can run. We need a place to take a stand." Finnian veered to the right and toward a large group of boulders.

"We can't defeat knights." Tomas stayed a bit behind Finnian.

"We have to do something. We've avoided their trap, but there are still too many. I think the ones to the left aren't knights though. The clinking sounds vanished a few minutes ago."

Which made sense. The spells on those suits of armor would burn out most mages. They'd need to keep their use limited. Lizeth felt a little less terrified. Not a lot, but she'd take it.

"There's some caves to the right." Maurial was having no problem keeping up with Finnian's increased speed and sounded as relaxed as if she was out for a stroll.

Finnian looked where she pointed but shook his head. "They could trap us there. Too many ways to kill people in enclosed spaces, especially ones we don't know how to get out of. But those boulders themselves might help." He turned even more toward them.

They reached the massive pile of sharp black boulders and Tomas took over barking orders for their defense. There were two more people with shorter bows and they and Arcadia climbed up on the rocks but had to stop about ten feet up as the sharpness of the rocks made climbing higher impossible. The pile of boulders was almost a small mountain and would keep anyone from coming behind them.

"Can't they get on top and drop things on us?" Lizeth forced herself not to pant—princesses did not pant. But she was extremely glad they stopped running. Princesses also supposedly didn't sweat and that was a horrible lie.

"This is a carven range. Those rocks are huge and would take days to climb. They're also slick and not easy to get traction on without special tools." Finnian nodded to the black rocks appreciatively. "Don't see these very often." There had been a slight pause before 'very' which made Lizeth think it was going to be 'in our time'.

"Glad you're more of a woodsman than we'd heard." Tomas nodded to Finnian and turned toward Lizeth. "Hope you have some good defensive spells on hand, a shield would be nice."

Lizeth smiled while her mind furiously searched for non-augmented spells that might be used. Unfortunately, since her spell singing gifts had shown up at five years old, she wasn't as trained in the non-augmented spells as she wished right now. Even if she could sing spells, exposing herself as a spell singer wouldn't be a good idea. Augmented magic users were almost exclusively found in royal and noble lines—explaining that this Larking person had that ability, and it had never been mentioned, would be awkward at best.

They might find themselves facing both the knights *and* this group in battle.

A deflect spell might slow their attackers down. She wished she could think of anything more aggressive instead of defensive, but nothing came to mind. And Tomas had asked for defense. She still wasn't sure about Finnian's choice in joining them, but it was where they were now and listening to the boss was a good idea.

Not to mention, if this group had a plan for fighting, she could throw them off by trying to blast people unexpectedly.

A game she and her sisters used to play against their magic tutors—when they all were still young enough to train together—came to mind. Moving spell blocks. It was actually Nevaine's idea, but Lizeth had modified it. Piallen had been too young to do much but throw them around. It wasn't a wonder that the staff was often nervous around the young princesses.

The almost invisible blocks were each two feet square, and she could only call up ten at a time, but once up and running they reacted to energy against them and blocked it. They were simplistic spells, and they would also react to block projectiles coming from their side as well. She glanced up toward the archers. She might be able to restrict the blocks from their arrows, but that would also potentially let higher aimed arrows from the enemy get through. She chewed on her thumbnail in thought.

Scruff tapped her head. He hadn't gotten down from her pack yet, which might be a good idea for now. "You thinking of your spell blocks?"

"Yes. I don't know what else."

"Good. No matter what, no singing." He climbed down her shoulder to peer into her face. "I'm serious. No. Singing." The look in his wide eyes scared her almost as much as the shapes of people she could now see running toward them.

"Agreed." She turned toward Tomas. "I have spell blocks. The thing is they will react to physical action from either side. No firing arrows when they're up and everyone needs to stay behind that rock." She pointed toward a large boulder on the edge of their clearing around the boulder mountain. It would make a good line for the spell.

"I've seen those blocks of hers work well." Finnian lied so quickly and with such surety that Lizeth scowled at him. She hadn't used that spell in at least ten years—but he was keeping their ruse up with the gifts of a professional con man.

Tomas nodded. "Aye, we brought you on board for your skill and experience. Everyone stands down until Larking says."

Lizeth gave a tight smile and set her spell. She could see the blocks as they formed but no one else would see them; magic left an image to the spell castor. At least the non-augmented spells did. She rarely saw anything with her spell songs.

It looked odd to have a group of fighters approach, and she and the rest of the gang standing there waiting. If there were any magic users in the group almost upon them, they would immediately know there were spells in place just by feel.

Judging by the volley of arrows that preceded the attackers once they were clear of the tree line, Lizeth figured they didn't have any magic users.

She held her breath as her blocks zipped to stop the arrows. Thank the stars the spell worked; the flight of arrows all dropped harmlessly to the ground in front of them. She really wished it would be safe to use her spell singing; there were only twenty attackers and they weren't in armor nor terribly well-armed. The archers were using old battered bows and the swords carried by the rest looked of poor quality.

One simple song could have stopped them immediately.

Her thoughts must have been clear to Scruff even though he couldn't see her face as he tapped the side of her head. "Don't even think it. The blocks are good. Focus on them."

Lizeth didn't answer him but kept feeding magic energy into the blocks. There not only were no magic users with the people facing them, they seemed extremely confused by what in her time would be a common spell.

They fired two more volleys of arrows before finally stepping back into the forest to have a loud debate.

"Can we go out and get their arrows?" Arcadia was still on the rocks with the other archers, so she was asking if someone down on the ground could go out.

Lizeth shook her head. "I wouldn't recommend it. The spell will react to any movement toward it as something to be blocked. The blocks will stay in a line, but no one should cross them. I don't think we want me to drop it right now." She wasn't up to explaining the way the spell blocks worked at this moment.

"They don't seem to be much of a threat," Finnian said to Tomas and Maurial. He still had his sword out, but he wasn't in a fighting stance.

Lizeth mentally appreciated that he had such faith in her magic, but she wasn't sure how long she could hold the blocks active. Not keeping up on her non-augmented magic lessons was going to be really hitting her here. She agreed with Finnian about the condition of the people still yelling at each other in the forest though. They really didn't seem to know what they were doing.

"They're bounders, sort of like cheap mercenaries," Maurial's voice was loaded with scorn. "No one with an ounce of common sense hires them." She raised her voice to make sure the people in the forest heard her.

"Aren't they working with the knights though?" Lizeth wasn't sure, but it would be odd that two separate groups would be after them. One of the spell blocks flickered, then came back. That wasn't a good sign. She focused more magic into that one, but they could cascade into collapse at any time. As kids, she recalled easily keeping them up for hours—this wasn't a good turn of events.

"They get hired to run along and stall people if the knights have to back down. Like carrion dogs. As I said, no one with any sense hires them." Maurial kept flexing her grip on her sword—she looked like she wanted to go charge them all single-handedly.

The bounders' reaction was yet another round of arrows.

Lizeth cringed as two of the blocks flared as they moved to block the arrows—slowly. They did it and all ten blocks were still up, but something was draining their magic far sooner than it should. Lizeth moved sideways to be closer to Tomas and Maurial. "There's something messing with my spell. It should hold for hours, but it's faltering." She hated to admit it, and she certainly wasn't going to mention how long it had been since she'd cast this spell—but they needed to know.

"The bounders rarely have any mages with them, but they could have spell trinkets." Tomas didn't snarl quite as much as Maurial did when mentioning the bounders, but he didn't look happy.

Lizeth didn't know of any trinkets that could sap magic energy, but it seemed like there were things in the past that had vanished in her time.

Or things that changed because of the damaged timeline. Lizeth forced that thought into a small, dark hole. They would fix the timeline and return to a safe world. She had to believe that.

"Do I drop the spell, or wait until it falls on its own?" Lizeth had never had a spell fail on its own, but augmented magic worked differently than the non-augmented kind. It would take more than a few trinkets to disrupt one of her spell songs.

"I'd suggest we prepare to charge and have her drop the spell. I've never seen this happen to her spells before." Finnian was honest about that.

"There are only twenty. The day we can't take out twenty bounders is the day I retire." Maurial's grin said that day would be a long way off.

"Agreed. At my mark, drop the spell. I'll flag our archers." Tomas waited until Lizeth nodded then raised his hand and dropped it.

Lizeth released the spell, Arcadia and the other two archers started shooting into the forest, and Maurial led the charge following the arrows.

Lizeth started to follow, but Scruff smacked her in the head. "Let the stronger fighters go first, you need more sword training." He kept his voice a whisper, but Finnian nodded as he ran by.

Maybe this was her Challenge, getting used to not being able to do things. Seemed a bit extreme to be pulled back in time for that though. She didn't like it, but she stayed put as everyone except she and the three archers charged forward.

She had no doubt that the five of them could do some serious damage to the twenty bounders, but as she watched, the bounders' numbers doubled and they roared as they ran forward.

Chapter Nineteen

Twenty against five was one thing, forty or more against five was suicide.

"They're going to be slaughtered! Where did those extra fighters come from?" Lizeth didn't really think Scruff had an answer, but he did. Sort of.

"Mirror me. At least a hundred." He jumped to the ground and ruffled his fur.

Damn it. Mirroring was another non-augmented spell, but a lot trickier than her spell blocks had been. She'd be making a hundred copies of Scruff. Which meant he would be charging forward into a messy and uneven fight. "They'll figure it out."

"Maybe. I'll keep my movements threatening and if my history is right, and it probably is, my people were seen as a threat in smaller villages."

There wasn't time to argue, Finnian and the others were in danger of being overwhelmed. She cast the spell and a hundred Scruffs came out from the rocks. They all moved slightly differently, but she couldn't make them function completely on their own. Scruff gave a roar and led the charge.

Lizeth wanted to do more, but the magic needed to keep the mirror spell up was draining her badly. Still when one of the bounders got past the others and ran for her, she managed to throw her knife at him before he got within striking distance. The liquid 'thunk' as it went into his chest almost made her throw up. He went down, but she couldn't do more. Fighting was one thing in theory, something completely different in real life.

Scruff and his mirror gang did their job though; half of the bounders took off yelling as the grigeens got closer. Tomas started to join them, his face white as the grigeens swarmed past him, but Finnian yelled something to him and his people and they stayed.

Lizeth twitched as the draw from her spell started to blur her vision. Not that it mattered. A minute later the mirror Scruffs hit the remaining bounders and it was clear they weren't real.

Luckily, by then the archers and the fighters had done enough damage to the remaining bounders.

"Keep one alive," Finnian yelled. Tomas looked ready to argue, but Maurial quickly dispatched her current fighting opponent by knocking him out with a punch to the head.

Within a few moments, the bounders had all run away or were dead. Except for the unconscious one that Maurial was dragging back. Lizeth glanced at the opponent she'd gotten the lucky knife shot into—he was dead. At first, she was surprised then she saw that he'd already been injured—seriously, from the amount of blood not coming from her knife wound. She turned away quickly and forced her stomach to stay in place.

A princess would throw up, a hardened mage traveling the land wouldn't. There was no way she was going to grab her knife though.

Finnian jogged up to her, stopped at the body, and removed the knife. At least he wiped it off on the dead man's tunic before handing it to her.

"Thanks." She couldn't really tell him she'd rather leave it behind, not with the others coming up to them. But she barely touched it as she put it back in its sheath.

"We have to get out of here. There will be more coming." Arcadia jumped down from her rock and gathered as many arrows as she could.

Janus had been on the edge of the fighting but shook his head. "They won't be back until the knights can recharge, as least a day. I've seen these bounders fight before." He nodded to Tomas before he could respond. "Before I joined you. We're safe here."

Lizeth really had no feelings about the members of this gang. Maurial seemed friendly, but it was hard to tell with the rest. Janus was making the hair on the back of her neck rise. He seemed far too calm about this entire thing.

"I think we need to move." Finnian watched Janus. "The bounders will be back, or someone else working with those knights. There were survivors who saw that the grigeen invasion was a ruse."

"That's another thing." Janus folded his arms and gave an odd smile. "I've never heard of a spell like that. Nor of whatever shield you were holding up. Where did you learn your magic?"

Lizeth had no idea what to tell him. She learned it far in the future in another land and had no idea how mages were taught normally—especially non-augmented magic users.

Finnian had been helping gather arrows but turned around and handed the arrows he'd found to Arcadia. "Where we're from it's rude and potentially dangerous to ask a mage what school they followed. That information could get into the wrong hands and be used against the mage." There was a low, dangerous tone to his voice, and his hand rested on the hilt of his sword.

Lizeth hoped he knew what he was talking about. She'd find out how he knew later when they were alone, providing they survived whatever was going on. She'd never heard of such a thing, but judging from the looks on the faces around them, including Tomas and Maurial, the others had.

Janus raised his hands and gave a weak smile. "No harm meant. I was curious. But you're right, we can't have our pretty Larking giving away her secrets, can we?" His light blue eyes were flat.

Lizeth wondered if he was related to the nathrachas she'd sent into the air a few days ago. She flashed her haughtiest of smiles, one that even the chancellor cringed under if she sent it his way. "I *do* understand. It can be hard for some people to keep track of simple things like courtesies. Do not worry yourself, I learned my spells appropriately." She managed to glare down at him even though he was almost as tall as Finnian.

Janus pulled back for a second and something dark flashed through his light eyes. "I would have no doubt. Forgive me for overstepping." He gave a small head tilt and took a step away.

Tomas shook his head. "Don't question magic users, Janus. If she turns you into a toad, no one is going to help you."

That was interesting. Janus seemed to have been with this gang for a while, yet Tomas didn't look like he liked him at all—even before this issue came up. So, why was Janus still with them? She had no idea how gangs worked, but maybe Janus had skills that came in handy.

Maurial secured the injured bounder and then threw him over her shoulder. "I'm ready. We probably want to question this one soon or I'll have to knock him out again—too many times and there won't be anything to question."

Tomas nodded but didn't seem concerned. He hadn't been the one saying he wanted to question the man. "Where to? Our job is to the north, but I'd rather not travel for two days while being followed." Tomas held up a small map to Finnian. "Our job is here. Sorry to have mislead you two in our earlier communication. Couldn't take chances."

Finnian studied the map, looked around at where they were, then scowled. "I can get us there without being tracked. But you're really looking at a job in the haunted city? Might not have agreed had we known." He started to hand the map back, but when Tomas waved for him to keep it, he tucked it in his cloak.

"Ah, so you'd sneak into the capital for five hundred dubars each—as was originally offered—but not some mostly empty city with a questionable reputation?" Tomas grinned.

At least now they knew what they job was supposed to be, and what it really was. Lizeth felt better about that, but not about Finnian recognizing the location so easily. She might have, at some point in a long, boring history lesson, heard of something called the haunted city. She *was* interested in the Laiandran people—but ghost stories were never her thing so she probably would have stopped listening early in the lesson.

So, how did a vaguely educated former soldier-woodsman know what it was just by seeing it on a map? She'd glanced at the map before Finnian put it away, and there were no names. She stored that aside to join the growing pile of questions she had for Finnian.

Scruff jumped up on her pack and took a moment or two to adjust himself. Then he tapped the top of her head. "I believe we're moving." His tone was imperious.

Lizeth didn't say anything to him but followed Finnian and Tomas. Maurial was right behind her and seemed to be lost in her own thoughts.

Lizeth started to pick up speed to catch up with Tomas and Finnian, but Arcadia caught up to her before she could get to them.

"Haven't had a chance to thank you for that blocking spell. We could have been picked off that rock easily if you hadn't blocked those arrows." Arcadia was thin, with short dark hair, and a sharp narrow face. She looked stern until she smiled. It also made her look younger.

"Why would you and the other two go up there?" Logically she'd realized they were risking themselves as there was no coverage on those rocks—but she thought they knew something she didn't.

"It's what we do. Archers do best with a leverage location and Tomas expects us to take care of things." She shrugged. "It's the job."

Lizeth really wanted to ask her what made her join this type of life. She doubted any little girl or boy went to sleep at night wishing they would join a gang of thieves and risk their life on a regular basis. But, considering that Lizeth was supposed to have made the same choice, asking would be odd.

"Can you tell me about your adventures? I expected you both to be older. I know most of this group isn't aware of the exploits of you and Groun, but I was at Clocksberg five years ago. I saw the fighting from a distance. They said you were amazing with a bow." She grinned. "One of the reasons I started studying it."

Lizeth had years of training to not show panic under pressure. And she was using all of it right now. The bow was strictly Piallen's weapon in their family. Nevaine could use it under duress, Lizeth almost always shot something she shouldn't. This was a problem—she and Finnian where stepping into the lives of two real people with real reputations. If Arcadia wanted to share archer techniques, this entire ruse was going to fall apart.

Scruff coughed. "Larking won't talk about it, but she tore a hole in the muscle on the back of her right bicep a while ago. She can still fence, but archery is a thing of the past." He dropped his front paws to Lizeth's shoulder. "It's a sore point with her that the healers couldn't fix it. Now the damage is permanent."

Lizeth watched as sorrow and pity crossed Arcadia's face. It was a good thing that both Scruff and Finnian could make up lies so fast and so well. She gave a struggling smile. "It's true, but I can speak for myself, you know. Don't feel bad for me. That part of my life is over, but I am still fighting."

Arcadia nodded. "The magic probably helps, I'd think. Those were impressive spells."

A wind went through the group, cold and unwelcoming. And if Lizeth's instincts were right—not natural. "They've got a magic user after us." She slowed down and tried to feel where the wind was coming from. Boan had tried teaching her more useful magic, such as the search spell that was still flowing among them. Lizeth hadn't paid much attention, even knowing that she'd be facing the Challenge at some point. She never thought there would be magics she couldn't spell sing to defeat. Looking back, she realized how much she'd counted on her spell singing abilities to take care of everything.

When they got back home, she was having Boan teach her all he knew about non-augmented magic.

"They aren't close. That wind has traveled a distance. It's a searching spell, not strong enough to let them know where we are, but it will start showing them our general direction unless it's stopped. I can block it, but I have to be behind all of you. And I'll have my focus all on that spell." All magic took focus, but her spell songs were so ingrained she didn't need much.

Unfortunately, not training well in the non-augmented spells was becoming a bigger issue. Both her sisters had weaker augmented magic than she did so had done far more training than her on the non-augmented side. She was going to face a lot of ribbing for this when she got back. She swallowed the lump in her throat at the thought of never seeing her sisters again. This would work. They would get back and everything would be fine.

She wished she believed herself more.

Finnian started to drop back to her but she waved him off. "You can't stay with me. You need to get us to the city without being seen."

Arcadia nodded. "I can stay back with her."

"Me too. I might not be as big as all of you, but few people live to face a guardian grigeen a second time." Scruff growled.

Lizeth couldn't see him since he was still on her pack, but she knew he was probably poofed up. In his mind, he looked fierce when he did that. She'd never had the heart to tell him it made him look soft and cuddly. He was probably also baring his fangs—those were at least impressive. Didn't take away from the cuddly poofing though.

"Don't let her drop too far behind. Two days of travel are ahead of us." Tomas nodded and he and Finnian continued.

Janus looked ready to drop back as well, but a snarl from Scruff got him moving with the rest.

"Is there anything I should look for? I've never worked with a mage before." Again, Arcadia's grin made her look younger.

Lizeth was only twenty, but somehow someone in Arcadia's line of work looking to be close to her own age was disturbing. She gave her a grin to cover her thoughts. "Not really. You and Sorlin need to make sure no one sneaks up on me. And that we keep following the others. I won't really see much of what's around us while I'm in this spell, so you'll need to nudge me from time to time to stay on the trail." She took a deep breath to calm and focus herself. Unlike her block spell, she would need to do all the work, not just set it and feed it magic. She would be reaching out for the spell that had already found them once and actively disburse it each time it sent a tendril their direction. They were lucky that the people using the spell tipped their hand by using it while still so far away. It warned Lizeth they were still being followed with enough warning to counter it.

"So, this group doesn't usually have a mage?" That could be important to know. Whoever was after them might not have worried about being detected if they weren't expecting a magic user. Her mother had always said to know what your enemy expects and make sure that's not what you give them.

"Not since I've been in it. Four years this spring. Tomas doesn't trust them." Arcadia's eyes widened. "No offense."

Lizeth waved her hand. "None taken. Okay, I'm going into my trance now. You two keep me from walking into a tree." She took a few more deep breaths for good measure, and then slipped into a spell trance. She had to fight a bit more than she expected and again swallowed the thought of how easy it would be with her spell singing. One song and their route would be masked to all but the highest level of magic users. And even they would have a difficult time with it. Not being able to access that magic was like having a heavy new sword and having to make do with a paring knife instead.

But eventually she got into the space in her head that she needed for the trance and sent out passive waves, searching for any spells that might be coming their way. The trick with this spell was to be subtle. If the spell caster pointedly went searching for magic, they would be spotted by whoever was following them. But wafting along in a disbursed, unforced circle that *happened* to be drifting around their group, would be hard to pin down.

The spell was twofold: one to search, then, if anything was found, to confuse the searchers. Again, it had to be subtle. When she'd first been learning it, her immediate reaction was to go after the spell caster directly. And each time she got magically smacked down for her troubles. Being subtle and not attacking when the following spell was found wasn't as easy as it sounded.

She let her mind drift as she continued her indirect searching.

That her thoughts landed directly on Finnian wasn't a good thing. She'd noticed that she watched him far too often, even when they were in this group—he stood out. There was a mystery about him that she wanted to solve and she feared that it wasn't only curiosity that was making her feel that way.

She was attracted to him.

That thought almost jerked her out of her spell weaving. Not that she found him attractive—he was. But that she was *attracted* to him. That wasn't going to work. She might not marry Trion when she got back, since he seemed to have eyes for her sister, but she would be expected to make a match with another person of royal blood. Augmented magic flowed strong in the blood of the Astarious royals, and for the safety and propriety of the kingdom, they needed to continue that.

Then why was she going through images of Finnian in her head? Especially when he wasn't aware anyone was looking, there was a vulnerability in his face. It vanished quickly, but that softness in those moments was her downfall. She gave herself a few more moments of studying him in her mind's eye. Then shoved all of those images, thoughts, and feelings into a mental dark box and slammed it shut. When they got back to their own time, she was going to make a point of never being where he was—at least until she was an old married woman.

A sharp poke hit one of her spell tendrils. It wasn't strong after the initial stab and was coming from behind. Lizeth let her magic gently engulf the tendril and smother it. The spell tendril immediately sped up. She'd been too direct in her response. She waited to the count of ten, then gently reached out again. As if her own spell had accidentally come across this other one.

It took four tries before she finally disbursed the searching spell. She shook herself free of her spell trance and touched Arcadia's arm. "Can you tell Groun and Tomas to change direction a few times? They are still following."

Arcadia had jumped when she touched her, but then nodded and jogged up to the front of the group.

"Are you okay in there?" Scruff asked from his seat on her pack.

"Yes, this is harder than I'd expected." There was no way she was admitting that to anyone else. "I'll go back in once Arcadia gets back."

"I am perfectly fine protecting you." Scruff sounded a bit miffed.

"From walking off a cliff? I know you can protect me from most things but you're not big enough to keep me on the trail."

Scruff snorted as Arcadia came back.

"They're adjusting direction. Don't worry, I'll make sure you don't go the wrong way."

Lizeth gave her a nod, then went back into her trance. Focusing too much on her spell would make it become too noticeable, as Boan would say, too sharp-edged. She needed this one to stay soft and fluffy. Odd visual, but imagining the spell as a group of slow-moving clouds helped.

Since she banned thinking about Finnian, she mentally pulled in the big problem—her Challenge and what was wrong with the oracles and the timeline. If this issue were still connected to her preordained Challenge, then she should be able to connect the dots and figure out a solution. Deep thinking was more Nevaine's thing than hers, but she was smart enough to be able to push through.

Or not.

Try as she could, the connection wasn't there. Which in a way did resolve one thing. She'd still been trying to figure out her Challenge. That had to take a lower priority. Right now, being stuck in a past that might be unraveling the future with each second, and staying ahead of whoever was looking for them, were more important than her Challenge. If she got Scruff, Finnian, and herself to the future, and the future was as they left it, she'd count it a win. Whether or not she solved her Challenge. If she didn't resolve her Challenge, she couldn't be queen. That thought prickled a bit, but saving all of them was more important.

That acceptance was an odd thing. Her life had been directed to the Challenge and becoming a Queen of Astarious. She had never thought much beyond that. But if they could fix the timeline, restore the oracles, and get home? She'd give that all up. Knowing that was strange, yet freeing.

This time when the searching spell appeared she diffused it on the first try. Even managed to make the diffusion look like it came from a completely different direction. That felt good.

She'd had to block the searching spell five more times before they came to a halt.

Finnian had been calling her name for a while in her head before she realized that he was standing in front of her and had been calling it aloud. And that they were no longer walking.

"Fi—Groun, what's wrong?" She shook her head to clear away the vague thoughts that the spell trance had left behind. "It's night?" The sky was a dark blue with fading streaks of color on the horizon.

"Almost. Arcadia couldn't wake you, but we stopped walking ten minutes ago." He peered into her eyes, but then nodded at what he saw, or didn't see, and pulled back. "We're heading into that village down the hill. There's an inn on the edge that Tomas is familiar with."

The idea of being around a lot of people and having to keep up her identity ruse sent a shiver down her spine. Not to mention any interactions here could do damage to their own time. It was bad enough they were traveling with this group. "Wouldn't it be better to camp out in the wilds?"

"There are advantages and disadvantages to both. We made good time today and I'm assuming that you blocked the search spell. But we do have another day on the road. A long one. Rest would be good, not to mention if we're among others we might not be as noticeable to whoever is trying to find us."

A wave of fatigue hit Lizeth as if his words reminded her of the day she'd had. She'd admit, if only to herself, sleeping on a nice bed would be preferable to a bedroll on the rocky ground. She looked down toward the inn. Two stories tall and probably built a hundred years ago. Judging by the appearance, she might find a bed, but the word nice wouldn't be something attached to it.

But he had another point, the searching spell would have a difficult time trying to find them in a crowd. Even the rest of the village could cause a problem for it. Over the last few hours, she'd learned more about the spell caster behind the searching spell. Not who they were, but their skill level. It was high enough to be annoying and would have found them hours ago if Lizeth hadn't been blocking, but they weren't strong. The inn and the mass of people in the town would stop them for a bit.

And she needed to rest. That blocking, on top of her other two spells, was really hitting her now. "Agreed. We should be safe there."

"Oh, Tomas understands our *situation* and will make sure we get our own room and a single bed." Even in the darkening sky, the blush on Finnian's face was clear. "Sorry about that, but I figured if we were involved it would keep unwanted attention at bay. Not to mention an excuse for privacy."

Lizeth was glad she'd worked through some of her Finnian issues and quickly made sure her attraction was still locked up in the tiny black box in her mind. "I understand, but you still have some explaining in general to do. A lot of it."

"I'm sleeping with you two, by the way. I overheard someone up there mention the stable for me." Scruff was flapping his tail as he climbed down on her shoulder. "We stick together."

"Which might make it weird for our supposed situation." Finnian's blush was gone.

"I'm a sound sleeper?" Scruff suggested.

"Works for me." Lizeth *thought* she'd dealt with the Finnian issue, but her relief, knowing Scruff would be with them, made that glaringly obvious that it wasn't true. She wasn't afraid that Finnian would try anything—she wasn't completely certain that she trusted herself.

Chapter Twenty

Everyone was silent as they walked down to the inn. Not out of being secretive, but from what she saw, general fatigue. When she'd first gone into her spell trance, the sun had been high, probably a little before the midday. Given where it was now, sinking fast, they'd been walking without a break for about five hours. Her stomach grumbled and reminded her she hadn't had much to eat.

"Don't worry, Tomas says the food is much better than the appearance of the place." Finnian walked alongside her and Arcadia drifted a bit ahead. "He did warn that the clientele was mostly thieves and cutthroats—which is why it's at the edge of the village and not in it."

"Sounds lovely. They have food and beds, that's what I'm focusing on." She looked around. "I take it no one else followed us in a non-magical form?" There was no sign of fighting on anyone and most likely had there been an ambush she would have been pulled out of her spell. Then again, considering how long Finnian might have been trying to get her to come out of it, she might not. That could be a problem.

"Not a one. We changed directions a few times but didn't see anyone." He lowered his voice. "I recognize where we are from maps. In our time, this village is a massive city. A bit different than now."

Another thing to talk to him about when they were alone. How he knew so much about Laiandra. They were a closed country and didn't allow for outsiders—from anywhere. "I might need to take breaks tomorrow. I sunk a bit too deep this time and could have an issue if we are attacked and you can't get me out of the trance." Since tomorrow would be an even longer day, that was extremely likely. She had a feeling Tomas didn't stop for breaks much, if at all.

"I'll tell Tomas that for the safety of your spell, we need to stop. But will that leave us open to being found?"

That was an extremely good question. Since she'd never been in a situation anywhere near this one, nor used a lot of non-augmented magic, she had no idea. She finally sighed and also kept her voice low. "I'm not sure. Maybe a quick break. Pop me out of my trance, let me grab food and take care of necessities, then I'll drop back in." She looked up. "And we're here. I really hope that Tomas is right about the food—this place looks pretty bad." It looked worse than bad, it looked like it was about to fall down on itself. It was two stories high, with grungy gray plaster on its sides over the wood frame. The varying shades of plaster, even in the dim light, indicated that instead of doing a full replaster, they'd simply slapped more on the old.

She was about to suggest something in the village, but from what she could see, it wasn't in much better shape.

"In my experience, some of the shabbiest places are the most welcoming." Finnian held the door open for her to enter. "Where's Sorlin?"

Lizeth reached up; her pack still felt like he was on it. But his spot was empty. The pack had a new lump from what she could feel. "Inside my pack."

"Staying here until we get to our room. Grab some food for me. I don't trust this place." Scruff spoke from inside the pack as she felt him nestle in deeper.

Then she saw a patron walk by with what looked like a well-worn grigeen fur vest. Keeping him hidden was probably a good idea.

Tomas waved them down from a corner—one large enough for all of them and far from the rest of the people. It was still early, so there wasn't a lot of drinking going on, and not a lot of folks—yet. She had a feeling that eating and getting to their rooms quickly would be the best plan.

Maurial sat down next to her.

"Where's the guy?" Lizeth hadn't noticed that the body Maurial had been carrying wasn't with them anymore until now. That spell trance was messing with her observation skills.

"He died while we were walking. Dumped him a few miles back. I might have hit him too hard." She didn't seem too upset.

Finnian scowled. "It would have been good to find out what he knows."

"Eh, bounders don't know much—or at least normal ones don't. They get told where to go, cause as much havoc as they can. If they live, they get paid; if not, usually there's no one to miss them." She waved down a barmaid. "My two friends and I would like three ales and three plates of your roast." She grinned to Lizeth and Finnian. "My treat."

The barmaid looked to the rest, took their orders and left.

"You don't have to do that. We can pay." Lizeth was touched at Maurial's generosity.

Finnian, however, gave a short laugh. "You frisked the body."

"Aye. And our friend was carrying far more than a bounder should. I'd say they weren't normal thugs. I figured I can share, especially since it was because Groun wanted to question him that I got the funds." She grinned as the barmaid dropped off three tankards.

Lizeth usually didn't drink ale, but she had tried it a few times. The deep, dark, but clean tasting ale served in the palace was nothing like the claggy tasting murky drink before her. She didn't spit it out, but it was only due to years of decorum training. "Interesting." She slid her tankard over to Finnian. "I shouldn't drink after running that spell all day. Thank you though."

Finnian took a huge drink of his and wiped his mouth. "That's good stuff. Thank you again." He tipped his head to Maurial.

Lizeth thought he was simply being polite, but he quickly finished his tankard and started on hers. He either enjoyed it, or he was a far better actor than she gave him credit for.

Maurial nodded and downed her drink in a single swig. Granted, she wasn't a small woman, but even so, that was impressive. She waved the barmaid back and handed her the empty tankard. "Another." She nodded to Finnian but he shook his head. "Just one more then, for now."

The food arrived and, while not exotic—a slab of meat, some potatoes, and a collection of rather sad vegetables—it tasted far better than it looked. Of course, it could be more from hunger after walking for hours rather than any skill of the cook. She didn't care at that point. She inhaled the food, then worked on finishing the pile of bread on the table.

Tomas was smart; he waited until all of his people had some drink and food in them before discussing the plans. He kept their names and the direction they would be going silent, but passed around the map.

Lizeth didn't like the look of the places they would be going through—especially when she would be in a spell trance. If this map was like one from home in terms of how elevation was marked then they would be climbing some pretty steep mountains. There was no way to complain about it without sounding like a spoiled princess though.

"Is there any way to go around those mountains?" That was less spoiled princess and more person-who-would-be-in-a-trance. She hoped.

"Not unless we want to add another few days and possibly run into whoever is trying to find us." Finnian kept his voice low but Tomas nodded in agreement.

Lizeth chewed the side of her thumb as she looked the map over. He was right. There was a wide road that went across the plains—and would take forever and be out in the open. "Just make sure that I have more watchers when we start going up. One false step and I'm gone." She trusted both Scruff and Arcadia, but she wanted another human walking alongside her. The depth of her spell trance today was still eating at her.

"We'll make sure you have more people with you," Tomas said. "Now finish up. We leave at first light." He glanced down the table to Janus and Rilkin. "That means no all-night drinking."

Rilkin shrugged and finished his tankard. Janus looked annoyed but nodded. "This better be worth it." He smiled as he said it, but his words were oddly weighted. Dhlin, the mostly silent last member of the group, scowled, but sat his tankard down.

Tomas watched them for a few moments, then went back to his meal without responding.

Lizeth watched Janus. He kept watching Tomas, even as he went back for more food. There was something extremely unsavory about Janus, something that she couldn't explain, but a wrongness that was there. She'd make sure he wasn't one of the ones walking with her tomorrow and warn Finnian to be wary of him.

They finished their food mostly in silence with Lizeth ordering extra to take back for Scruff—her excuse was that she would get hungry in a few hours because of the strain of running her spells so long. She could have told them it was for Scruff, but she didn't want to bring him up in here. No one questioned it and the barmaid even gave the tray a metal cover. Finnian led them to the small room that Tomas had assigned them. One thing about being with the group, it kept her and Finnian from making too many fumbles with money and the way things were handled. Finnian had been on the road a lot, but it had been in their time. Lizeth had never gone past the Hart woods that surrounded the palace unless she'd been with her parents, a full entourage, and guards.

The room was an excellent reflection of the building itself: small, dark, and cold. A tiny fireplace sat in one corner with a few twigs and one skinny branch. It would warm the place briefly, but clearly wouldn't be enough for the night.

She opened her pack to let Scruff out and stood back as he ran for his plate. He almost ate the thin metal cover as well but Finnian snatched it from him.

"Thank the stars, I was starving." He looked around. "Water?"

Finnian used the metal cover to hold water from the water skin and refilled it twice.

Scruff finished the entire plate in under three minutes.

"Much better. So, what's the plan for tomorrow? And why did you have us join these people in the first place? I get you had possibly been exposed, but couldn't you have found a way that didn't have us joining a gang of thieves?"

Lizeth laughed and folded her arms. "I was going to ask him the same thing."

"They knew we were there when they first came up. I was watching Arcadia and Janus—both kept glancing exactly in our direction. All they had to do was point us out." He shrugged as to why neither of them had done that. "Plus, I figured the village we were going to was a bad idea once I heard about more knights being there. There had been a lot there when I snuck in, but it sounds like more joined them after the fact. I don't think we want to be found by them, no matter what we're calling ourselves. I was hoping that by sticking with them, for a little while at least, we could leave behind anyone after us."

Lizeth held off his comments with a raised hand. "It doesn't matter now, we're with them. We've no idea what we're supposed to be doing in this time so maybe traveling about will point that out." It sounded lame even to her, but the truth was, if she thought too hard about being trapped in the past, she'd probably start screaming. For a few days. She knew the oracles were in trouble, and her parents had taught all three sisters to rely on themselves—but right now she would really like at least a hint as to what they needed to do to fix things.

"Oh, forgot to tell you what we're after. Tomas filled me in while we walked since he'd lied about the destination in his letters to the real Groun." Finnian smiled. "The ghost city has a shrine to the oracles. Laiandra hasn't followed the oracles for decades in our time and might not now. But they did at one point. I thought perhaps we could say that your family followed them, and you would like a closer examination. The treasures that Tomas is after are a bit off from the shrine, so no one should object to us going there afterwards as long as we do what we need to do to help with the job first." He shook his head. "He's being closed-lipped about the particulars of what this thing is that we're after, even to his regular crew. But there must be something big if this Groun and Larking have the reputation they do."

"Don't get cocky about your decision, you had no idea where this gang was going when you signed us up." Scruff stretched. "What are we going to do if the real people you're pretending to be show up?"

Lizeth figured that was becoming less likely the further from the meeting village that they went—especially if Tomas had never told them where the job was. "Or we run into someone who knows them." That was far more likely in her mind. "I agree that being with Tomas and his people might help us for now. But we should separate once we finish this job." She really hoped that he was right about there being some hint in the oracles' temple, but either way, they needed to go on their own.

"I believe that the real Larking and Groun were detained in that village we were going to. When I snuck in to liberate the clothes and weapons, I heard the guards outside a stockade. They had two notorious criminals in lockup."

"Which could bring other questions if word gets out that you two are locked up." Scruff cleaned a few straggling furs. "Or dead."

"We'll have to figure out something if that comes up—or someone claims to know us," Lizeth said. "We need to be ready for it though. Possibly say that I put a spell on two unsavory types in the village when it looked like Groun and I were going to get caught to make them look like us." She tilted her head. "Something like that might work. Hopefully it won't come up, but is another reason to take off on our own as soon as we can. We can always claim a magic glamour if pushed."

"Yes, this plan was a risk," Finnian admitted. "But I have a feeling that at least some of those knights were looking for us—the real us. When we first were thrown back here, they showed up too quickly for us being out in the middle of nowhere. They could have arrived chasing those Stiklins that followed us through—but again, how did they know to come out that far? Tomas has a much larger map that I was able to look at—we were far from any civilization when we were pulled through. And if it's true those knights can't travel far? Coming after us was a risky move for them."

"You're right, actually." Lizeth ran her fingers through her hair and wished she had her imported brushes from home. "There'd be no strategic point for them to be out that far—that we know of. There could be things going on here that don't involve us." The fact was, this entire Challenge was a disaster. She'd wanted to travel when she was younger. Right now, if they got back, she was never leaving the palace again.

When they got back, she corrected herself. Exhaustion wasn't helping her stay positive about the whole situation.

Finnian set up their tiny fire while Lizeth pulled out every blanket they carried. She took the heaviest one and curled it into a nest for Scruff on the floor near the tiny fireplace—there would be barely enough room on the bed for she and Finnian, let alone him. Then she dumped the other three blankets on the bed.

"I can take the floor as well." Finnian looked stoic as he removed a single blanket.

Lizeth hadn't missed how tired he looked. His eyes looked bruised from fatigue. "Are you planning on ravishing me in my sleep?" she asked bluntly with her hands on her hips. Having him on the floor might keep her thoughts away from him, but having him be exhausted tomorrow wouldn't be a good idea. Tomas hired one of the best swordsmen and a well-known mage for this job for a reason. Finnian was a good swordsman, but he wouldn't be if he didn't rest.

"What?" Finnian spun from where he was putting down his blanket. "Of course not! How could you—"

"Then you'll sleep on the bed like a normal person." She cut him off. "This is an odd situation for me as well, but the fact is we need to be rested enough to survive another day, and have another day to find our way home." That was her father's mindset. Do whatever was needed to live to fight another day. Or in this case—live to figure out what they needed to do. "That means food and water—and rest."

Under her continued glare, Finnian put the blanket back on the bed. "Is she always like this?" he asked Scruff.

"Sometimes, but I like it—a lot of her parents' traits are showing in her right now. Might be just what we need."

Lizeth relaxed her stance and went to the small washroom. Finnian had the tiny fire going and Scruff was ensconced in his nest when she came back.

"How long before I can start using my spell songs? I know, not around Tomas or his people. And my voice still sounds off to me, but using the non-augmented magic is slow. If we get ambushed, I might not be able to pull out a successful spell in time." Her voice actually sounded horrific to her ears, and she still didn't understand why the two of them didn't hear it.

"You need to keep from trying a spell song—it might land us in a far worse situation. But, for what it's worth, your voice sounds fine to me." There was a sadness in Scruff's voice that she didn't like. He wasn't lying to her, but also not telling her the entire truth.

That was not a good sign and she wished she'd paid more attention that week when Boan had been teaching her of song magic illnesses. Finnian nodded and shrugged. Not helpful, but since he wasn't a magic user, he wouldn't be.

"Well, I'm going to bed. Just remember, don't let me walk off a cliff tomorrow." She took over a side of the bed, wrapped herself in one of the blankets and closed her eyes.

"I'll be there in a bit. Just need to check my weapons." Finnian's voice sounded distant and vague, and Lizeth let herself drift off. She was hoping that even though the oracles said they couldn't reach out anymore, maybe they'd try to send a dream or something to her.

Either the oracles really were cut off or she was too exhausted to have even noticed a dream. There was a small window in their room, but everything was dark when she woke. Judging by how thin the curtain was, had it been daylight, they would have known. Scruff was softly snoring on the floor. Finnian was good to his word and had gotten on the bed but was curled as much as he could be away from her. He didn't snore so much as grumble in his sleep, as if he were having an argument in his dreams.

The fire had died so long before not even an ember showed.

Yet she was wide awake. Her grand da used to say that waking in the middle of the night meant someone was thinking of you—or something was horribly wrong. She never liked that saying as it seemed that there was no way to know which it was in a given situation.

She would adhere to Scruff's banning of her song magic, but she could still use the calming and focusing techniques she'd learned for the heavier spells. Even though the room was completely dark, she still closed her eyes and took slow, deep breaths, while thinking of a calming image. For her it was a tree she'd climbed into with an armload of coloring books as a girl. The palace had been turned upside down looking for her, but she'd been happily ensconced with Scruff, snacks, and enough art to keep her entertained for hours. That feeling became her focus point when Boan had started teaching her the calming techniques.

The calming and awareness came from her first, a tiny point in space right above her head. Then she gently pushed it out. If there was anything out of place, she should notice it. Nothing in the room caught her notice. After a few minutes she pushed out into the hall and the rooms beyond this one. At first she thought there was nothing there either. She didn't want to push outside of the inn as that could leave her unaware in their room. Not to mention a threat outside of the inn probably wouldn't have awoken her, unless there were knights pounding on the inn doors—which would be noticeable, and the inn was completely silent.

She was pulling her consciousness back—maybe this time it was just someone was thinking of her—when the stabbing feeling came.

She fought to not lose her focus but narrowed in. An attack. Not stabbing, but someone was setting the inn on fire.

Chapter Twenty-One

Lizeth pulled her consciousness back into herself—the faint smell of smoke was now creeping into the room. She knew it wasn't from someone's room fire. The feeling she'd gotten had been evil. Whoever it was had just started but she sensed their intent—they wanted to kill everyone in the inn.

She wasn't sure about how that would work, as once the fire got larger, people would wake up and flee.

"Finnian, wake up." She kept her voice down and shook him. He didn't stir. She hopped out of bed and rousted Scruff. "There's a fire, but I can't wake Finnian." She went back to Finnian.

Scruff sniffed and cracked open the door. "No sign of smoke, but I smell it." He ran back to the bed and jumped on Finnian's chest. Aside from a sleepy grunt, Finnian didn't wake up. "Something's wrong with him." He leaned to sniff Finnian's mouth. "Elderbane. He's been poisoned."

Elderbane was a common enough plant but had to be boiled in a particular way to become a poison. It was mostly tasteless and didn't kill, but rendered the victim unconscious.

Lizeth grabbed their belongings and shoved everything in the packs. She'd leave them behind if she couldn't get Finnian up, but even without them she wasn't sure she could carry him out. "Why him and not us? You're certain about not using song magic?" There wasn't a non-augmented spell she could think of to lift Finnian's unconscious body—but there was a spell song she could use to do it. At least to get them out of there before the place burned down. The smoke still wasn't strong but the hairs on the back of her neck were standing—someone did this with murderous intent and they probably poisoned Finnian as well. "The ale? That's the only thing he had that you and I didn't." She'd had that single sip—it was lucky for her that stuff tasted nasty. "Everyone else drank it."

Scruff ran out to the hall and started pounding on the doors. Tomas had gotten five rooms besides theirs, but none of the doors opened even with Scruff yelling as well as pounding.

Lizeth didn't have a choice. She took Finnian's arm and sang a spell to counterbalance the poison. Elderbane wasn't deadly, but it could knock someone out for a day or two. If the building they happened to be in caught on fire—it would be deadly.

The spell song wasn't that hard but the gruff sound of her voice made her have to work harder than she normally would. It should have been immediate, but she couldn't get the song to come out right. She fought for crucial seconds, willing it to work, before Finnian finally opened his eyes.

"What happened?" He was groggy and kept rubbing his head. "Is that blood in your eyes?"

Lizeth wiped her eyes but there was nothing coming out. Her eyes felt fine, maybe they looked bloodshot because of the smoke? That was a stretch but this wasn't something she could deal with now.

"We think everyone was poisoned with elderbane, probably through that vile ale. Someone is setting the inn on fire. I had to use a spell song to wake you." She had no idea how they were going to wake everyone else up, and she wanted him to know why she couldn't do it for them since she'd exhausted her ability right now by waking him. Maybe Scruff was right about not using spell songs—she was already getting a massive headache from the small one she cast.

"I thought Scruff said not to?"

"He did, but there was no way he and I could carry you out of here. But I can't do it for the others."

Finnian went to his pack and started digging. "Elderbane? We're in luck. It's an easily countered plant—if you know what to use. First rule of being a woodsman, always carry antidotes." He held up a bag of herbs. "Sprinkle a bit on everyone's faces near their nose and mouth. I'm smelling more smoke now; we have to move." They were lucky the fire was moving slowly but that wouldn't last.

Scruff was able to help, so they managed to get the herbs on everyone on this floor. After Finnian kicked in the doors.

Finnian grabbed Tomas as he stumbled from his room. "It's a trap. We've all been poisoned—get everyone out."

They ran down the stairs while Tomas checked to make sure everyone in their group was with them. There had been a few other people on the floor and they came running down as well.

Lizeth almost slammed into Finnian's back when he came to a halt at the bottom of the stairs. The door out was blocked by piles of furniture and three hulking brutes waving massive swords.

"You're not going anywhere." The first one was probably part troll, a species that Lizeth had never seen outside of picture books as they exclusively lived in the massive mountain forests to the east. Or at least did during her time. Not being in the deep forest didn't seem to be slowing down this guy. Actually, the two behind him, a male and a female, looked to have trollish blood as well. The more she looked, the more she guessed they all might actually be full troll.

"If this place catches fire, you're trapped too." Lizeth glared and again wished for her spell songs.

"Not sure why you have red eyes, been crying? Good idea—you're going to die. We can get out, but none of you will." The troll woman grunted and flashed her fangs.

Lizeth would worry about her eyes being that noticeable after they got out of here. Right now, she drew her sword. There was a chance that the exhaustion from the spell song she cast to wake up Finnian could mess up non-augmented magic as well, and she didn't have time to take that chance. Scruff had gotten back on her pack as they ran down the stairs, but he jumped off now.

Tail lashing, he stalked the three troll-breeds, ignoring Lizeth's calls to come back.

"I knew trolls were stupid, but not this stupid." Before anyone could stop him, he leapt onto the face of the first troll.

At that moment, the slowly building fire on the second floor burst into full flame, the innkeeper came running out from a back room and attacked Maurial and Dhlin, and the troll Scruff landed on started screaming and trying to pull Scruff of his face.

Which resulted in a fire at their backs, a dead innkeeper, and a troll so panicked that he ran face first into a wall. Scruff jumped away from him a second before he slammed into the wall and made to leap for one of the two remaining trolls. They both looked at him like he was a fire-breathing dragon, dropped their weapons, and crashed through the window to the side of them.

Scruff grinned and came running back to jump on Lizeth's pack. "Follow them."

Tomas took the lead. The glass, like most everything in the inn, was cheap and shattered nicely. It still took longer than hoped to get everyone out, but by then the village was awake and people were running over.

"I don't think we want to stay and answer questions," Finnian said to Tomas as the wary villagers approached. They'd been running forward but seeing people come out of the window made them slow down. The trolls were nowhere in sight.

"Agreed. This way." Tomas led them out around the back of the inn. At first the other people who'd also been trapped there started to follow—Maurial convinced them that wasn't a good idea.

"We should go back; we did nothing wrong." Janus mostly kept to himself and right now he sounded like he was whining.

"Someone tried to kill us," Arcadia said as she looked back behind them. She had her bow out and her quiver of arrows was in easy reach on her back. "Why would we run back to give them another chance?"

"Not to mention that we do need to get this job done. There's a brief window of time for us to get in and get out." Tomas kept running even once they got to the forest. "I know of some caves we can hide in until morning." He glanced back over to Finnian before he could bring up the issues with caves. "Don't worry, I know them well and they have three entrances. We'll keep guard but they are hard to find if you don't know them well."

Finnian nodded and kept following him.

Scruff hung onto her pack but he was humming to himself. She wasn't sure why that troll reacted like he did, but Scruff was pretty smug about it. Something she'd ask him about when they weren't running for their lives. The villagers hadn't followed them, but whoever set that plan in motion—or rather whoever paid the Innkeeper and those trolls to do so—would eventually know their targets had survived.

Janus kept drifting back until he was the last in the group by a growing distance.

"If you take off right now, I'll see that you never work again. I have many friends in the thieves' guild who will make your life hell. You can leave *after* this job." Tomas hadn't looked back and pitched his voice to only carry as far as it needed.

Janus sped up and stayed closer to the group but didn't say anything. It was a good thing no one followed them from the village as they weren't being as quiet as she thought they should be as they ran. At some point she'd ask Tomas about Janus. There was something extremely unsavory about him and honestly, as long as he didn't sell them out to whoever tried to kill them, she'd be glad if he left.

Tomas ducked to the left and toward a lump of darkness. As they got closer, he slowed down in front of a solid rock face. Unlike the sharp black boulders of before, these looked old and worn—at least from what she could see. Lizeth's eyesight was better than most, even in the dark—a gift from her mother's side of the family. And even she didn't see any sort of entrance.

Tomas waited until everyone was together then walked through the rock. Lizeth followed him, with Finnian right behind. The spell on the entrance tingled as she went through. It was an old one, probably at least a few hundred years at this point, which meant even if she were to cross in to Laiandra in her time, it would be long gone. These types of long-running spells were rare and hard to pull off. They were tied to a place or thing, like this one was, and would keep going even when the spell caster was dust. Depending on the stretch of the spell caster. She'd heard tales of them continuing up to five hundred years—unless another, stronger magic user shut them down. This one felt close to five hundred years now.

The feel of this spell was almost welcoming and not a threat to anyone. Its purpose was to hide the entrances for these caves. But she couldn't tell much more beyond that.

Tomas stood at the entrance until everyone was in. "Okay, these are the nilfam caves. Yes, you thought they were myths, and no, they will not work for you if you come back here without me. Do not go out until I okay it or you won't get back in." He lit a small torch—seemingly just by touching it. "No, I don't have magic, this cave system and I are friends. Groun, could you start a fire? This torch is the only one I've been able to get to light." He patted the cave wall. "I think the spell is fading. It's an old one that my father introduced me to."

Finnian shrugged off his pack and knelt down by the pile of branches. He didn't have magic, but he had serious woodsman skills and soon a nice fire lit the cave. There was a tiny hole not too far off to the side for the smoke to go out. Not only were there spells on this cave, Lizeth would bet the cave itself was made with magic.

Lizeth took off her pack as well and Scruff nestled back on it once it was on the ground.

"I thought these were a myth?" She'd actually never heard of them, but by Tomas' words, anyone from here would have.

"As you can see, nope. But they've been around long enough to be like a myth." Tomas stopped and paused as the light from the torch and the fire filled the cave. "What's wrong with your eyes?"

Lizeth forgot about that. They still didn't feel bad, just tired. And sadly, her pack hadn't come with a mirror.

Finnian was still fussing with the fire but Scruff started nodding. "That happens sometimes when she's exhausted. There were a lot of pulls on her magic yesterday."

Lizeth nodded. "Yes, it's nothing bad. Just need to rest."

"I've never heard of a magic user's eyes going red." Janus folded his arms and glared. "Maybe she caused that fire and it's showing. There are fire mages, you know."

If Lizeth already didn't like or trust Janus, this accusation would do it. "I'm not a fire mage, and why would I try to kill you all? And the last time I checked, you weren't a magic user—so your knowledge is secondhand. At best." She looked around the group. "Let's end this now; do any of you think myself or Groun were involved in what happened? Why would we have saved you if we'd tried to kill you?" She turned her extremely-annoyed-princess glare on everyone except for Finnian and Scruff. Scruff stood next to her flinging his tail about in reinforcement.

A few did look sheepish; Janus had brought up things they might have been thinking but weren't ready to say.

"Janus, you are always accusing others of evil doings without grounds. Back off, or I'll change my mind and you can leave now." Tomas had his hand on the hilt of his sword.

Janus shrugged and stepped back but still looked pissed. "She's the only magic user and magic had to have been used—how else could someone knock us all out?"

Finnian turned and took a step toward Janus. "They—and considering that he attacked us, it was most likely the innkeeper, either on his own or working for someone—used elderbane to take everyone out. Since Larking and Sorlin were the only two who didn't drink the ale and they weren't affected, I'd say it was in that and not the food. I carry dried elfswort as a general antidote when I travel. Larking was able to wake me and she, Sorlin, and myself saved your sorry ass by dusting your face with it. I wonder if that was a mistake." His hand slipped to the hilt of his sword.

For a moment, it looked like Janus might start something with Finnian as his hand drifted to his sword as well. Then he held his hand up and grinned. Not a friendly smile, but it was something.

"No harm, I was wrong. I apologize. Thank you for saving us." He even took a step backwards.

Lizeth quickly looked to Tomas and the others—all of them looked surprised at his reaction. Maybe Janus had been involved in the attack somehow and was now trying to defuse the situation.

Finnian released the hilt of his sword but didn't return the smile. "Apology accepted." He turned and came back to where Lizeth and Scruff were.

Tomas narrowed his eyes at Janus, then shook it off and turned to the rest. "We still have a few hours before morning and we need sleep. The magic of this place will keep the entrances hidden, but I still want to leave someone awake at all times."

"I can take the first watch," Maurial said. "I don't really sleep much." One by one the others took the spots. Tomas refused Lizeth, Scruff, Finnian, or Janus offering to stand guard based on recent events.

Finnian looked annoyed—she had a feeling he was used to being trusted—but Janus looked relieved. She was honestly glad for some more sleep. The spell song she'd used to wake Finnian took far more out of her than she expected.

She set their blankets away from the others against a far wall; the fire wasn't large but the walls of the cave reflected the warmth and heated things up quickly.

Finnian did a bit more glaring at Janus, who ignored it, then came to join her and Scruff.

"That was fun." Lizeth kept her voice low but had no doubts that the others could hear them if they wanted—the cave wasn't that large.

"I wish Maurial hadn't had to kill the innkeeper. I know why she had to, but he must have been who was paid off to do this." Finnian adjusted his blankets. "It would be good to know who hired him and why."

"Maybe he was doing it on his own?" Lizeth shook her head as soon as the words were out of her mouth. "Of course, burning down your place of business isn't a great idea, unless someone is paying you heavily. Sorry, my brain is slow. I have a massive headache."

Scruff had been adjusting his nest but came over to her immediately. "Red eyes and a headache?" He dropped his voice to barely a whisper, just loud enough for her to hear. "You used a spell song to wake him." It wasn't a question and his tail lashed in annoyance.

"There wasn't a choice." She kept her voice as low as she could. "Could you have carried him out? I couldn't have—not to mention I had no way to wake the others."

"Understood, but this might have made things worse. A lot worse." Scruff turned to Finnian who appeared to be pretending he couldn't hear them. And failing. "Do you have any dried hassa leaves in that collection of yours?" He'd returned his voice to a low but not quite whispering level. Probably a good idea as people tended to pay more attention when others were whispering.

"I do, but what do you want them for? They are more used as a seasoning than anything medicinal."

"They actually will help with a magically induced headache. Larking needs to sleep and she won't be able to if her head is pounding."

"Ah, makes sense." Finnian dug through his pack and came up with a small container. "It's powdered, but should work."

Lizeth was aware that although they were trying not to, most of the others were paying attention. Janus had gone to the furthest part of the cave away from them and had already laid down with his back to everyone.

Scruff sniffed the powder. "That'll work nicely. Just need a large pinch in water."

Finnian took out a battered metal cup, poured in some water, and added a healthy pinch of the gray powder. He handed it to Lizeth.

It smelled better than it looked, which was a plus. Still, she held her breath as she drank it. It didn't taste bad, almost like a roast chicken. "I don't know how this is going to—" She froze as the world started spinning. Luckily, she'd drunk the entire thing as the cup tumbled from her fingers. "I feel weird." She blinked as Finnian and Scruff both split into doubles of themselves.

"What did you do to her? Hassa leaves shouldn't do that." Arcadia was the closest to them and looked up in alarm as Lizeth wobbled back and forth where she sat.

"Ah, but for this type of magic fatigue, they will. Now if they were in a stew, and if she wasn't so badly exhausted from the spell use, she'd be fine," Scruff said before turning back to Finnian. "Catch her. She'll be going to sleep now."

Lizeth opened her mouth to disagree. For one thing, she'd never been given hassa leaves for magical backlash, and second, she felt fine, just a bit dizzy. A moment later she found herself in Finnian's arms. "Oops," she said, then passed out.

Chapter Twenty-Two

Lizeth didn't recall dreaming. Well, she felt that she'd had some dreams, but she wasn't sure of what. Her room was still dark, with only a low banked fire lending a glow. That was odd; the fire in her rooms usually stayed all night on cold eves like this. Maybe the spell on it was having trouble. She'd run a check on it when she got up. Low-level long-running spells could glitch and she couldn't recall the last time she checked this one.

She took a deep sigh. She'd slept well. Maybe she'd even be early for her training with Boan. The moment her hands went to her sides to push her up—and she hit hard stone under her blanket instead of her soft bed—she realized where she was.

The pang of loss that followed was sharp and startling.

The feeling of a normal day being snatched from her was swift and harsh. She hadn't given herself time to grieve for what might be gone forever, and it now seemed to be hitting her. Little things she took for granted in the day-to-day life as a princess in a palace now felt like a world lost.

She tamped those feelings down. Not that ignoring them forever was a good thing. They'd come out one way or another, but she knew they wouldn't help her now. She was fighting to maintain the world she'd been taken from. To do that, she needed to focus. She didn't like placing too much hope in one thing, but this abandoned oracles' temple was the first real possibility since they got here. She'd spent most of her Challenge running from things—it was good to be running toward something. She let herself calmly take in the acceptance of this new reality. Nevaine had been turning to meditation and focus training—mostly to get her extremely active mind to slow down—but was finding she liked it.

Lizeth tried it now. After a few minutes, and no noticeable changes, she opened her eyes and sat up.

There wasn't any movement from the sleeping forms around her. A shape that looked to be Tomas sat up against a rock, but was mostly still aside from a soft scraping sound as he sharpened a knife.

"You're up? Good. It's time we get moving." Tomas rose to his feet. "Wake up folks, you won't have any sunlight in here, but the sun is up."

Lizeth would definitely look into these caves in her history book when she got back. They'd never been mentioned in any studies she'd done, but there had to be something. The Astarious library was the size of the massive throne room and crammed with books, scrolls, and even ancient clay tablets kept under protection spells and glass. There must be some information in there about these caves—mostly who made them. In her time, Laiandra didn't allow magic—it had been outlawed, with magic users kicked out of the land or killed, not long after the mysterious canyon opened. But obviously, they'd had some strong magic users in the past.

Tomas' words acted like an alarm and everyone started stirring and getting to their feet. After ablutions in a creek behind the caves, a change of clothes, and an uneventful and unexciting breakfast, they headed out.

Finnian again took the lead with Tomas next to him as Lizeth, Scruff, Arcadia, and Maurial took the back of the line.

"No worries, I'll stay between you and the cliff edge once we get to the mountains." Maurial grinned as they started through the forest. "It would take a lot more than a wee thing like you to push me over the edge." She was clearly one of those people who loved mornings. Lizeth didn't hate them as much as her sister Nevaine did, but Piallen was one of those early risers who was ready to go at the first sign of morning. Sometimes even before the sun. When she was little, she used to run around like a puppy urging her sisters to get up and play. Nevaine usually grabbed her and sat on her to make her stay still.

"What's wrong? You look sad. Although it's nice to see your eyes normal again." Maurial asked as they walked around a particularly large tree.

Lizeth hadn't realized that she'd been that transparent and would have to work harder to keep her feelings to herself. "I was thinking of my sisters. I left them a while ago and I miss them." Might as well keep it as close to the truth as possible.

"Ah. That I understand. For me it was five brothers. Haven't seen them in years." She nodded toward the rest as they'd slowly drifted further behind. "We need to keep up the pace. It's not safe to be too far away from the group."

Arcadia had been setting their pace and shook her head. "Sorry about that, I was off wool gathering. Must not have gotten enough sleep." She started walking faster, but clearly not enough for Maurial, as she pushed them more. They were quickly only a few feet behind Rilkin and the rest of their little gang.

Maurial didn't say anything but she watched Arcadia out of the corner of her eye. "We'll need to keep up close behind them as we go into the mountains. Larking? When will you need to go into your spell?"

Lizeth swore to herself. She should have set it the minute they came out of the cave. "Ah, now, I'm afraid. If you have any questions while I'm under, ask Sorlin. Unless it's an emergency don't bring me out for at least two hours." Ideally, she'd prefer to take a break every hour, but each break would be another chance for the searching spell to find them. She hadn't felt anything from it yet, but it was still sloppy of her to have not set it immediately. She was glad that her eyes had returned to normal, and that her headache was gone, but she still felt out of sorts. Forgetting to set the spell the moment they'd left the caves wasn't good. Nor was it like her.

Scruff didn't chastise her, mostly because he probably didn't want to call attention to her failure, but she knew he'd give her grief later. With a nod from Maurial, Lizeth took a deep breath and settled into her spell trance.

The spell trance slid on quickly, but this time she fought to keep more anchored to the world around them as she automatically kept pace with Maurial. She'd lost herself too deeply yesterday and that was never a good thing with magic. Arcadia, Scruff, and Maurial would be keeping an eye on her, but if something came up quickly, they might not be able to wake her in time.

It made for a disjointed trip—at least in the beginning. Part of her mind was focused on searching for the spell that she knew was probably still tracking them. A spell song would have allowed her to track the follower and maybe give her a clue as to whether they were following herself, Finnian, and Scruff, or Tomas and his gang. Sadly, she couldn't do that and was lucky she was able to block them.

The other part of her, the part that was fighting to remain anchored in the current place, was hearing bits of low conversation as Maurial, Arcadia, and Scruff discussed food. Food was one of Scruff's favorite topics, mostly the eating of it, but he loved to share stories about great meals he'd had in his past. Arcadia and Maurial were probably going to quickly regret this topic of discussion.

Whoever was behind the searching spell was spreading out their range. Or running all day at a full level yesterday had exhausted the spell caster behind it. The tendril of searching that drifted their way was far less focused than before. They might not have an idea where they were, so were sending the spell out in a wider circle. A weaker spell, but covering a larger area. Had she the time and energy, she might be able to pinpoint where they were by the use of a circular spell—which was why Boan always pointed out that they were a bad idea. Sadly, she didn't have the time nor the energy for it.

She wouldn't be able to track them, not on the road like this, but she might be able to mess with them a bit.

Circular spells had more against them than just being able to find the caster—although that was the biggest problem. They could be tricked into feeding on the circle itself and going into a spiraling loop that would smack back into the casting magic user. If done right, they looked like a spell failure but could slam back and knock out whoever created the spell out for a bit.

She mentally cracked her knuckles and looked for the next wave of the searching spell. It came a few minutes later. She mentally grabbed onto the wave as it passed them, then linked it back on itself. Even though the spell went out in a circle, not every part of it went at the exact same time. The delay was incredibly small, but if one looked hard enough, one could tie a slightly faster portion onto a slightly slower section. The spell would keep winding its way backwards as it searched itself.

It took a few tries, but eventually the spell started following itself.

"Is she supposed to be smiling in that trance? She's got a serious grin right now." Maurial's voice was distant but clear. Lizeth felt Scruff climb down from her pack and put his two front feet on her shoulder.

"Aye. She's most likely done something devilishly sneaky to our followers and is feeling smug about it." He patted her head. "Good job, now don't get overconfident." He climbed back onto her pack.

Lizeth would have loved to have told him what she did—the others wouldn't understand it, but he would. At the very least, when she got back home, she'd have a much better appreciation for non-augmented magic.

With a sigh she settled back into her trance spell. She had looped one wave back to the sender and it should slow them down, but it wouldn't be enough to get whoever was following to back down.

She couldn't really see while in the trance spell, just vague shadows and images of the real world around her. But she could tell when they started climbing up. One thing she could sense was the energy of something. Psychic energy of things, as opposed to people and animals, was a field that Piallen had started working on and Lizeth had joined in the classes out of curiosity. The energy given off by a mountain for instance, could tell a person the age and any dramatic events that had happened.

This mountain was old—extremely so. And if she could see it clearly, she knew that she'd see massive, sloping hills.

The wave of anger from the mountain that hit her almost knocked her off her feet. She felt Maurial's hands grab her arm. She nudged Lizeth back to the center of the path. *"We don't mean you harm. We are passing through."* She focused on the words and sent them to whatever had pushed her.

Images of fire, destruction, and death came back from the mountain. They might not be words, but they were clear.

"I am sorry that happened, but we won't do that."

She would do it—not the others, her.

"Did magic users do what you showed? I will not do that." Everyone around her were shadows, but they seemed to be fine and not under threat. They might not know how much danger they were in, but she did. This mountain had a strong spirit and could come down on them all quickly and violently. Something bad had happened and mountains had long memories.

Then images of her home appeared in her mind. The palace, her sisters, and her parents. The colony of grigeens. Anger built up in the mountain.

"No, those are all good, not bad. No one will hurt you." She felt odd arguing with a mountain, not to mention she seriously doubted any of the people traveling with them could hurt it. She might be able to, but not without using song magic. If what happened to her yesterday with a small spell song was any indication—she wasn't trying any spell songs until she got home. Whatever had happened to her on the river when they were fleeing the knights had done something to her

spell singing ability. She mentally sent that as well as an image of a bird that couldn't sing. Somehow this mountain knew what she was, so she needed to make sure it understood that she wasn't a threat.

Pressure built in her head and she again staggered into Maurial.

"You probably should keep a hand on her right now." Scruff's voice was faint and distant. "She might be fighting back against our followers."

Lizeth couldn't respond, but feeling hands on both arms felt good. Arcadia had obviously agreed with Scruff's assessment as well and had taken hold of the other side.

The pressure increased and stole her breath. Then suddenly it left.

"*I told the mountain you were on the side of good. Get to the temple.*" It was definitely the voice of the oracles, but it vanished as quickly as it came. And before Lizeth could ask any questions.

A moment later an image of a beautiful spring hillside came to her, then her ability to sense the mountain vanished.

Even though she'd sat in with Piallen on some of her trainings for this type of interaction, this had been the first time she'd tried it. Considering how closely she'd come to being killed, along with the others with her, she didn't want to try it again.

She ignored the voice in her head that pointed out the mountain could have still killed them whether or not she'd been in contact with it.

Scruff patted her on the head. Grigeens sensed things in nature that others didn't, so maybe he'd picked up on the infuriation of the mountain they were climbing.

Lizeth wanted to tell Finnian and Scruff about the mountain and the message from the oracles. The oracles might not be able to directly help, but hints were extremely welcome and knowing that the temple would at least help them was a start.

She forced herself to think happy, non-threatening thoughts as they slowly made their way up the mountain. There was one more attempt by the searching spell, but either she'd weakened it by turning it back on itself or the mountain didn't like it either and had blocked it.

Then Maurial was shaking her arm and Scruff was patting the side of her face. She took a breath and released her trance spell. She was the one who set the breaks, but it was still an odd feeling to let go—even for a short period. She felt completely exposed.

Lizeth would have liked to have discussed the entire mountain spirit situation with Scruff, but the place they'd stopped was too small to do so without others overhearing. The entire theory that non-sentient things could communicate was fairly new in her world—and therefore not trusted by many—there was no way it would go over well in this one.

The break was brief, snacks and water were given to her, and Tomas asked how their pursuer was doing. She didn't go into detail but she did explain that she'd looped their spell back on them.

"So, they aren't following us anymore?" Tomas asked.

"Sadly, all that did was slow them down. They've hit once since I looped them an hour ago." She was proud of slowing them down—Tomas and the others didn't look as impressed. "That's far fewer times than they had been hitting us."

"That's nice. We'll be back on the trail in a few minutes." Tomas nodded and went over to Dhlin.

Finnian came and sat next to her. "For what it's worth, Sorlin and I are impressed."

Scruff looked up from shoveling nuts in his face like a deranged squirrel. His mouth was too full to speak but he nodded.

"Thank you, Groun." She shook a finger at Scruff. "And you did have breakfast, I saw you."

Scruff swallowed. "True, but it's always good to eat when you can on the rough trail. Mountain travel makes one hungry."

"Even though you're riding on me, not walking?" Lizeth shook her head. "Never mind." Arguing with Scruff about most things was difficult, but about food it was impossible.

Tomas put his things back in his pack, which got everyone else to doing the same.

Tomas and Finnian had started back on the trail when yells came from around the bend.

Chapter Twenty-Three

Lizeth stopped trying to get into her trance and drew her sword. Scruff had already jumped onto her pack, but he leaped down to a boulder near her. The rest of the gang stood ready with weapons out. Charging forward to meet whoever was coming wouldn't be a good idea—the path led to a blind corner.

The yells kept coming but at first there was no sign of their attackers. Giving your victims warning was a unique way to fight, and one she doubted that her more fighter-driven sisters would agree with.

Tomas nodded and Arcadia, Dhlin, and Rilkin grabbed bows and took positions on boulders around them. Not as high as the ones they'd used on the black rocks, but it still would give them a better shot.

The ground shook as four massive beasts came running around the corner. They looked like pictures she'd seen of ancient creatures, mathidos, that used to roam the lands long before her people arrived. Long trunks wrapped in chains with spikes swung ahead of the massive furred bodies. Their shoulders were a foot taller than Finnian.

They weren't the ones yelling though. Each beast was ridden, awkwardly it seemed to Lizeth, by a chain mail clad fighter. Those four were the ones yelling and waving long pikes.

Arcadia shot the leader in the neck and he tumbled off his beast.

Lizeth braced for the rest to keep charging, but the massive creatures stopped suddenly, tumbling the three remaining riders to the ground.

Scruff was in full poof as he stalked toward the riderless beasts. "You go back where you came from." He lunged forward with his fangs bared. The four beasts paused, then turned around and ran back the way they came. Lizeth wasn't sure who was more surprised—herself or Tomas and his gang. Jaws literally dropped.

Scruff was looking too smug as he turned back toward Lizeth and missed the attacker near him quickly jumping to his feet.

Arcadia shot the man before he could throw his pike, or stab Scruff with it, but her aim was off because of the odd angle and only got him in the shoulder. Unfortunately, his chain mail must have been reinforced as the arrow bounced off.

Scruff scrambled behind Lizeth as the three attackers ran right for her. Or him.

All three archers fired but there was now a magic user in play as the arrows all stopped and dropped about a foot in front of the three attackers.

If they had magic, then not having that spell up when they made their charge cost them a man. Not to mention, similar to yelling to warn people they were coming, it was a really bad idea.

Lizeth blocked the first attacker, a woman about the size of Maurial. A pike against a sword wasn't a great idea. Unless you were willing to throw the pike. Lizeth pushed as she blocked and the woman stumbled back.

Finnian, Tomas, and Maurial took care of the other two attackers. Like the arrows, about half of their blows were blocked. It wasn't consistent, which made it difficult to counter. The spell, whatever it was, dropped as the attacker swung their pike, then closed up again.

Lizeth kept fighting with her attacker as she looked for where a magic user could be hiding. It was doubtful that it was one of the three fighters. Holding a spell while in combat was difficult for even an augmented magic user. And while these three were all big, they lacked the confidence of Finnian, Tomas, or any of the others in the gang.

Which meant there was someone else out of sight casting spells. They'd need to maintain line of sight for the blocking spell they were using. It seemed similar to her magic blocks, only not as well used.

A glint of light came from a set of tall trees high on the ridge before them. Not terribly close, but if that glint was of a looking glass, the mage would still have line of sight. While maintaining a good distance to run away if their plans failed.

She might be able to hit them with a spell, but that would leave her vulnerable to the woman with the pike. She clearly wasn't the best fighter around, but she was persistent enough that she would be able to take Lizeth down if she went to cast a spell. Another advantage to spell singing –she could have fought and sang at the same time and had, in fact, trained for it. Non-augmented spells wouldn't work in this case.

"Arcadia, can you hit that tree? There's someone in it." She yelled back to the archer.

Arcadia grinned. "If I can't, I don't deserve this bow." She took her aim and fired. Nothing happened. The weird blocking was still affecting their own people. Arcadia scowled, took a deep breath, aimed, and fired again. The scream as the mage tumbled out of the tree was a good sign.

The attacker facing her blanched as the mage fell, their magic protection vanished, and she swung out wildly with her pike. "We die free!"

Lizeth blocked the wild swing. She had a feeling that the people attacking them thought they were someone else completely as the other two yelled the same cry before they were run through by Janus and Tomas.

Lizeth didn't have the heart to do that. The woman before her looked seriously terrified. So, she threw a non-augmented spell at her to slow her down, then reversed her sword and knocked her on the head. The woman looked confused as her pike fell from her fingers and she tumbled to the dirt. The hit alone wouldn't have been enough to knock her out but the spell gave it enough kick to do so.

Janus ran over to run the woman through. "You have a sword for a reason."

Lizeth blocked his sword with her own. "And I know how to use it, and when not to use it. Don't you think this entire attack was odd?"

Finnian came over but didn't get between them.

"It was an attack. You fight back or you die." Janus stepped back but still held his sword ready.

"And understanding who and what is attacking you can make sure it doesn't happen again." Lizeth looked around to the others as they came closer. "Am I the only one who thinks this is extremely abnormal? The animals they were riding were ill-prepared for facing battle and ran as soon as they were able." She'd ask Scruff later how he knew they'd take off when he challenged them. For now, let the others think that had been part of their plan. "Their mage was far enough away that it limited the functionality of their spells—and cost them a fighter right at the start. No serious mage would do that if they were committed to a cause. And then their cry? 'We die free'? Why did they think we were going to capture them?" She pointed to the woman at her feet. "I, for one, am tired of not knowing who we're up against. These people were probably not with the people chasing us, but wouldn't you like to know why they attacked us?"

Finnian stepped forward and quickly bound the woman's wrists and ankles. Then he picked up her pike. "The chain mail is decent, even without a spell enhancing it. But this pike is crap." He easily snapped it in half. "I'd like to know what is going on." He threw the pieces of the pike into the shrubs behind them.

Tomas rubbed the back of his head. "Not our standard procedure, but being followed *before* we do a job isn't either. I say we see what she has to say when she wakes up." He pointed to Maurial and Dhlin. "Pat down our friend and the three bodies." He squinted up toward the tree line. "I'd like to see what that magic user had on them, but it looks like there's no trail on this side."

Rilkin stepped back from the first attacker. "Not much on him but this trinket. No weapons besides another badly made pike." He held up a necklace with a small golden shape dangling from it. "Not even real gold."

He was about to throw it away when Finnian narrowed his eyes. "Can I see that?"

Rilkin tossed it to him. Finnian held it up, but didn't touch the pendant itself as he looked at it. "A glarkin. These were followers of Velaix. Check to see if the others have the same thing. They won't be wearing it—not yet. It will be in their clothing." A look of disgust crossed his face.

Lizeth glanced over, but the cheap trinket didn't look at all familiar. The god Velaix sounded vaguely familiar but it wasn't a major deity and not someone who was followed by any country she knew. Her education was primarily focused on the closest countries, their best friends, and their worst enemies. Laiandra was one of the latter, but in her time, they had no public religion. Hopefully, that meant these throwbacks didn't move forward.

"They're all dead, the followers of Velaix, I mean." Maurial looked pale but didn't step closer. "Nasty people, but they were killed during my grand da's time. Why would anyone bring their religion back?"

"That's a good question." Tomas scowled down at the still unconscious woman. "I never followed religions; I don't like the idea of having to listen to something other than myself. But the followers of Velaix were a nasty bunch. These don't seem to be like what the stories said though." He had a sharp face and it got even more so when he was trying to sort something out.

"These were probably acolytes trying to prove themselves in battle—that's why they weren't wearing the necklace, but had it with them." Finnian shook his head as he studied the necklace. "Long ago, in another life, I was an academic. The followers of Velaix were a source of study for all military training. Ironically, because of their fighting prowess."

"Something that even as new fighters, these four didn't exhibit. I've seen first-year cadets do better than these," Tomas said.

"I still don't like that they're back—whether or not they know what they're doing." Maurial glared at the unconscious woman fighter. It was clear that she would be more than happy to take care of the still-alive part. "They did human sacrifices. And the people they took were alive when they were offered up to be tortured. Barely. I know I don't have book learning, but they are horrible."

"Is it safe to toss these?" Rilkin held up two of the pendants to Finnian. Finnian still had one and while Arcadia had patted the unconscious fighter down for weapons, and nodded that there was a pendant, she hadn't removed it.

"Yes. They're dead and hopefully removing them will upset the rest of their bunch when they find them. But hide them somewhere, don't just toss them." He handed the pendant he held to Rilkin. At a nod from Tomas, Rilkin darted into the forest. "I think we should leave the one on our guest. It could help her speak more freely if she thinks her deity is still supporting her."

Tomas stepped closer to the bound woman. "I'm fine with interrogating her, but might I remind you that we're still on a timeline, still being followed, and right now we don't have a magic shield running." He looked pointedly at Lizeth.

"Good points." Lizeth quickly mentally reached out for the searching spell, then shook her head. "No sign of it. I don't want to go into my trance until we talk to her." She looked up to see that everyone, including Finnian and Scruff, were looking at her.

"You took her out, you talk to her." Tomas folded his arms. "Not that we might not ask questions too, but you're part of our gang for now—follow through."

Lizeth looked at the woman. Talking wasn't a problem for her—as a princess everyone in the palace always wanted to talk to her. Interrogating a prisoner was something new however. Part of her had knocked the woman out simply because she couldn't stomach killing someone who was so overmatched. Knowing the type of person she probably was, or was trying to be, by hearing about the followers of Velaix, made her less sympathetic in that regard. The fact remained; this was an odd attack. While it could have been a coming-of-age training—although all four were not kids and easily older than Lizeth by ten years—she did still think finding out for sure was a good idea.

She took a deep breath and channeled her sister Nevaine. As a kid, Nevaine used to interrogate her teddy bears as to what they'd done while she was in lessons. That behavior had only intensified as she grew up. Lizeth took out her water pouch and poured a small amount on the woman's face. She sputtered, tried to move, then opened her eyes.

Yup, pure terror. Lizeth tamped down the surge of sympathy that rose when the woman realized where she was and with whom. This woman would have killed her, Finnian, Scruff, any of them simply because she was trying to prove her worth to some deity. Lizeth couldn't forget that.

"Why did you attack us?" Lizeth lowered her voice. Scruff and Finnian kept stating that her voice sounded normal to them, but she still heard a roughness even when she spoke normally. Lowering it made it suitably grave. At least to her ears.

"No, no, no. You were to kill us all if we failed. We failed. Kill me!" The last came out in a wail.

Lizeth bent down closer to her. "You aren't dead. That should mean something to you. Now, who sent you after us?" There was more doubt now that anyone had sent these four after them specifically, but she'd started this. And Janus was still looking ready to kill the woman.

"I die free!" The woman rolled around but she was tied too well to even hurt herself, let alone kill herself.

"Oh, this is ridiculous." Scruff stomped over with his tail poofed and fangs bared. "You will talk and talk now or my people and I will haunt your spirits into the afterlife. You know I speak the truth." The snarl he added was a nice touch but for Lizeth it was hard to take someone as soft and cute as Scruff as a danger—and she knew how deadly grigeens could be.

"Aye! Velaix smite me before the ravages of this foul beast!" The woman closed her eyes and yelled. After a few moments of nothing happening she peeked her eyes open. "I am still breathing."

"Yes, for now." Lizeth sighed. "But we won't let you go on to your reward until you tell us why you and your friends attacked us. We can keep you alive a long time, you know." Normally threatening to kill someone would be more of a logical choice—since this one wanted to die, keeping that from her seemed the better option.

"You are a cruel mistress, as foretold." She nodded. "I will speak. The great god Velaix has reawakened and is demanding sacrifices. You of the golden hair, great beauty, and voice of the gods were foretold to be coming and deemed the best first sacrifice."

Lizeth looked to Finnian, but he scowled and shrugged.

"But you were trying to *kill* me. Don't you need to bring your sacrifices still alive to your god?"

"I failed! I fell to the battle lust and failed again." The rest of her words were lost as she wailed and sobbed. It would have looked more dramatic if her hands and feet weren't tied.

Finnian stepped forward with his knife—handle first. "I don't think we're going to get anything more from her."

"True." Lizeth nodded and he knocked the woman out again.

"We should kill her. We don't want her rallying her people after us." Janus raised his sword.

"Seriously?" Finnian blocked him from moving closer. "This woman *wants* us to kill her. And she has nothing more to tell us. We leave her for her people to find." He tilted his head. "It's not good that they targeted Larking's appearance, but I don't think these are real followers of Velaix. They might think they are though. They'd have made a great delaying tactic if they managed to seriously injure or kill one of us." He shook his head. "I think someone set them up to slow people heading toward the lost city."

"I don't want to kill her if we don't need to." Lizeth agreed that someone had put these people in place. There was no way they could have won.

"I don't like leaving someone behind like her. Janus is right, they could follow us." Maurial wouldn't look at the woman.

Lizeth folded her arms and did her best haughty princess stare. "You truly think they are a force to even be considered remotely annoying? They didn't even hit anyone. Leave her tied, but leave her alive."

Tomas folded his arms and faced Lizeth. Finally he nodded. "I hire people for their skills, it's stupid not to listen to them. We leave her as is. Now, time for your trance? We need to make up time." He nodded to Maurial and Arcadia to stay back with Lizeth.

"I'm ready." Lizeth waited until they had started walking up the trail before she slipped into her trance. Like before, she was able to keep partially aware of the world around her as she searched for the spell hunting them. There was little conversation from the people around her this time however. Before she'd gone into a trance, she'd seen some of the trail beyond the immediate bend—lots of curves.

Most likely everyone would have their hands on their weapons and be moving silently.

Her thoughts kept drifting back to that woman and her words. Were these new followers just keen on getting a blonde sacrifice? She was the only golden blonde in this group, Janus was blond, and so was Maurial, but it was a much darker shade on both. But the voice thing disturbed her. Again, it could have been a made-up reason and they lucked out that she was a song mage. Or for some reason, was someone after her specifically? That was such a disturbing thought that she almost missed the searching spell reaching out.

Her shields were up so they rebuffed the spell, but still she wanted to be aware of the frequency of the attacks in case she needed to adjust her shields and she'd almost missed this one.

She also needed to speak to both Scruff and Finnian in private. Finnian knew an awful lot about an obscure defunct religion, and how did Scruff know those beasts would run when he stood up to them? And did he think that somehow those people were after her specifically?

Getting them alone wasn't going to be easy until they separated for the temple. This treasure that Tomas was after would need to be dealt with first since it had a timeline of when the path would be clear and that's what they'd been '*hired*' for. But after that she, Finnian, and Scruff could go pay their respects to the fallen temple. And really hope there was something there to help the three get back home.

A wave of hopelessness folded over her. What if her parents had never made it back to the palace after she'd vanished? What if her sisters were attacked and the palace fell? If the chancellor was really working on a plot to take over the country, he would have had resources to control the army. Removing all legitimate claims to the throne would be his first action. And what about the rash of dead bodies? She didn't even know if they were her countrymen or intruders, but someone had killed them with a purpose. Were the Stiklin involved? Some had followed them through to this time, but there could have been many more still inside the palace.

She never should have left. Ignoring the fact that she hadn't had a choice in leaving was part of the whirlwind of doubt and hopelessness. She knew that logically, but an evil voice said she could have stopped it.

"Is she okay?" Maurial wasn't talking to her but about her. "She's crying."

Lizeth felt Scruff put his front paws on her shoulder and sniff her face. "She's working through some things. Magic users aren't like the rest of us. I'd leave her be." He went back to his spot but not before patting Lizeth on the cheek.

She hadn't realized she was crying, but hearing that did get her to push back against the sorrow. It was easy to let it spin out of control, but she didn't have time for that. She took a deep breath and focused on the task at hand.

Her spell had successfully blocked three more spell tendrils from their followers when Maurial grabbed her arm and brought her to a stop.

"Halt! We have a problem." Tomas' voice seemed far away until Lizeth shook herself free of the spell. They'd come further than she'd expected if the massive hill behind them and the open plain before them was any indication.

It was hard to see what Tomas was pointing at until she stepped a bit away from the rest. The plain was open and at the center of a mountain ring of which the mountain they'd climbed down was the smallest. But the plain wasn't empty. In the center were the crumbled remains of a settlement sitting atop a hill. And surrounding that settlement was a line of knights, the afternoon sun glinting brightly off their armor.

Chapter Twenty-Four

"We can't get through them. There's simply no way." Janus scowled. "They knew we were coming." He turned to glare at Finnian and Lizeth. "I wonder how?"

"Why would we have done it?" Finnian snarled back. "We have a stake in this too. You're the one who spent time in the village with the knights. Maybe they paid you off to sell us out."

Tomas stepped between the two men. "Fighting each other isn't going to work. There is a huge reward waiting on the other side of that line of knights—I'm not giving that up."

Finnian and Janus glared at each other for a few moments more, then Finnian stepped back and released the hold he had on the hilt of his sword. Janus held his stance a bit longer, and then also backed down.

Lizeth watched Janus carefully. He was so unsavory; she knew he had to be up to something awful.

"We now have until the end of day after tomorrow to get the treasure and take it to the meeting point. Both of which are behind that line. I need ideas, now."

Arcadia looked around. "Might it be better to find somewhere more private to discuss things? We are on an open, if not often used, trail."

Tomas flushed at her words; he was more out of sorts about the knights being there than he'd been trying to let on. He'd gotten detailed information—most likely from whoever hired him—and the knights were unexpected. "Agreed. Let's go back up the mountain a bit. There were some shallow caves off the trail." He looked up into the sky. "It's getting dark enough to camp for the night, or at least a few hours. Crossing in the dark would be a safer idea."

"Once we figure out how to beat all of those knights, you mean." Rilkin wasn't happy as he continued to look through a long-glass.

"There is easily twice the number we see milling around the ruins. Are they looking for our treasure?"

Tomas held up his own long-glass, then shook his head. "If so, they are completely in the wrong area. Which is good. We'll have to be stealthier than I'd originally planned, but once we get around the knights, we should make it in and out without a problem." His grin indicated he was already spending the payment they'd be getting for this treasure in his head.

He still hadn't said much as to what they were looking for, and Lizeth didn't want to ask since no one else had.

Finnian had a smaller long-glass and he studied the area then handed it to Lizeth. She looked but wasn't certain what she was looking at. A lot of ruins and knights. She gave it back and he put it away as they all went back up the trail.

"I predict we'll have our trinket, give it to the emperor's men for the war, and be on our way to being rich within three days." Tomas led them up the trail.

Lizeth gave Finnian a worried look. There had been a war between Laiandra and Astarious, a horrible one, centuries ago, but she'd seen no signs that they were anywhere near a war zone.

Janus gave a rude snort as he followed Tomas. "That war is stupid and costing good people their lives. We need to stop expanding. Astarious isn't going to fall over and surrender to us just because we want them to. We need to build our country from within."

Lizeth carefully schooled her face. She had been about to reset the trance, but Janus's words caught her. They were obviously far beyond the battle lines, but being here during the time of that fight wasn't good. The chances for messing something up horribly increased.

"This item we're supplying will make that happen. Think of it, Janus, their land is lush and fruitful. They have more magic users than you can shake a stick at, and with this bauble, they will fall to our empire. Or so the propaganda says." Tomas shrugged. "Not that I plan on going there. Once we're paid, I'm getting a place far from the borders. A huge place with tons of servants and lots of land around me. Maybe a wife or two." He grinned at Maurial who remained walking next to Lizeth. Arcadia had gone ahead.

Maurial blushed but didn't look upset at his implication.

Lizeth kept the panic from showing. Her mother always said to keep the emotion for times of peace; in times of war, focus on the reality and the options. The main point was that they weren't near the border. The second point was that they might find a way to sabotage whatever the bauble was that Tomas was going to sell to the emperor's mages. Preferably without Tomas or the emperor's people realizing it. She didn't want Tomas and his people after her, Finnian, and Scruff, nor did she want Tomas' gang in trouble with the emperor. But hypothetically, a long hidden magical relic might not work after all of this time—she'd have to make sure that she pointed out that she had no reference to it and couldn't confirm that it worked. When they found it. That the empress's knights were swarming the ruins at the same time the emperor's people had hired Tomas to find the item didn't bode well for the unity of Laiandra.

The cave Tomas found, or rather cavelets, were really a series of small indentations that went about ten feet into the rock face. They weren't great but they were large enough to hide in. As long as they kept watch and didn't light a fire.

Tomas quickly set up a guard rotation, still keeping Finnian, Lizeth, Scruff, and Janus out of it. Finnian looked ready to argue but then shrugged it off.

Once everyone was settled, Lizeth leaned into Finnian's arms as she turned toward Tomas. "I need some time apart from everyone, for my magic. Groun will protect me." She took Finnian's hand in case she'd been too subtle.

Tomas raised an eyebrow—clearly he thought it was for other things than magic. Which was what she was hoping—magic might allow for some privacy, but not as much as if they thought she and Finnian were up to something else. "Just don't go far. It will be completely dark soon and I'll want to head down not long after."

Lizeth got to her feet with Finnian right behind. "We'll be back. Sorlin will keep an eye on our things. If something goes wrong, he can find me." She gave a small smile. She'd rather have Scruff with them for this discussion, but she also wanted him to listen to the others when they were gone. Not to mention that him staying behind reinforced the romantic rendezvous idea.

Scruff settled in on their packs, after a few circles to make sure it was comfortable, and nodded as if they took off frequently.

Finnian took her hand and they left the cave.

"We need to talk," Lizeth whispered once they were a little distant. Finnian led them further back into the trees.

"I gathered." He dropped her hand and found a small clump of shrubs. "This will work as long as you don't mind sitting on dirt." The sky was darkening, but still light enough that she could see the smirk on his face.

"It's rough for a princess of my renown, but I shall try." The space was small, but hid them from anyone on the trail or coming from the caves. Not really decent enough for a romantic entanglement in her mind, though.

She quickly shared her plan—which she didn't really have beyond stopping the emperor's being able to do whatever he was planning with whatever item Tomas was trying to find.

"That's vague, but I agree with it and will try to help where I can. I hope those followers of Velaix don't cause a problem—or even better, that they're fake. Reading about Velaix when I was younger left a horrible impact on me."

"That's another thing. I had an extensive education—including area religions. I'd barely heard a mention of Velaix."

"And your education was based on what limited information the Laiandran empire let escape. They were embarrassed by the Velaix episode of their past and tried to suppress it. Not to mention, history is written by the winners. Your people paid attention to other things when they beat Laiandra."

Lizeth shook her head. "We didn't win. The canyon caused both sides to have to stop fighting."

"But do you know what happened to Laiandra once the battle was cut short because of the Canyon from God? That's what they call it by the way. It doesn't look like it out this far away from the front lines, but the empire spent a lot of money on the battle. The goal was to expand not only through Astarious but into as many countries as they could. That plain out there that we need to cross is a desert now, but a hundred, maybe two hundred years ago it was lush farmland. Mage battles between warring overlords destroyed it. There are pockets like this all over Laiandra. The emperor and empress never stepped in because the mage warlords paid them tithes. That ended when the warlords destroyed each other. Not only is the land damaged, but their magic users were weakened by the strongest dying."

Lizeth took the information in, but now, more than before, she questioned where this had come from. She couldn't think of a single university that could have taught him that. She was about to ask him about that when the soft crunching sound of stealthy footsteps was heard on the other side of the shrubs.

Finnian grabbed her arms and pulled her in for a kiss. At first it was awkward as she hadn't been expecting it, but it quickly changed. Then it was definitely not awkward and she felt him responding to her as much as she was to him. This was a bad idea. Really bad.

"Ah, sorry, didn't mean to interrupt. Thought I heard voices and wanted to make sure we weren't being stalked." Arcadia had a short knife out, but she smirked as Lizeth and Finnian broke apart.

Lizeth really hoped she didn't look as completely confused and radically happy at the same time—because that's what she felt. A quick glance said the same look was on Finnian's face but he recovered quickly.

"That's okay. It might have been us. We were discussing some issues." Lizeth smiled and let Finnian help her to her feet. There was a shock at the touch of his hand, one that definitely hadn't been there before. She tried to ignore it, but a part of her refused.

Arcadia nodded but still had her knife out. "Yes, *talking*." She winked.

"Are you on guard rotation right now? I thought it was Rilkin?" Finnian kept his voice level, but Lizeth was getting to understand him well enough that she knew he sensed something was wrong.

"Actually, I was looking for Rilkin, but he seems to have wandered off. I can escort you two back to Tomas—he's talking strategy now." She finally put her knife away but she wasn't smiling.

Lizeth grabbed Finnian's hand. "We don't need an escort if you need to keep looking for Rilkin. Between Groun's sword and my magic we're fairly able to protect ourselves." She almost felt like Arcadia was challenging them. Being as she was one of the first, along with Maurial, whom Lizeth felt accepted them into the group, that was disturbing.

"I was joking; you two don't need protecting." Arcadia looked around the trees with a shrug. "And if Rilkin has wandered far away, he can deal with Tomas' anger when he gets back. I've done what I can."

Finnian squeezed Lizeth's hand but he did narrow his eyes as Arcadia turned and headed out of the forest.

Lizeth really wanted to talk about that kiss. She'd shared kisses before. Growing up she had her share of harmless boyfriends.

This kiss had been radically different from those. She felt this one deep in her soul.

And she shoved it into the same dark box that her suspected feelings for Finnian went in. Having casual boyfriends as a teen was different than when she would be an adult heir to the throne. She needed to focus on finding a suitable spouse. One that had royal lineage and magic.

It was too bad she hadn't met Finnian when she was younger though.

There was still no sign of Rilkin as they approached the cave, but Tomas stood near the entrance scowling into the night.

"You didn't see him?"

Arcadia shook her head. "Found these two though. Figured you wanted them back."

"Aye. We'll leave as soon as Janus gets back. I sent him out after Rilkin as well."

Arcadia shrugged and went inside. "I didn't see Rilkin anywhere, but maybe the great Janus will have better luck."

Tomas rolled his eyes after she passed by him. "Those two have never gotten along. Hoped that would change, but it's been a year now, so not gonna happen. At least they usually focus on killing others rather than each other."

Lizeth was about to go inside the cave—she agreed with Arcadia about Janus, there was something extremely off-putting about him—when the sound of someone running through the brush stopped her.

It was Janus and he had his sword out. "Someone killed Rilkin. Single dagger strike through the heart from behind." He held his sword at Finnian's throat before anyone could react.

Chapter Twenty-Five

"What are you doing?" Tomas kept his voice low and didn't move. Neither did Janus or Finnian. Lizeth was about to take the risk that her spell magic would work without destroying her and had a nasty spell song ready in her mind.

Finnian didn't look concerned. "I'd rethink your implication. I'd also look down." Finnian only had a dagger, but it was poised at Janus's stomach.

"These two go out and Rilkin is killed?" Janus licked his lips as he looked down at Finnian's dagger, but he didn't back away. "And he was killed with something like that."

"Why? You keep accusing us, but why? There's absolutely no reason to think we would do anything to stop this job." Lizeth flexed her fingers. Maybe she could brush Janus back far enough with a non-augmented spell to throw him off balance and keep him from Finnian.

"Because I don't think you're who you are claiming to be, for one. Haven't since we met you, but I wanted to see what your plans were before I brought it up."

Tomas narrowed his eyes. "You should have come to me if you had doubts."

"I have lots of doubts about this job, one of which is if we should even be doing it. I'm not running to you with everything." He didn't lower his sword, but his stance relaxed. "Isn't it convenient that the great Groun and Larking are running around in disguise? I get it when they were fleeing the village, but why haven't they dropped their glamour?" He turned to Lizeth. "You're exhausting yourself with that spell trance, yet you still have the ability to keep up a glamour spell? I've known some mages in my life and that can be a tricky thing to pull off. Not sure what your plan was at that inn with the fire, but it failed. So now you're taking us out one at a time on guard duty?"

Tomas watched him for a few moments, then turned to Lizeth. "He does make a point about the glamour—I'd wondered about that as well. Enough of us know what you two really look like, so while pretending to be far younger and prettier than either of you really are might be fun, I can't figure out why you'd waste magic on a glamour."

Lizeth thought quickly. The problem would be that she had no idea what the real Groun and Larking looked like. And she couldn't think of a good reason why she couldn't tell them.

"You might as well tell them the truth. It's embarrassing, but it's better than me having to kill Janus." Finnian looked to Tomas. "Neither Larking nor myself killed Rilkin nor sent the innkeeper and those trolls to kill everyone. I swear on my grand babies' graves." He gave Tomas a nod.

Lizeth scowled once her brain caught up to where she'd heard that phrase—in a book on Laiandra. A common phrase to indicate the speaker was offering unborn future generations if they were lying. It was handy that Finnian knew so much, but it was also a growing concern for her. One that Scruff caught as well as he sat on their packs with narrowed eyes and a lashing tail. He could have been glaring at Janus. But she had a feeling that glare was aimed at Finnian.

But it wasn't an issue they could deal with right now—certainly not with Janus holding his sword at Finnian's throat.

"I didn't want to tell them, but fine." Lizeth turned to face Thomas. "I might have broken the glamour spell. We were rushed, trying to stay away from the knights, who we weren't expecting, by the way." She channeled her best excuses-for-Boan voice as she got into her tale. "And now I can't take it off. One of the reasons I need to go to the abandoned oracle temple is to see if the waters under it will help release it." She gestured to herself with a wry grin. "I didn't look like this even when I was this age, so it's been fun. But I'd like my old self back."

Arcadia smiled. "I'm sure it doesn't hurt being stuck as a lovely young woman. 'A gray and craggy crone' was how I'd heard you referred to. And Groun as a 'skeletal twig of a man with deep sorrows on his face and stringy gray hair'. I'd say you made a good choice of what to get stuck as." She shrugged and turned to Tomas. "Before I joined you, I had also worked with magic users. Glamour spells are tricky and can get stuck. They warn new mages not to change into anything they don't want to spend their lives as. And I can attest that they were not anywhere near Rilkin." She glared at Janus. "Unlike someone who obviously was where Rilkin was."

Lizeth let herself relax a bit. Having Arcadia back up her story definitely helped.

Janus glared at everyone. "I *found* Rilkin, I didn't kill him." He lowered his sword and cautiously stepped back from Finnian's dagger.

Finnian stepped back as well, but he didn't put away his dagger.

Tomas watched them both before shaking his head. "Maurial and Dhlin—follow Janus to Rilkin and bury him properly. But quickly. Someone killed him and they might be doing so to make us fight among ourselves or something else. But we need to get down to the ruins within the hour."

Finnian gave Janus one final glare then stalked over to Lizeth. "Let's make sure we're ready to leave." Together they went to their packs.

There were a lot of things that Lizeth needed to talk about—and she couldn't bring up a single one. She did flash a smile to Arcadia for coming to their rescue. She was glad her doubt about her was wrong. Her thought process wasn't working as great as she'd like, so it was handy that Finnian pointed her toward a creative lie.

Her thoughts were mush because Finnian had muddled her brain with that kiss. She knew why he did it, but her reaction, and that it felt like it was returned by him, were not what she needed right now. If Tomas and his people thought they weren't Groun and Larking, they wouldn't hesitate to kill them.

"Not sure what those clothes did to you, but shoving them around like that isn't going to help," Scruff said as came up next to her as she rearranged her pack for the third time. "Thinking of strangling a certain person? Me too. That Janus is wretched. He's most likely the spy, if anyone is."

That hadn't been who she'd been frantically trying to work out of her head while she packed, but that was a good enough excuse. She wasn't admitting her reactions to Finnian to anyone until they were back home and she was safely married. And possibly already had grandkids.

She'd always been logical about her attachments since she knew the boys she flirted and dallied with couldn't be anything more. They were safe and she focused on men like Trion—attractive, suitable, and stable as her marriage goal. If she thought about it, she wasn't even sure she liked him—he was just the next step toward queen-hood.

Finnian certainly couldn't be anything more, but that wasn't stopping her from mentally fluttering about every time she looked over at him.

Scruff narrowed his eyes as he followed one of her glances. "Oh no. No. No. Push that thought out of your mind." He dropped his voice to a hiss. "Did something happen out there?"

She tried to look affronted as she shook her head.

"Oh, no. It did." His tail lashed more. "We can't deal with it now, but you have obligations. *That* can't happen."

Lizeth shrugged. "It's nothing. I'm fine, I'm keeping things under control. It was to fool anyone who came upon us." And she might believe that in a few years. How Finnian had gone from an annoying woodsman she hung in the air to someone she now had to pull back from wasn't something to deal with, or talk about.

"Well, just you watch it, young lady." Scruff ruffled his fur in order to look larger and fiercer. Which didn't work on her.

"You think the oracles' temple will hold any help for you?" Arcadia came up from behind as Lizeth finished packing.

Lizeth schooled her face before turning around. "I hope so. The oracles guide many things. As much as I don't mind looking like this"—she flashed a smile—"it is a drain. Not to mention, our reputations will be at stake if we no longer look as we did. I'm not sure I want to go through this age again." Since she really was only twenty, she tapped into some of the conversations she'd heard in the kitchen among the older staff. They missed their youthful looks, but enjoyed who they were inside more now.

"True." Arcadia looked to Finnian with a crooked grin. "But there are some advantages."

Lizeth fought the blush she felt creeping up. "Yes, there is that."

"Who did you base your glamour spell on?" Arcadia's smile had dropped and her eyes were darker.

Lizeth felt the truth almost come out but fought back with a smile. "A young couple we'd come across near the border a few months ago. Farmers, I think." She took a deep breath. Had Arcadia tried to use a truth spell? Supposedly none of the people working with Tomas were magic users aside from herself. But that tug had been noticeable and distinctive. "I think Tomas is ready to leave." She stepped around Arcadia and fought off the shiver she felt. If Arcadia were a magic user—and one who was hiding it from these people even though she'd been with them for a year—that was extremely bad news.

Maurial, Janus, and Dhlin had come back and were waiting silently outside the cave. They'd buried Rilkin shallowly, if the time was any indication.

Lizeth had only known Rilkin a few days and probably hadn't said more than one or two words to him. But his loss still should have more meaning. She sent a silent farewell and followed Finnian outside.

The way was dark, but Tomas seemed surefooted as he led them down. Lizeth knew her eyesight was better than most, but she was impressed at how well he did. There was an almost full moon, but it kept hiding behind clouds. The group followed him exactly, staying close enough to see each other.

Lizeth didn't want to take the chance of not being able to see while she set the spell searching spell, so she heightened her general awareness of magic instead of going into the trance. A tricky spell and another that would have worked so much better as a spell song. It would ideally let her know if magic was around and the general direction it was coming from. Hopefully she'd sense the searching spell in time to block it, but doing it this way did leave things more open for others to find them. It was that or stumble off the trail in the dark. She was willing to take the magic risk.

Finnian had stayed next to her. "No trance?"

"No, it's too dark to try that." She didn't want to point out her superior vision. Not that it mattered about him knowing, but she wasn't sure who to trust in this group now, and her mother had always said to keep some advantages secret even among friends.

They reached the plain as Tomas waited a few moments in silence. He pulled out a slip of paper that had glowing lines on it. It looked like a piece of map, but he put it away before she could see much of it. Then he led them along the base of the mountain. There were few knights to be seen, and most far from their side. Hopefully, that stayed.

There were low mutters but nothing voiced loud enough to understand. With her better eyesight, Lizeth could see why he changed direction, even though she couldn't see what was on the magical paper—normal paper didn't glow. The place they came off the mountain trail was a longer route across the open plain to get to the ruins. He was using the backdrop of the mountain to hide their passage from being seen by the knights in the ruins. Even when they crossed the plain, the location of the moon coming up would cast enough shadow to at least make them less noticeable. If the moon stayed away from the clouds.

And that was his plan. They got to the narrowest part where the ruins were closest to the mountain base and Tomas stopped. Clouds were still drifting across the moon and he held his hand up for everyone to wait. When the clouds moved and the moon made a shadow across the face of the mountain, he got them moving.

Now she understood his insistence on a certain time. It was interesting that he hadn't expected the knights to be there, yet had a plan, and a bit of a magical map to help, when they were.

As they jogged toward the ruins, she saw there was another advantage to coming in from this side. The ruins weren't well covered by the knights at this section. There seemed to be far fewer than earlier, but most were at the front—the way they would have come in from the mountain trail. Tomas took another peek at his map, so small it fit in the palm of his hand, and led them around a fallen tower. Whatever that map was, it was good. Magical maps that could adapt were hard to make and usually extremely old. He had to pause every once in a while, but it led them around the debris. Hills of noise-making rubble were piled on either side of the thin trail the map led them on. Even with her eyesight, Lizeth would have been hard-pressed to find a silent way through.

A part of Lizeth would have liked to have seen more of the ruins up close as even the remains of the tower they passed was unique in design. It didn't look anything like the bulky and boring designs she associated with the Laiandran people.

Tomas quickly led them past it.

She did wonder how she and Finnian were going to find the oracles' temple before daybreak—obviously without Tomas' map. He had no problem with them going to look for it—after they found what he wanted. But he wasn't going to help them. If she was certain that going there would get them home, she'd break off and search for it now. Since there was no way to know what going there would do, and that they might need Tomas and his map to get out of these ruins, she made certain to stay with them.

Even when she spotted the arch of the oracles' fallen temple in the distance. The arch should have been on the front of the temple itself, but there was no building behind it—or rather not a standing one. Most likely the dark pile behind the arch was the collapsed building. Even with her improved eyesight, climbing around the rubble looking for something from the oracles wasn't going to be easy in the dark, and without disturbing the knights. The knights had a skeleton crew on guard, but she'd seen how many were out here. The rest were sleeping somewhere and could easily be called to help.

She made a mental note where the temple was and paid attention to everything around it. She nudged Finnian and pointed toward it.

"Good spotting." He held up his long-glass and seemed to be making notations of his own.

Tomas picked up the pace and they passed the temple. With the number of ruins here, and that it seemed like many had broken down to absolute rubble, it was amazing how silent they were.

Until Janus misstepped.

Tomas held up his fist and everyone froze. Tense moments passed as they waited for the knights to head their way. When that didn't happen, Tomas glanced at his mini map again and quickly headed out. Janus shook his head and followed.

Lizeth started watching Janus more than Tomas. If he was trying to get them captured by the knights, he might *accidently* slip again. She wasn't the only one as Arcadia kept her hand on her dagger and dropped back to stay closer to him.

Maurial was right behind Tomas but kept glancing back. That she was almost exclusively glancing back to Janus reinforced Lizeth's concerns. They had a traitor in their midst as they were crossing enemy territory. Exposing him now would increase the risk for everyone, but after they were safe, Lizeth had a feeling he would be taken care of.

The sound of a single pair of metal clad feet walking slowly brought all of them to a halt as Tomas raised his fist.

The knight didn't seem to be looking for them, at least not them specifically, as his pace was steady but not trying to be silent. He wasn't wearing his helmet as he probably felt he was safe, as well as it really would have made seeing anything in the dark almost impossible. He also wasn't yelling for back up. Which she felt he probably would have done had he known they were out here. The best thing to do would be to wait until he finished this section of his search, then move on after he left. Attacking a single sentinel when you hadn't been found was one of her father's rules of stupidity. Also known as—how to get yourself killed without trying hard.

Tomas motioned down and everyone crouched. The knight wasn't that close, but the silence of the ruins carried the sound of his boots well. He was starting to leave their area, when Arcadia silently got up, drew her bow, and fired. The arrow slammed into the back of his head and he collapsed. He might have been silent, but the sound of all that armor crashing as he fell was not.

Chapter Twenty-Six

Tomas swore softly and led them racing across the ruins in a different direction than he'd been headed.

Arcadia put back her bow, but Lizeth saw her smile as she did so.

"What in the world did she do that for?" Scruff's whispered words came from right next to her ear and wouldn't be heard by others.

"No idea." Lizeth kept her words low but didn't want to say more. Not to mention that at their increased pace, keeping her feet, and not making too much noise while doing it, wasn't easy.

The pounding sound of knights in armor running wasn't what she wanted to hear, but she wasn't surprised. The clatter from that knight collapsing was probably heard back in the village they'd run from.

Tomas ducked into the ruins of what was probably once a huge building, judging by the debris everywhere. At least it still had walls and a roof—sort of. He motioned for them to stay down and when Arcadia pulled out her bow and turned to face outwards, he ripped it from her hands.

There was fury on his face as he glared at Arcadia. She reached for the bow but even though he was shorter than her he kept it away. "I will snap it." The words were low and quiet but full of intention. Lizeth knew he'd do it.

Arcadia flexed her fingers, then nodded and moved back. "I panicked." The words didn't ring true and Lizeth recognized the finger movements Arcadia made. Sorcerers often used their fingers and hands to direct and guide their spells.

Lizeth swore under her breath. She'd been focused on the spell searching for them and missed Arcadia's sorcery. She could be a mage, but finger movements were rare with magic users. Lizeth closed her eyes and gave a hard push to her own magic searching spell. Arcadia glowed in her mind's eye. And a trail led from her to the searching spell.

Lizeth had been blocking it, but Arcadia had been creating it?

She wasn't sure what to do. This was a horrific place to challenge Arcadia and she had no idea how strong of a sorceress she was. Now that she saw the trail, she realized that the searching spell had neatly masked any sorcery residue from Arcadia that Lizeth might have picked up on.

She had a bad feeling that she knew who'd killed Rilkin. Why she did it wasn't so clear. Even though Tomas was being cagey about what they were after, she guessed that Arcadia knew. She might have wanted it for herself, but her goal seemed more to make certain Tomas and the rest of them didn't get it. Considering that whatever it was, it was supposed to help the emperor in the fight against Astarious, that most likely meant that Arcadia was secretly working for Astarious as a spy—or she was working for the empress. From what she'd heard from the people around her while they'd traveled, Lizeth gathered that the empress and emperor were roughly on the same side against everyone else, but one wouldn't mind if the other were out of the picture.

The choice was made for her when Maurial stabbed Arcadia in the arm with a thin dagger. It was so thin that it almost looked like a needle, and it looked to be coated in something.

Arcadia lunged for Maurial but whatever had been on the thin blade dropped her before she took two steps.

Lizeth wanted to ask if Arcadia was dead, but a slow rise of her chest told her no. Maurial wiped off the blade and put it away. Then she kicked Arcadia a few times. She'd made the same connection of who killed Rilkin as Lizeth had, and Maurial seemed to have been friends with him.

Tomas handed Arcadia's bow and quiver to Dhlin, the only archer remaining.

Then the sound of knights grew closer to their hideout.

Lizeth held her breath and a nasty spell at the ready. If she collapsed after using a spell song, so be it—they were running out of options.

Everyone around her had weapons drawn as they waited in the darkness.

"I don't see anyone, and a damn long-bow archer could have gotten him from outside the perimeter. Everyone move back, and increase the border guards."

The voice was close enough that the hairs on the back of her neck rose. Lizeth took some deep calming breaths; this could be it. The people she was with were excellent fighters, but there had been dozens of knights out there earlier. Even if her spell songs worked, they might not make it if it came to a full fight.

There was more discussion among the knights, but not loud enough to hear, then they moved away.

Lizeth had clenched her hand so tightly around the hilt of her sword that it hurt as she released it. That was interesting. Before this adventure, she would have never thought to be ready with both spell and blade—if she even had a blade with her. Now it was automatic. She doubted her Challenge had dumped her in the past just to get that point across, however.

"What do we do with her?" Maurial kicked Arcadia one more time. Maurial was normally loud, even in everyday speaking, but her whisper was such that no one outside the collapsed building would have heard it.

"Tie her up, gag her, and leave her. Not sure who she's working for, but hopefully it'll take the knights a while to figure it out." Tomas had the same whisper.

Lizeth still thought there was a good chance that Arcadia and the knights were both working for the same person—the empress.

But unless they were expecting one of their spies out here, it could take them time to sort it out. Hopefully.

"If we kill her, she can't tell them anything." Janus came close and held up his sword. "We know she killed Rilkin."

"That drug I gave her will keep her out for a day or two. If we're not out of here by then, we're already dead." Maurial stepped back. "I want to pay her back on an equal field. At another time."

At a nod from Tomas, Janus backed down.

Lizeth watched Janus carefully. Even though Arcadia had been shown to be the traitor, that didn't mean there couldn't be two. They might not even be on the same side. Maurial and Finnian tied and gagged Arcadia and neither were gentle about it.

Tomas looked outside their shelter, then turned right. It was roughly the same direction he'd been headed before the encounter with the knight, but Lizeth followed him along with the rest.

A strange sound came from all around them after a few minutes. Everyone's hands dropped to their weapons—aside from Tomas.

"Ghosts." Scruff whispered in her ear. "Ignore them no matter what they do."

Everyone, including Finnian, seemed to know about them as they didn't slow down, even when faint images began appearing alongside them. Rather gruesome ones as none of the spirits trapped here had died of old age. A chill hit her as a decapitated man walked through her, but she ignored him as best she could.

One spell she had in her arsenal, that she really thought she'd never use, was singing souls to sleep. It was mostly done as an act of soothing for the survivors, but this was also the first time she'd seen real ghosts. These souls were definitely not happy. She made a mental promise; she would sing them free when she found her way home. If the stories were true, something had trapped them here, and someone was probably using them to keep people away. Possibly from whatever it was Tomas was searching for. She'd let them move on to the next life, or heaven, or wherever they belonged.

Providing she could get free from here.

A wave of warmth flowed over her and the pitch of the ghosts' moaning changed.

"Agreed." A woman warrior with the look of someone who drowned, stood in front of her. "Safe passage." Even though the ghost stayed motionless in front of her, Lizeth felt a ghostly hand clasp her elbow then all of the ghosts vanished.

Scruff was back down near her ear immediately. "What did you do?"

"Nothing." She kept her voice low but still saw the others turn back to her. She couldn't explain now, but clearly the ghosts heard her mental pledge to set them free and accepted it.

Tomas raised his fist as knights could be heard marching toward them. They weren't that far away but there was nothing to hide in that she could see. And the moon was making them far too visible.

"What's that? Damn it! Stop it!" The knights were fighting someone, but it wasn't clear who.

Then the howling of the ghosts came from the same direction as the sound of the knights. "Don't look at them!" Sounds of knights running away were a wonderful thing to hear. Tomas nodded and took off at a faster pace. The ghosts had bought them time, but they still needed to get away from the knights.

They jogged for another fifteen minutes without sight nor sound of the knights. Maybe this had all been the ghosts' area and the knights figured they didn't need to patrol since the ghosts would take care of anyone coming through. Lizeth said a mental thank you to the ghost who'd met with her as she followed the others. She would let them move on. Considering how old the ruins looked, those ghosts might have been haunting here for a long time. It was cruelty that kept them here.

Tomas halted the group in front of a deep crater. A large, dark pit that, even with her eyesight and the moon not being covered by clouds, still looked too dark. And deep.

He motioned for them to move in closer. "The thing we want is at the bottom of that crater. I assume we have Larking to thank for removing the ghosts. Good thing, as they've led many explorers to their deaths. I figured that it would be better if you didn't know. But thank you, Larking. Once we get the object from down there, a portal will open. There's a powerful mage working with the people who hired us. He can't get the object directly as there are layers of magic around it, but if we break it free, he can come get the object and give us our reward."

"And then we have to fight our way back out through the knights?" Dhlin wasn't happy and neither were the others. Lizeth didn't blame them. She, Finnian, and Scruff would be separating—after they got paid, to keep up the ruse. Hopefully, that temple would have a way home and dealing with the knights wouldn't be an issue. It would be for everyone else though. Riches were useless if you couldn't live to spend them.

"No, the mage will give us coverage to leave. We'll have to move quickly, but we should be able to get out without being seen." He turned to Lizeth and Finnian. "Still staying here after the job? The mage's coverage won't protect you in that temple."

"Yes. I need to, for my family." Which was true, she needed to make sure the future wasn't the one she'd seen before and that her family was safe. She wasn't as good at the way of whispering they used but she tried to keep her voice as low as possible.

"What is this thing?" Dhlin asked as they slowly descended into the crater.

"You'll see," Tomas said as he lit a small torch from a fire stone and scrambled down faster.

The term hole wasn't accurate; it was a pit. There had been a building here and more of it remained than most of the ruins they'd seen. But it was inverted on itself—somehow the pit was made of the exterior walls of what was once a massive hall. Only heavy magic could have done that, and Lizeth didn't know any spells that could even come close. It appeared to have happened hundreds of years ago, yet the sides still exuded magic residue as they made their way down. She shivered as it reached out to her.

"Stay focused. I feel it too—bad magic." Scruff had stayed with his two front feet on her shoulder.

Lizeth tried, but it was hard. How could a spell that old still be calling? The answer came as a tendril twisted toward her until she smacked it aside. The spell was old, and the only way it had stayed alive as long as it had was feeding off magic users who ventured down here. A pile of skeletons along the trail, all without any sort of armor, attested to its success in the past.

"Not this time." She stuck to non-augmented magic but sent a reverse spell to the walls around them as they descended. It wasn't strong but was slowly sucking away what magic remained in the walls.

There was still residue, but it was no longer reaching out to any-one. The fact that someone was strong enough to have created such a spell, and vicious enough to make it self-feeding was horrifying.

The path wasn't clear and there were times of scrambling over debris piles as well as walking sideways to get through partially col-lapsed ledges. Still the bottom was not in sight.

Lizeth was about to light a torch of her own with magic when the sound of loud flapping wings and a horrific scream filled the space.

Chapter Twenty-Seven

The shadow that followed the sound made Lizeth wish that Tomas' torch had gone out. A long serpentine head with vicious teeth and white eyes snaked toward them.

"A drake! Aim for the mouth and the throat." Tomas yelled as the time for being silent fled.

The drake hovered near them but Dhlin couldn't get a shot in. The creature wasn't that far, and Dhlin didn't have Arcadia's skill, but the creature seemed to move away at every arrow.

Lizeth tried to sense any spells guiding the monster but since the entire place was spelled, nothing was clear. "Magic?" she asked Scruff. He might not be able to tell any better than she but his intuition was good.

"My thoughts exactly. Don't use a song though. This place will make it worse and you're not up to it."

She bristled a bit at that. She should be the one to decide what she was up to or not. But she still used a non-augmented spell of revealing. Drakes were little more than myths in their world, and even this far in the past, it shouldn't be here.

The drake turned to her and raised its head to swallow her. She released her spell and the drake vanished into smoke—it had been a spell. She let her breath out slowly. That was close. Even though that wasn't a real drake, it could have hurt or even killed her if the spell behind it was strong enough. Whatever was down here, someone really didn't want anyone getting it. That it was something that could turn the tide of the battle against her own people made her sick to her stomach.

Tomas started walking again, but Finnian softly called out. "Give her a moment. This place is full of magic and that spell drained her."

Lizeth smiled, took a few deep breaths, and then nodded to move on. She was grateful for his stepping in, though. Since she was the only magic user, no one else would know how this place felt.

They made it to the final level above the ground—that they could finally see. The ledge winding down to it was only about a foot wide and looked to be crumbling as she watched. The drop to the bottom was at least two stories down and the floor was filled with nasty-looking sharp rubble.

And there was an increase in magic around them. This felt different though—it was dark sorcery. For the most part sorcery and magic used similar spells. However, magic was something given at birth—or at least the potential for it was. Whereas sorcery was mostly learned. Sorcerers also used gestures and spoken words to augment their spells. Or so Lizeth had been taught. No one really talked of sorcerers or sorcery much in the palace.

Lizeth had only met one sorcerer in her life before Arcadia—a woman who lived in a cottage in the woods favored by the grigeens, Gliandra. The grigeens were her friends and they kept others from coming out to see her and messing with her spells. She'd come into the palace once, right after Piallen was born, to wish good life and place some sort of blessings on all three royal daughters. Lizeth was only four at the time and didn't recall much except that Gliandra scared her.

Like mages, sorcerers could follow light or dark paths. The one here was so dark it almost took her breath away. And, because it was sorcery and not magic, unlike the spell of the drake and the one on the walls, this spell was recent and fresh. Sorcery had to be maintained in the long term, more so than magic. And it could also be more powerful than magic—even augmented magic—if the sorcerer were strong enough.

"We need to stop." She kept her voice low but she needed Tomas to hear her. Luckily, he had excellent hearing and trusted her enough to stop even though his goal was within sight. "There's dark sorcery here—something evil." If she could have done it without falling off the ledge, she probably would have stepped to the side and gotten ill. The feelings that came with the sorcery flowing around them were awful.

"Magic is magic. Can't you stop it?" Dhlin said louder than he should have.

Tomas carefully stepped past Dhlin at a wider section as he moved back to be closer to her. He didn't say anything but watched around them carefully.

Lizeth kept her voice low. "Magic and sorcery are different things—we work differently. My spells might not have an effect on the ones used by a dark sorcerer." Not to mention she didn't think she knew of any non-augmented spells that could fight against what she was feeling. Violence, hatred, and death all flowed around her. The worst was the glee that all of those things brought to whoever was behind it.

"We can't stop now; what is the spell going to do?" Tomas glanced to her as he continued looking around them.

"Kill you all where you stand." The deep voice echoed around the chamber.

Everyone already had their weapons out and Lizeth was seriously thinking of using a spell song.

"Who's there? Show yourself!" Tomas yelled into the air, but nothing more came.

Because Tomas had moved to where Lizeth and Finnian were, Dhlin was in the lead. He started firing arrows into the air and yelling.

There was nothing there and he seemed to be firing randomly. Then a crack of lightning appeared from the ground and slammed right into Dhlin's chest. He was dead before his body hit the ground.

"What do you want? And us dying isn't an option." Finnian stepped forward without his sword and arcs of lightning crackled between his hands.

At first, Lizeth thought that he'd been hit the same way Dhlin had, then she realized the arcs were coming *from* Finnian. And they felt like sorcery. Her eyes went wide, but she tried to keep her surprise hidden. No one thought Groun was a magic user and he'd been around for a long time. She certainly hadn't thought that Finnian was a magic user.

Tomas, Maurial, and Janus all looked to Finnian then her.

She shrugged and tried to look calm, as if this wasn't totally unexpected. "He doesn't like to let people know. But, yes, he's a sorcerer."

How in the world he had any sort of magic or sorcery—now that he'd done something she could tell that's what it was—the entire time they were traipsing through this adventure and she never knew was going to sting for a long time. That he hadn't told her was a different issue—but even worse.

"Ah, young one. Your sorcery will taste lovely when I take you—not much training there, but the knowledge of spells and the potential you will give up will be delectable. Not as much as your blonde spell singer companion, but never fear, I will enjoy all the abilities you both have. Once I get those abilities, I will be free to roam again. Being trapped here for a thousand years has been awkward to say the least."

Scruff started swearing under his breath and Lizeth felt his tail lashing as he sat on her pack. Had she a tail it would be lashing as well. First Finnian had sorcery of some sort, and now this evil sorcerer knew she was a spell singer. Tomas and the other two didn't seem to know who to look at.

"You can't sing a spell song. The risk is too great. I didn't want to say it before as I hoped things would change. I do hear the roughness in your voice—you overextended and damaged your magic. Every time you cast a spell song until you have had time to recover, you risk losing your ability to sing. Forever." Scruff kept his voice low and spoke quickly. "However, telling you before could have made things worse."

But his words rang true. Somewhere inside she knew he was right. Being in denial had been nice. But if this was where she lost her spell singing magic, then so be it. Tomas, Maurial, and Janus weren't really friends—she still didn't trust Janus—but none of them deserved to die down here. Not to mention that if the voice was telling the truth, just by she and Finnian coming to him they might unleash an evil sorcerer on the world. He could have a weapon to win the battle for Laiandra, but then that land would fall as well. Then the rest of the world.

"Or we all might die and take down thousands with us. Sorry, Scruff, I don't have a choice." She looked up to see the other three watching her. Their ruse was probably pointless right now, but she tried. "It's a nickname for him. You heard our friend, I'm a spell singer. Groun is a sorcerer, and Scruff has his own powers. Non magic users probably want to stay behind us." There was a hell of a lot of things to deal with, but first they needed to survive.

A dry wind swirled around them as the other three got behind her and Finnian.

Janus stopped near her as he passed. "You're not really Larking and Groun, are you?" For the first time since they'd met him, he didn't sound snarky or judgmental.

She was going to lie, then gave it up. "No, we're not. But we can still try and save you." She lifted her chin and reminded herself who she was. "Now, shall we?" She did pull out her sword, it felt better than going into battle without it, even though she was already running through spell songs in her head.

"I'll follow you anywhere." Finnian smiled with far too many emotions for her to sort out right now. One hand held his sword, the other was crackling with power. She wasn't certain if it was the same sorcery the voice had taken out Dhlin with, but it was impressive.

"Are you planning on hiding forever? What's wrong, were you horribly injured when you were trapped here?" Lizeth took a few steps down the ledge as she taunted the voice.

Scruff clutched her pack hard and Finnian stepped behind her.

A crack of lighting hit under Finnian's feet and he fell from the ledge.

Lizeth sang the spell she'd used when she first met him. It slowed his decent but the timber of her voice had enough distortion that she couldn't keep him in the air. He started drifting down.

"It's okay." Finnian shouted as he landed and sent an arc of lightning into a rock. The entire structure shook. A short arc snapped back at him and he stumbled but blocked most of it with his sword.

"Why are you afraid of us?" She took another two steps down the ledge. Ideally, she might try to float herself and Scruff down like she'd done for Finnian, but she wasn't that confident in her ability to do so. Even with her voice at full strength, floating others was much easier than herself.

"He's afraid that we're going to take his treasure. The weapon must be the only thing he has anymore." Finnian took a few steps toward what looked like a cave made out of rubble.

Lightning blasted him backwards, but unlike the attack on Dhlin, it didn't kill him. It looked like he knew enough to have a shield up.

A rumble shook the walls, but it wasn't the same as before. It was...laughter?

"Weapon? Boy, there is no weapon but me. I was trapped here long ago by beings who didn't understand me, but who couldn't kill me. The people who sent you to get me want to use me to destroy their enemies. You will open the portal at this end, I will take all of the magic from you and your woman, then you will die. If you open the portal quickly, your deaths will be quick. Take too long and you will beg to die. I will go through the portal and destroy those magic users as well, then feast upon the war they are involved in."

Lizeth tilted her head as the sorcerer rambled. Her voice might not be working the best, but having music training almost her entire life left her with exceptionally good hearing.

She ran down the ledge, the edges crumbling as she went, but she moved faster than they could fall. As she ran, she sang at the top of her lungs, trying to adjust for the variance in her voice as she sang a spell of reveal and containment. A tricky spell under textbook circumstances—running down a ramp with a damaged voice as she cast it was something else. But she knew exactly where that sorcerer was.

The tunnel that Finnian had faced was close, but not right. A large throne-like pile of rocks a few feet over from it was the hiding spot. As she sang, an image flickered in and out. Then finally held. Tall, cloaked in shimmering white, an old man with long white hair and a kindly face. Not what she was expecting, but looks could be deceiving.

"What did you do?" Arcs of lightning flew out from his fingers only to bash themselves into a shield the confinement spell threw around him. His eyes went red and his jaws grew longer. Whatever he really was, it wasn't anything Lizeth had heard of before.

Chapter Twenty-Eight

"A glouthlin? Seriously? You were all killed. Long ago." Finnian came forward but stopped next to Lizeth. She might not have a clue what this sorcerer was, even the name didn't sound remotely familiar, but Finnian's research helped him again.

"I survived." The jaws returned to normal, but his eyes stayed red. "Now, you will die." An arc of lightning grabbed Finnian as a portal of light appeared behind the sorcerer.

Lizeth had a brief flash of hope that maybe the oracles had stepped in, but a group of ancient-looking Laiandran mages crowded through the portal. They tried to pull back once they saw the sorcerer, but he flung Finnian against the wall and spun on them.

"Thank you for opening that side with your magic, but I have more places to consume and people to kill." He turned to the mages, now trying to climb over each other to get back out of the portal. They'd obviously been expecting their battle-changing weapon—not envisioning that weapon to have plans of his own.

The sorcerer lashed out at all of them, muttering a spell that burned Lizeth's ears as he did so. The mages all screamed as everything was drawn from them and they collapsed into dried husks. The sorcerer raced down the portal.

Lizeth ran to Finnian where he lay on the floor. Maurial, Tomas, and Janus did as well.

"Come on, grab him, but we need to follow that thing," Janus yelled as he also tore through the portal.

Tomas shrugged and took off after him. Maurial picked up Finnian. Then she and Lizeth ran toward the portal.

"Faster!" Scruff called from atop Lizeth's pack. "It's closing! That sorcerer has to be stopped!"

Maurial picked up speed and Lizeth followed at her heels. The portal closed down a few feet behind her as she raced out. Close enough that she felt a push of wind behind her.

Tomas and Janus were swearing as they looked around. Maurial joined in but didn't put Finnian down. Lizeth couldn't even swear.

She'd never seen an actual battle scene outside of the history books that always made them look more honorable and less gruesome. But that's what this was. She didn't recognize the land around them, not on this side. But her exemplary eyesight spotted the flags on a line of knights charging across a field below them—it was the flag of Astarious and they were racing toward knights bearing the flag of Laiandra. Crossing a plain that she was pretty sure should have a massive canyon down the middle of it.

"We're at the front." Tomas' eyes were wide and he looked lost as no one disagreed with his assessment.

"And we're really good targets for any archers down there." Scruff jumped off Lizeth's pack. "Follow me." He jogged back to a thin line of trees. It wouldn't hide them from anyone who came up this far, but they were far enough back from the cliff overlooking the battlefield that it should keep anyone down there from seeing them.

Maurial gently put Finnian down but she looked as confused as the rest. "Someone sent us here with magic?" She turned to Lizeth. "Could you send us back?"

Lizeth ran to Finnian. He'd hit that wall hard but there were few injuries to show for it beyond some bruising on his face. And hands. He'd put them up to protect himself but both hands looked bent wrongly now. They weren't just broken, they were shattered. "No, I couldn't. Even if my magic was in perfect form, which it's not, I couldn't do that. I don't even know anyone who *could* do that." Terror built in her chest as she turned back to Finnian and gently put her hand on his chest. He was still breathing and she felt his heart fighting for life, but there was something wrong inside him. Considering how hard he was slammed into the wall, there were probably many things wrong with him.

"How are we going to get out of here?" There was a shrill note of real panic in Maurial's voice.

"I don't know, but I need to heal him." Lizeth was already crying. She knew healing songs but wasn't sure they would be strong enough. Or that her voice would hold. She might not be able to save him this time.

Tomas waved Maurial to where he and Janus stood a way off. "Let them be. We need to assess the situation. Stay in eyesight of each other, but there must be a way down from here that doesn't go out to that plain." He nodded toward Lizeth. "I hope you can save him." Then the three moved off.

"I'll keep watch, you fix him." Scruff sounded more upset than she'd heard in a long time. Even though he and Finnian poked at each other sometimes, he'd clearly come to trust and like him. Scruff didn't wait for her response but stalked a few feet away and started a circle. Grigeen magic was limited and mostly nature-focused. They didn't have spells so much as they *were* magic. But if he walked the path enough times, he would successfully make a shield. Not as strong as Lizeth could create, but it would mean that she could focus her energy on healing Finnian.

She nodded her thanks and returned to her assessment of Finnian. She gently brushed back his rich hair and put one hand on his forehead and one back over his heart. Under her breath she sang the song of guidance for healing. It was a simple one and was designed to lead the healer to where the injuries were, but not heal anything yet. It still took her five tries to get the spell song right and she still couldn't get the pitch exactly as it should be. Fighting not to cry wasn't helping as it made her tighten her throat. She took a deep breath, swallowed her tears, relaxed her throat, and sang it once more.

This time it worked. That was the good news; the bad news was that the song revealed extensive damage all over Finnian. He might not look bad from the outside, but inside everything was broken or bruised.

Lizeth fought her panic down and pulled in her magic. First thing was to reach him. It would be painful. Right now, being unconscious was saving him from a lot of agony, but she needed his help. Even if he wasn't a sorcerer, the best person to heal someone was themselves. His being a sorcerer increased that.

She softly called to him with a song. Luckily, it worked on the first try and she felt him stirring.

"What happened? Oh, gods, the pain. Let me die, please." His voice was inside her head.

Lizeth grabbed his arm; his hands were too damaged to touch. "No. You can't leave me." She opened her thoughts to him to let him see how she viewed him. The amount of emotion behind it startled even her. Times she'd been watching him do simple tasks that stuck with her even though she hadn't noticed what she was doing at the time.

He stopped fighting and did the same. Mind to mind was a tricky thing and could let more than was wanted out. But all she felt from Finnian was love. He'd seen her with her sisters in the gardens one afternoon over a month ago when he was crossing through Astarious to another kingdom. He then applied for the job as forester in order to see her again, knowing she would never notice him. He would die a thousand times to keep her safe.

"Too much." His voice cracked as he said it out loud.

"No, it wasn't." Lizeth sang the song of healing—which kicked in after the third time. Her throat hurt and her voice sounded to her like nails on a slate. But slowly she felt his body respond. She latched onto his feelings for her as he got to know her and his admiration grew to something more. Those feelings helped her knit his bones and stop the bleeding. She fell forward, barely catching herself before she fell on him.

"Stop now, I'll be fine." He still sounded too hurt to stand.

"No, you won't be. We're at the front. We have to run. You have to be able to run because I'm not leaving you." She could tell that, while he didn't seem ready to die at the moment, there was no way he could walk, let alone run. She forced herself to sit up and sang again.

Her voice was fading, there was nothing left. But she had to save him.

A flush of energy responded to her. Finnian's sorcery was trying to help. She worked alongside it and was about to dive in again when strong hands grabbed her own. She opened her eyes to see an awake, aware, and healed Finnian watching her as he held her hands.

"Thank you. I'm sorry that you saw what you did. I never would have—"

Lizeth cut him off with a kiss. She hadn't accepted how she felt about him before, but there was no denying what she'd felt from both of them. Logical or not, she was falling in love with him. A few more lingering kisses later and Scruff coughed.

"Not sure how that's healing him, but you both look robust and healthy. Tomas found a way down away from the front and he and the others are waiting for us at the top of the trail." He shook his head. "I told them you were still healing and they needed to stay away." He paused. "You do realize that when we get back, and we will, the oracles might not accept this as a successful Challenge. We didn't have a choice, but Finnian and I joining you ruined the clause of no assistance."

Lizeth had sort of figured that. Even if Scruff knew he was being sent along from his elders who worked closely with the oracles, Finnian couldn't have been planned for until it happened.

Finnian got to his feet; a bit stiff, but healed, and held down a hand for her. Lizeth took it with a smile. "But I doubt I would have survived here without you two. If they don't accept this Challenge, so be it." Survival and getting back home were much larger issues. She didn't let go of Finnian's hand as they followed Scruff. There could be nothing between them when they got home—so she'd enjoy what they had while they were here.

Tomas and the other two stood at the top of a trail. It was steeper than the cliffside overlooking the battle front but had the advantage of not leading down to certain death—she hoped.

As happy as she was about saving Finnian, and the feelings they both had, there was more than a healthy dose of terror floating around. She was good. One of the most powerful spell singers in centuries. Yet, she knew deep inside that she couldn't stop that sorcerer alone. Even if her voice hadn't been damaged.

"Glad to see you up and about." Tomas nodded as they approached. "I'd really love to know who you two really are, but maybe after we get out of here and find a pub. A few hundred miles from here." He shuddered as the sounds of horses charging each other and catapults flinging massive rocks echoed on this side of the mountain.

"We can't leave." Lizeth pointed back toward the fighting. "There's a good chance we won't survive, but Finnian," she smiled as she used his real name, "Scruff, and myself—I'm Lizeth by the way—have to stop that sorcerer." She couldn't tell them more, nor probably even explain it to Finnian and Scruff, but she knew that sorcerer, and what he would be able to do if left to continue, was her Challenge.

"There's no way you can beat him. I've heard of the glouthlin sorcerers, they were unstoppable." Maurial looked like she was debating picking up Lizeth and Finnian and running away from the front with them.

"Then who stopped the rest of his breed?" Finnian patted Maurial on the arm. "I grew up hearing the stories too. Something killed the rest of his kind and trapped him for hundreds of years." He squeezed Lizeth's hand. "I don't have near the power in the world of magic and sorcery that she does, but I think the two of us," he nodded to Scruff sitting on a rock, "the three of us, at least have a chance."

"We have to try." Lizeth smiled to all of them. "But you three should save yourselves. Get as far from here as you can. If we fail, things will go horrible quickly."

Surprisingly, it was Janus who shook his head first. "Sorry, we're not leaving. At least I'm not. I don't have magic beyond a few simple spells of protection that can only be used in times of great need, but as part of the Illusterati I have to help. It's what my people do. Something is wrong in the timeline. I was sent to join Tomas' gang two years ago when there were warnings of a terrible tear, something was disrupting things, but never saw what needed to be fixed until now." He held up his sword. "I'll protect the three of you with my dying breath."

Lizeth hadn't heard much about the Illusterati, but by the widening of his eyes, Finnian had.

He gave a short bow. "I'm honored to be in your presence." He shot Lizeth an odd glance, then turned back to Janus. "My parents followed the teachings of your people. They died when I was sixteen, but it made an impact in my life."

Lizeth realized that was another truth about Finnian—he wasn't from Rashia, he was Laiandran. There had been enough hints along the way, but she was focused on getting them home—and ignoring her feelings for him—so she hadn't put them together. He looked back again and she smiled and nodded.

Tomas turned to Maurial. "Are *you* actually who I think you are?" He didn't seem angry, just a bit overwhelmed.

"Aye, that I am." Maurial also gave Janus a short bow. "And I think we need to help them stop this menace. How long would we keep finding work if that glouthlin is off destroying the world? Not to mention, there's now only you and I left in this gang of yours."

"So, what's the plan?" Scruff hadn't regained his seat on Lizeth's pack but was flapping his tail violently. "Six of us, against those armies down there and some sorcerer who should have been killed eons ago?"

"We can't go against the armies—that's suicide. We have to find the sorcerer, figure out how he was trapped before, and do it again." Lizeth still had no plan, but there must be something they could do.

"Most of my order aren't heavy magic users, and I have extremely little compared to you," Janus said. "But my order helped destroy the glouthlin sorcerers. They take magic from other sources to augment their own. This one took the magic from those mages that were trying to use him as a weapon—that was what he was planning on doing to you two. The good news is that he'll burn through that stolen magic quickly. So, we need to cut whatever other source he is pulling from."

Everyone looked at him. Lizeth was waiting for the easy part that he was implying.

"We don't even know where he is, let alone what magic source he's pulling from." Lizeth shook her head. "How can we stop what we can't see?"

At those words, the mountain shook and screams echoed from the plains. Tomas led them away from the trail to an area overlooking the battlefield. "I think we found him. Or rather the Astarious army found him."

Lizeth had to keep from running down there. Her people, no matter how far in the past they were, had their line shattered. An explosion had destroyed rows of knights.

The glouthlin sorcerer stood calmly in the middle of the field.

"I have demonstrated my power. I expect both sides to surrender to me within the hour, giving me access to all magic users in your kingdoms. Your royals will present them personally." His voice carried through a spell and judging from what could be seen, everyone heard it.

Lizeth and the others knew what he was, but even with almost destroying a third of the Astarious army, it looked like the Laiandran leaders weren't impressed. A group of at least two hundred charged forward, only to be crumpled like little toys before they'd gotten halfway there.

"Tomas. Will that path you found lead us to the battle front? We have to try to destroy him." She had no idea how to stop him, but they had to try.

"When we're closer you should sense where he is getting his extra power," Janus said. As they followed Tomas back to the path. "I'm not as familiar with spell singers as some, but you might be able to defeat him if we can cut whatever power source he's pulling from."

Lizeth couldn't tell him that she had no idea how much of her singing was back, so she nodded as if she was deep in thought. Finnian watched her with a concerned frown, however.

They got down to the bottom and Tomas pulled them close. "Maurial and I will keep any non-magic users off you all. At least until we can't." He gave a grim nod and shook Finnian and Lizeth's hands. "It's been an honor. Too bad we didn't get rich together."

Maurial took their hands as well. "May the goddess protect you." Then she pulled out a sword, a dagger, and threw on a brace of throwing knives. "We die fighting well. Good journey."

The two of them crept out to watch for any stragglers at the base of the trail. Janus followed, then turned. "Use your emotions. Whoever or whatever he is pulling magic from, they will be in pain and that could tell you who they are. Cut them free once you sense them." He nodded to both and kept going.

Lizeth looked to Finnian and Scruff but they looked as confused as she was.

The glouthlin sorcerer was closer to this side of the battlefield. He still looked like a kindly old man—but Lizeth recalled the mouth and eyes from before. They were still a distance away, when a breeze lifted her hair. A feeling of loss, hopelessness, and...the oracles?

She pulled Finnian down to whisper in his ear. "He's somehow draining the oracles. That's his extra power."

Finnian's eyes went wide and so did Scruff's.

"I can't do anything to stop that. My sorcery is mostly under-trained."

Lizeth continued to watch the sorcerer as they spoke and then she saw it. A thin stream of faded color feeding into the sorcerer.

She couldn't cut anything though, not before she attacked anyway. If her voice held. "You and I have to attack him together. I'll free the oracles."

Finnian looked doubtful but he nodded and briefly kissed her.

The only spell song that Lizeth could even hope to hold up against the sorcerer was the song of distraction and destruction. It had a more formal name but that was what she had called it. It was designed to confuse your enemies and then fling a massive force against them. She needed a distraction.

A snow bear. It would be fitting if that was her final spell. Unlike the housemaid, she doubted the sorcerer would faint, but he should be confused. She quickly whispered her intentions to Finnian, Scruff, and Janus, then she sang the bear into existence.

The sorcerer started and quickly recovered but it was enough for Lizeth to join with Finnian's sorcery and send a barrage of spells. Her voice held and the spells flew true, but there was a strain in her vocal cords.

The ground shattered as the spells from Lizeth and Finnian slammed into the sorcerer and pushed his spell back onto him. The force crumpled him in on himself in a way Lizeth really hoped he couldn't come back from. The extra magical power he'd been draining from the oracles was severed as they attacked and he was pushed into the ground. Way into the ground.

Lizeth's thought had been to create something similar to what held him before, only much larger. It looked like their spell worked a little too well, as what was left of the sorcerer was soon out of sight and the hole continued to grow and a wind filled the entire area.

Lizeth, Finnian, and Scruff were across from the other three. Tomas was helping Maurial run, but she was clearly injured.

"We have to help them!" Lizeth yelled to Finnian. After what they'd been through together, she didn't want Tomas and Maurial to be hurt—they had become friends.

Janus was closer to them and he turned back. "Go! I will protect them, I promise." He sent a shield over Tomas and Maurial as they ran for the Laiandra side. "Good luck wherever you end up!" He scrambled away from them as the ground opened up further.

The spot where she and Finnian had slammed the sorcerer into was folding in on itself and taking everything nearby with it. The horses were getting out, but many of the knights were being pulled down after the sorcerer. But even if she wanted to, she couldn't stop it. That sorcerer should be dead by the force of the combined spell she and Finnian hit him with, but she didn't want to count on it. The impassible canyon in her time started with the destruction of a vile sorcerer. He screamed as he was torn apart and swallowed by the earth.

Finnian grabbed her hand and they raced to the other side. Things were collapsing too quickly and they slid down a hill as the canyon grew.

Scruff jumped off her pack and started scrambling upwards. "Come on, we can't slide down!"

Finnian and Lizeth climbed as well. A chime rang in Lizeth's head. "*Thank you. That sorcerer had broken through to our temple and was draining our life forces. You have freed the oracles. Be safe."* Another chime and the world froze.

The world around them snapped back, changing right in front of them at an increasingly rapid pace. The plants in the widening canyon grew huge and died and more plants sprouted and the cycle continued over and over. Lizeth, Finnian, and Scruff stayed where they were and watched as the world sped around them. Then it stopped moving. The canyon looked right but Lizeth had never seen it from this angle before. They were a good thirty feet below the edge.

"I can climb up and get help." Finnian looked paler than before. He hadn't had enough time to recover from almost dying and having to fight again.

"We can all climb up together." She slipped a bit.

"You two climb together, I can take care of myself. Might need to leave your packs—you both look weaker than a pair of kittens." Scruff started up the steep incline.

Finnian took a few things out of his pack, stuffing them in his pockets then left it. Lizeth took hers off and left it. She had her weapons on her and there wasn't much else in it that she needed.

Lizeth tried humming and felt herself feel lighter. "Can you carry me on your back? I think I can lighten us, but we need to be together."

He nodded and they made their way up.

Lizeth clung to Finnian as they reached the top of the canyon. Her hummed spell continued to help make both of them lighter, but she couldn't do more than that right now. Her energy was gone, her throat felt shredded, and right now falling back into the abyss at the bottom of the canyon she'd created didn't seem so bad. At least her entire body wouldn't ache. The way to the top of this cliff seemed far longer than it had appeared and she was feeling how much that last fight had taken out of her. It might have only been minutes in length—but she felt like she'd been doing hard labor for a month.

The edge of the not-so-mysterious-anymore canyon crumbled as they worked their way up, but they eventually got to solid ground. They climbed even further to be sure and both stayed on the ground for a bit.

Lizeth tamped down the brief terror that ran through her if things had changed here. There were no monsters roaming, no massive fire ripping through the palace and forest that she could see. But she had no idea how they would fix things if they had changed the future. If they'd changed things for the worse—there was no way to go back and fix them. For good or bad, this was their reality now.

"We can't tell anyone about this." She couldn't look at what she'd made. She hated to have done it, but the suffering that had been all around her was unbearable. The canyon wasn't a great option, but it was better than the alternative. And it had destroyed that glouthlin sorcerer. And freed the oracles. She still wasn't sure what the connection to him in the past and the oracles in the present had been, and she wasn't going to try to guess. She'd do it again in an instant given the same circumstances. Even knowing what it had cost. Her voice had held for that final fight, but she didn't know what permanent damage she'd done to it.

Scruff had been a few feet behind them but he flopped next to her once he got to the top. "Agreed, none of us can say anything. Time is unstable. At least here and now. There are pockets..." He waved his paws. "Never mind. You did what was needed." He sniffed the air. "I think our timeline is as it was. No changes remain."

Lizeth wanted to ask him how he knew—but wasn't sure she wanted the answer. "Did you know that this was what would happen? What my Challenge was?" She watched Scruff carefully, but his furry face didn't give away anything.

"The high counsel of my people only knew something needed to happen and I had to be with you as you started your Challenge—he didn't tell me I would be included in it. That was why I came into the palace. If he knew more, he didn't tell. He certainly didn't let me know you would be an early starter. There hasn't been one of those in a thousand years." He shrugged and groomed the fur on the top of his head. If he knew more, he wasn't going to tell either.

Lizeth couldn't even raise her head. She was exhausted and heartbroken. What she'd had to do was horrible, and she hoped that Tomas, Maurial, and Janus survived. But there was no way her Challenge would be accepted with Finnian and Scruff along for the trip.

And she was pretty certain she'd fallen in love with Finnian and he with her. The sorcery was a bit of a shock, she admitted, and aside from Gliandra in the woods, there were no sorcerers in Astarious, but it was something she could live with. But he had no royal blood and was actually one of their enemies—technically, even though he'd left Laiandra long ago—it would still be hard to deal with. Therefore, whatever was between them could never be.

A new thought struck her as she finally sat up. That actually wouldn't be a problem since she'd broken her Challenge and therefore would no longer be in line for the throne. The law stipulated that the Challenge must be started before the heir-potential's twenty-first birthday. She had to be past that since they'd been gone a few days and her birthday was two days after she was taken, so she couldn't start another Challenge now. She laughed softly.

"We can barely move, and you're laughing?" Finnian was able to sit up now as well but he still looked pale. His wounds might have been healed but he hadn't fully recovered.

"I made an interesting connection. You two coming with me saved my life. And by doing so, saved the kingdom, since I could do what had to be done. But you also cost me my place in line for the crown. I'm twenty-one now, and don't have a successful Challenge behind me." As she said the words, she found she didn't mind at all, which was interesting since before the Challenge, being High Queen was first and foremost on her mind.

Finnian's face fell and he reached for her hand. "I am so sorry. I never—"

Scruff hit him in the shoulder and gave a shake of his head. "You *know* what that means? Sorry that I didn't make the connection sooner. It's been a rough few days."

"That we cost her the crown? That's an issue, Scruff." Finnian frowned.

"It means that thanks to both of you being dragged along, I am alive. The entire land is safe and protected...and I don't have to follow royal rules anymore." Lizeth waited for a stab of pain or loss, but there wasn't one.

She waited for Finnian to come to the same conclusion she had. Granted he hadn't said out loud what his feelings for her had been, but the feelings when she was healing him and the kisses they'd shared afterward had done so. Looking at him, she realized she could happily spend her life by his side. She might need to give him a few days to adjust to the idea. But if he didn't propose by then, she would have to do so. She got to her feet and dusted off her clothing as best she could. There wasn't much that wasn't dusty at this point.

"She doesn't have to marry a royal now, you slow thinking fox-monkey." Scruff also got to his feet and shook the dust off his fur. "Not that anyone needs to go running off getting married—you're both young. But I believe that's what she is alluding to." He gave her a wink over Finnian's shoulder.

"I...you mean—" Finnian was turning a lovely rose color when his words were cut off by shouts.

"Your highness!" A pair of guards came running through the trees. "Thank goodness we found you."

Nevaine and Piallen were right behind them and both ran past the guards and hit Lizeth with enough force that they almost all tumbled back into the canyon.

She held them both tightly. "How long have we been gone?" She wasn't sure that time wasn't different in the past, but she also wasn't sure what she could talk about to anyone. Scruff made it sound like information had to be limited or it could undo everything they'd just almost died fixing.

Nevaine gave her an odd look. "Four weeks. Your Challenge was only to be a week. Why are they here? Did they find you first?" She gave Finnian a scowl as he slowly got to his feet.

The minister of guidance made his way forward. "They must have. It is forbidden for any to accompany the Challenger on their voyage. No matter how extended the Challenge is."

Four weeks? It had been less than a week on their end. But being a few hundred years in the past probably did mess up time.

The minister was such a sanctimonious little man that Lizeth couldn't help but proudly step forward and stop a foot away from him. "Actually, minister, they came with me on my Challenge. Both of them. They risked their lives to save myself and this kingdom. Do what you will, I don't care. We did the right thing."

The minister turned red, then purple, then an unbecoming shade of rust. "Your parents will be told!" He spun, almost tripping over his long robes, and stomped off.

Four guards went with him, the other ten stayed with her. "Until the time as we are advised otherwise, we will continue to escort and protect *all* of the royal family." The captain gave her a small smile. He clearly wasn't fond of the minister either.

"Are you serious?" Piallen's rich blue eyes were wide as Lizeth's words hit her. "Then you can't be..."

"An heir to the throne." Lizeth hugged her sister and looped in Nevaine as well. "I'm okay with it. Oddly, extremely okay. The kingdom can be easily covered by two queens when the time comes. You don't need a third."

Nevaine was silent, but continued to scowl at Finnian. "Isn't he the woodsman you hung in the air?"

Finnian laughed. "I am. And I am honored to meet you, Princess Nevaine. Your sister has told me so much about you." He smiled and gave a nod to Piallen. "Good to see you as well, Princess Piallen."

"You can drop the princess part, with me at least, when we're out here." Piallen stepped forward and shook his hand. "Thank you for saving Lizeth."

Nevaine nodded at the introduction but continued to watch everyone closely. At least Piallen took Lizeth at her word—Nevaine was suspicious of everything.

"Our parents made it home, I gather? I apparently had no choice on when my Challenge started—or how long I was gone." Lizeth tried to keep her voice light. She had Scruff's word for it that this timeline had remained as it was—but she found herself holding her breath for their answers.

She also wanted to take Finnian's hand but wasn't sure how he'd feel. He looked like he wasn't sure either. Clearly, his being born in Laiandra would never be spoken of—at least not publicly and, even then, not until after they were married. He'd run away from them and that life. It had no bearing on who he was. The sorcerer bit would wait as well. Maybe he could compare notes with Gliandra in the woods.

"They arrived two days after you vanished. The seers explained that the oracles determined you were needed for your Challenge earlier than expected. The bodies we found were determined to be Laiandran spies who had been working with the Stiklin. The Laiandran empire responded to our inquires with a statement that they didn't send them. Still no idea who killed them though." Nevaine watched Finnian carefully as she spoke.

Lizeth would like to do so as well. Did he kill those spies? There had been magic attached to them, but sorcery and magic spells were awfully similar. Another point for a later discussion.

Piallen continued. "The sight mages saw your return so once we get back to the palace, they should be ready. We took care of the chancellor by the way. Or he did. When our parents came back, he suddenly confessed trying to take over the kingdom and then dove off the highest tower. Didn't land well. The Stiklin menace vanished when you went on your Challenge."

Nevaine narrowed her eyes. "I think there will be much to talk about after you are presented to our parents."

"There will be much to discuss, of that I am certain." Lizeth took Finnian's hand and held it when he lightly tried to pull away. "No. We face them together."

Scruff walked a bit ahead of them. "Might as well, lad. I don't want to see her mooning and sighing. Went through that when she was younger." He lashed his tail and jogged off ahead of them.

Nevaine and Piallen walked on her other side.

They approached the palace and trumpets heralded their arrival.

Lizeth looked down at her bedraggled borrowed clothing. "Can't I at least get clean and change?"

Piallen smiled. "Nope. You have to go in as you came back from the Challenge. They told us some of the rules while we were waiting. Apparently, our great-great-great-grand-da came back completely covered in mud. Had to stand there dripping while the queen paid him praise."

"That's wonderful." She glanced down to see Scruff had gotten his fur clean as they walked. "That's not fair though. You're going to make us two look bad."

He waved his tail. "I make everyone look bad."

The seers had obviously prepared everyone else for their arrival. Guards lined the path as they got closer and all of them kept at full attention with their eyes forward. Lizeth knew she was probably a sight to see but appreciated that no one tried to stare.

The throne room wasn't completely decked out. That, hopefully, would be much later, after she got to clean up and change.

"Scruff, don't let him leave." Lizeth kept her eyes on her parents sitting at the far end as she released Finnian's hand.

"Princess Lizeth Ariane Gosslia, approach the throne." The crier's voice was loud and devoid of emotion. That was fine, Lizeth found she had enough rampaging emotions for a few people.

She refrained from patting down her dusty clothes or messy hair one more time and strode forward. It was good to see that her parents were all right.

"Daughter, we see you survived your Challenge, even though it was far longer than expected." Her father had his official voice going but the tiny smile and wink said far more.

"And that you unfortunately began earlier than expected. We do ask forgiveness that we were not here and no official Challenge event was done." Her mother gave her a larger smile. "We were delayed." Those words were heavier than they should be, and even though her mother was smiling, Lizeth guessed things had not gone smoothly on their trip to Northalia.

Lizeth curtsied, then rose. This was it. She knew her parents would still love her and she'd always be their daughter. She simply wouldn't be a royal princess any more. The lump in her throat was larger than expected and required a few swallows before she could speak.

"Thank you, Father and Mother." She stood tall. "It was success-ful; however, it would not have been if two champions had not ventured forth with me when I was taken in. Finnian the woodsman and Scruff of the grigeens joined me, at great risk to their own lives, and saved myself and this land. I have broken the solitary Challenge agreement, but given the results, I would do so again without pause."

There. It was done, and she felt stronger now. She'd played at what it would be like being a queen in her youth. This was the closest she felt to what it really demanded. The irony would have made Scruff laugh.

A not-so-subtle gasp echoed through the throne room. While not decked out for pomp, most all of the local nobility, and visiting ones, were there in attendance as witnesses of her return. Clearly, that wasn't what they'd expected.

"Thank you for telling us. Would the companions step forward?" Her father didn't look shocked, but his face was locked into stoic mode so it was hard to tell. Her mother looked like she wanted to cry; her blue eyes were brighter than normal but she held her hand up near her face.

Finnian and Scruff came to either side of Lizeth.

"We know Scruff. Would you please introduce us to your other companion?"

Lizeth wanted to take Finnian's hand but he looked ready to run, so she just presented him. "King Keven and Queen Chila, may I present Finnian, woodsman of our kingdom and rescuer of wayward princesses?" She smiled and glanced at their clothing. Since they both looked like they'd been run through a mud pit a few times and left to dry, it was impossible to take this situation seriously. Her sisters were off to the left of the dais. Piallen smiled as Finnian was introduced.

Finnian's elaborate bow was courtier-worthy and Lizeth wondered if there were a few things he hadn't told her about his time in his original homeland. Or if it was something he picked up during his travels. Not that it mattered now.

"We are most pleased to meet the man who has rescued our beloved eldest daughter. Thank you, Finnian. And good job, Scruff." The king then broke into a full smile. "However, these companions didn't remove you from claiming the throne as an heir. The dictates say you cannot *ask* for help. Did you ask for assistance?"

Lizeth was confused. Even Scruff figured she was out of the royal running. "No. In fact I told them they needed to go back. Repeatedly. They sort of were busy saving me and refused to try. I'm not sure they could have anyway, but they wouldn't leave me. Finnian was even injured. A few times." She glanced over to him but he was doing a nice impersonation of a statue.

"They risked their lives, risking never coming back, to save you. That is not a violation of the dictates." The king nodded.

The queen looked at her two sisters. "However, neither of you should try it on your time of Challenge. The oracles can feel the intentions of anyone who went with the Challenger. We were already aware of these additions." She nodded to Lizeth. "Please step forward, Challenger."

Lizeth took a breath and stepped forward.

"Princess Lizeth Ariane Gosslia, we officially recognize you as having successfully completed the Challenge. You will be named first heir at the ball tonight."

Lizeth had gotten used to the idea she wouldn't be an heir. This struck her like one of Scruff's body hits. She was going to be a queen. Which meant...she turned to Finnian, but from the sorrow in his deep brown eyes he'd figured it out faster than her.

"You are all dismissed until this evening." The queen smiled and she and the king left the dais.

Lizeth walked back with Scruff and Finnian. "I really thought they wouldn't let me continue my status as heir. I can talk to them..."

Finnian turned to her with a sad smile. "No. I knew when I first signed up to be a woodsman here—you could never be mine. I also knew the risk when I fell in love with you. You will make an amazing queen." He gave the elaborate bow again and kissed her hand. Then strode off before she could respond.

"Scruff, catch him." She couldn't move. He'd said he fell in love with her. She felt the same but hadn't said it. The words stuck in her throat and tears filled her eyes.

The look of deep sadness in Scruff's eyes was almost as painful as Finnian's had been. "Lizeth, his heart is breaking just as yours is. Don't make things worse. It's the law. But I will go follow him." His tail lashed and his shoulders slumped as he left.

Lizeth watched until Finnian was out of sight. He'd kept a strong pace but it looked to her that his shoulders dropped the further he got into the gardens.

Nevaine and Piallen came up to her and each took an arm.

"Let's get you cleaned up for the ball." Nevaine's smile was the broadest Lizeth had ever seen, but there were tears in her eyes.

Piallen looked stunned. "But, he and you...there has to be a way."

"We can discuss it once we've gotten her to her room," Nevaine hissed as she flashed a fake smile at a noble who was a bit too close to them.

Lizeth let them lead her. She'd known it couldn't happen. But in the half hour to get to the palace a feeling of such happiness had over-whelmed her. To lose it now was horrific.

And he said he'd fallen in love with her.

"And no crying until we are in the room and the door is shut." Nevaine sped them up before Lizeth realized she was crying.

The door shut behind her, Lizeth let them lead her to a couch. "I...I should get clean first." She pulled at her filthy clothes. "This will make a mess."

Nevaine grabbed her in a fierce hug and both of them started crying. Piallen came to her other side and enveloped them both.

"He...he said he loved me." Lizeth got out between sobs. "I knew we couldn't then we could...now we can't. It's not fair!"

Nevaine pulled back and brushed away Lizeth's tears. "No, it's not. And I'll admit that an hour ago I would have said it was for the better. But you two really had it, I could see it in your faces. Whatever happened on your Challenge, you fell in love too. I am so sorry."

That kind of honesty and sincerity coming from Nevaine was painful and beautiful.

A soft rapping at the door broke into their talk.

Piallen got up first. "I got it. Whoever they are they can bugger off." Her hand was on a short dagger at her waist.

Lizeth gave a small smile at her youngest sister. There was nothing to fight in this situation, but she'd take it out on whoever dared to come to the door. Probably not with the dagger, but it really depended who was there and what they wanted.

"What do you—oh." She looked down as Scruff stomped in.

"He's leaving. I caught up to him outside the gardens. I'd find a better time or way to say it, but there is none. He truly loves you and staying in the kingdom would be too painful. Both for him and you." He tilted his head. "He will never forget you."

Lizeth choked on a sob and collapsed on the couch. "But it's not fair. We saved..." She let those words drop. She couldn't even tell her sisters what she'd gone through. What she and Finnian had gone through. At least not until they had completed their own Challenges. "I need to bathe." She numbly got to her feet.

"I think you can wait. The ceremony won't start for a few hours. You need to rest," Piallen said.

Nevaine shook her head. "Bath first, then rest. Things will seem better after that."

Lizeth numbly went to her room, with her sisters and Scruff trailing close behind. "Thank you, but I will be fine. Maybe order some food? It's been a long time since I've had real food." She forced a smile before she the shut the door. Then she sobbed. She'd been crying before, but these were great gulping sobs. The Challenge had changed her; she still wasn't sure if her song magic was gone or not, and there was no way to try while she was sobbing. Not that she wanted to. If it was gone as well as Finnian, she wouldn't be able to bear it.

She mindlessly dropped her clothes—they should probably be destroyed but they had served her well—and climbed into a hot bath. It took a moment of sheer bliss of being covered in hot water before her mind kicked in that someone had already set this up for her. She'd thank whoever it was later, right now she needed that warmth to settle into her bones.

She'd almost dozed off when a knocking came from the bedroom door.

"I wouldn't spend too long in there. Pruning skin isn't a good look for the heir apparent." It was Nevaine but most likely Piallen and Scruff were still with her.

"I'm fine." Lizeth rose out of the bath. She felt creaky and old but at least clean. "I'm going to take a nap if that's okay with you three?" She dried off and put on her nightgown and robe. It seemed like far more than a few weeks that she'd been gone.

"We had Margie bring up food. Eat, then nap." Yup, Piallen was still there.

Lizeth went through the bedroom and opened her door. "Fine." A cup of steaming tea was held out to her.

"Don't worry, it's just an herbal. We'll give you something stronger after your nap." Piallen grimaced. "It's probably going to be a long, boring ceremony." Piallen hated pomp even more than the other two and neither were fond of it. Lizeth briefly wondered what would happen when it was Piallen's turn for her Challenge. The ceremony surrounding the leave taking—the one Lizeth missed—was usually quite elaborate from what she'd heard.

Lizeth took the tea and ate the food—it was all wonderful, yet tasteless at the same time. Finally, she excused herself and stood. "I need a nap. Will one of you make sure to come back and wake me in an hour?" The subtle push toward them leaving didn't appear to be working.

Scruff curled up on a chair and flicked his tail. "Me too. I'm exhausted."

Nevaine and Piallen shared a look—they had planned on staying in the front room.

"We *will* be back to help you dress." Nevaine raised her hand. "It's a sister-and-younger-royal privilege. One hour." She and Piallen hugged Lizeth once more then left.

Lizeth stumbled into her room and collapsed into her bed.

The dreams that followed weren't pleasant. Images of what that sorcerer had intended—what she'd seen inside his mind as she and Finnian destroyed him—were going to haunt her for a long time. They were coming to life in her nightmares now. She finally fought her way to being awake, expecting to find herself with Finnian, Maurial, Tomas, and even Janus.

Waking in her own massive and soft bed—alone—was almost a shock. She took some deep breaths and focused on calming down.

And thinking.

In a short time, she would be officially presented in front of the court as the heir apparent to the throne of Astarious. She'd looked forward to it her entire life, but now a feeling of dread was replacing that optimism. There must be a way around this.

Maybe she could demonstrate that she'd lost her spell singing? Augmented magic was important to the royals. She sighed. But not essential. And even if she had lost her ability to spell sing, she would still pass the gift of it to any children she had. With some vague, unnamed royal she didn't know. Trion didn't even seem remotely appealing at this point.

Once she was officially presented, she would have to give a small speech of acceptance. And then claim her wish. The first heir was always granted a special accommodation. It had to be something within the realm of the king and queen's ability to grant.

Why couldn't she ask them to abolish a law?

Chapter Twenty-Nine

She flew out of bed and dug into her closet. The light, ethereal gown that she'd had made a year ago for her confirmation was shoved aside for her white leathers. They were still elegant, and much more suitable to who she was now. And she did feel like she was running into battle.

Yes, the king and queen had the power to change a law. But it took years of consideration, debate, etc. She needed it changed now. Finnian might already be on the road out of town.

Dressed, she ran into the front room and opened the door as Nevaine raised her hand to knock.

"I'm ready." Lizeth looked back to see Scruff stretching. "Let's go? There's a ceremony awaiting?"

He jogged over and tilted his head but didn't say anything. He smiled and went out ahead of the sisters.

The main hall was decorated to the extreme. At least from what Lizeth could see. She, her sisters, and Scruff all skirted around the main section through service corridors. But peeking through the partially opened doors gave her stomach a flip.

Her sisters gave her quick hugs, then went inside where their seating would be.

"Good luck." Scruff gave another smile as he darted in as well.

Lizeth joined her parents on the main dais a few feet above the floor. Her mother gave her white leathers a look; she'd helped Lizeth design the shimmering gown now in her closet. But then she smiled and nodded as the event was announced.

Lizeth listened to the accolades and comments that took place before her confirmation with a smile and appropriate nods. But she wasn't focused on the mass of people filling the throne room, not even the larger masses that clustered around the palace and that she'd be smiling and waving to soon.

The Challenge had changed her. She would take her place as queen when the time came, but she wasn't the same woman she'd been when she left. And there would be a huge hole in her heart that would never heal. Unless her wild plan worked.

Her father called the assembly to order. "We gather to confirm that Princess Lizeth Ariane Gosslia has met the requirements to be officially recognized as the heir to our throne." He paused while polite cheers filled the hall, then held up his hand for silence. "One gift is bestowed to the heir upon their success in the Challenge. Princess Lizeth, now heir to the throne of Astarious, name what you want and it is yours."

She looked around the room. She could ask for anything. The early days of hearing of this as a child, her mind had swirled with options. Her own private chateau on the lake, a retreat in the mountains on the western border, there were many afternoons spent daydreaming about it.

Now there was only one and it was related to the one person she knew wasn't in the crowd before her, nor even outside.

Her sisters were right in front. Piallen looking supportive and Nevaine with a small grin. One that grew as their eyes met—as if Nevaine knew what Lizeth was planning. Nevaine would never let anything stand in her way of what she really wanted. Nothing.

Lizeth tugged on the bottom of her white leather jacket and took a deep breath. This was a massive demand, and would change one of the first laws of the kingdom. But they said anything, and it couldn't hurt to try. If she was denied, she'd work on tearing through law books to find another way around. "My wish is that no royal heir be required to marry one of royal blood. Henceforth, all royal heirs, regardless of gender, can marry whoever they so fall in love with." The muttered comments, looks, and gasps were not surprising. The look of support from both her parents was. She figured her father would put up a fuss just on his love of the law if nothing else.

The king and the queen bowed their heads together for a few tense moments, then the king rose. "The Challenger's wish has been granted and will be entered into law. Henceforth, no one of royal blood of the kingdom is required to marry a fellow royal. They may marry who they wish."

It took a moment for Lizeth to find her voice. And pick her jaw up off the floor. "Thank you." She curtsied and then turned back to the crowd. "And someone please stop woodsman Finnian from leaving town!"

The rest of the ceremony was a blur, Lizeth was made official heir to the throne with all the rights and obligations that came with it. Including a new crown that, while gorgeous, didn't affect her the way she expected. Scruff came up on the dais and officially recognized her as heir and also newly named a guardian of the grigeens—a position that had not been held for over three hundred years. That was surprising and he hadn't mentioned a word of it.

Then came the standing outside on the balcony and all of the greetings, waving, smiling, and speeches. And all she could think of was Finnian. Had she made a horrible mistake? What if he professed his love for her only because he knew she couldn't marry him? That would serve her right. Changing a major royal law, then not getting to marry the man she loved anyway.

Her sisters vanished after the first few minutes outside—so much for sisterly support. The speeches continued by assorted dukes, duchesses, and various others. Lizeth faced forward and kept her smile plastered on.

"You're wilting." Nevaine came up on her left after about twenty minutes. A step behind, but close enough to whisper. "You might need to gracefully excuse yourself and go to your waiting room."

"Yes. I believe you are correct. Definitely wilting, not a good look for the confirmed heir." Piallen had taken the same position as Nevaine, but to Lizeth's right side. "It would be bad form if you were to collapse in front of the entire kingdom." She didn't smile but it was in her voice.

Lizeth reached back both hands to grab those of her sisters. "Thank you."

Nevaine called over the new chancellor. "My sister has had a long day and is still recovering from the Challenge. We will be escorting her to her rooms now."

The chancellor blanched, but Nevaine stared him down. "Is there a problem?" The tone was sweetness, but the look was I-do-carry-knives-you-know.

"I shall inform their majesties." He bowed and quickly walked to their parents. Lizeth got a quick glance at both of their surprised faces before her sisters spun her around and neatly away from the crowd. Nevaine looked down the hall twice before she was satisfied it was empty, then grabbed Lizeth's arm and led the way.

"I'm not sure what you two are up to, but concern for my fatigue is not it. If we go any faster, I will be running." Lizeth's legs were longer than Nevaine's but that didn't slow her down at all.

"You might be the heir to the kingdom, officially and all, but that doesn't mean you have to know everything." Piallen laughed.

They stopped in front of Lizeth's chambers. She was almost disappointed. Part of her had hoped maybe they were stealing off for a fun adventure with only the three of them like they'd done when they were kids. The two doors to her chambers were wide and ostentatious, and each sister took one door to open with a bow.

Scowling at their antics, she was still looking at them when she stepped inside. The room was filled with flowers; not surprising, since she'd seen most of them coming in before the ceremony. The one slightly bedraggled bouquet in the center of the room, ending in a pair of legs, was new.

She took a step forward as the flowers lowered. "I'm sorry I didn't have time to change into anything befitting your new station.

Your sisters are extremely insistent, and both are heavily armed." Finnian stood there. He was wearing fresh leathers, basic but solid. But his smile was gorgeous.

She heard the doors shut behind her, but the doors didn't block the cheers from her two sisters in the hall.

"Lizeth, I love you with all my heart." Finnian set aside his flowers and held out a ring. "I bought this in town. I can get something fancier later, but I wanted to propose today." The ring was a simple band with a small stone in the middle. "Lizeth, will you marry me?"

Lizeth held back for a moment, then threw herself at him, and he caught her and held her tight. "Yes! A thousand, million times, yes!"

Epilogue—Eight months later

Lizeth's parents, and most of the court, had wanted at least a year-long engagement to give it the proper planning—preferably several. Lizeth fought with them regularly about it, but didn't want them to have negative feelings about their future son-in-law, so she compromised at eight months.

Finnian had adapted extremely well to living in the palace and had picked up a position as a swords master and was training young nobles to fight. His chambers were at the other end of the palace and he'd been holed up there with his friends from the guard and the master forester as his wedding party since yesterday morning.

Lizeth and her sisters had been together since the night before that and as much as she loved her sisters, she was ready to get this over with.

"I can't pin this on if you don't hold still." Nevaine was getting testy as she worked on getting Lizeth's hair, veil, and flowers just perfect. The veil wasn't hard, it was the intricate flowers that were to be woven between the hair and the veil that was tricky. "I will stab you. Unintentionally of course." The flowers were all secured to the hair with tiny pins.

"How many do I need? I think I'm going to fall over because my head is too heavy."

"Then your groom can carry you through the rest of the ceremony." Piallen finished her makeup and stood back to admire her work.

The gown was amazing. Long-waisted it was mostly white but light-colored gems winked all along the skirt. The bodice was fitted with long gossamer sleeves that went well past her fingers. Finnian's engagement ring shimmered through the fabric. They'd picked matching wedding bands and he'd tried to get her a nicer ring. She refused.

Piallen and Nevaine stepped back, then both ran forward and hugged as best they could.

The clock struck noon then, the wedding would be at half after the hour, but it would take almost that long to get Lizeth, and, more importantly, her long train down to the waiting area and in place. Most royal or noble brides dressed downstairs for that reason, but she wanted to be in her rooms.

"Wait a moment." Piallen patted her pockets and came out with a light brown envelope. "This was delivered for you. She said blessings on your marriage, but she didn't like being around a lot of people." She handed it to Lizeth.

Taking it, she realized it probably didn't start brown, but was old. Her name was written in flowing black ink that looked ancient as well. "Who gave this to you?"

"The old lady in the forest, Gliandra. Snuck up on me in the hall. You can probably wait and open it later."

Nevaine looked in agreement with that as she bent to pick up the train.

"No, this traveled to get to us. I can feel it." There was an odd tingle, a sense of familiarity. but Lizeth wasn't sure where it was from. Before either could stop her, she gently opened the envelope. The script on the letter inside was the same as on the front.

She read the words silently. *Lizeth, I hope this letter finds you, as I have given it to one of the remaining members of our order. I know you and your companions were from a different time and if you are reading this, then you made it home. I wanted to let you know what happened to Maurial and Tomas after you left.*

Lizeth stopped reading and started to fold the letter. She didn't need sadness on this day. Scruff had climbed onto a statue behind her to read over her shoulder.

"Keep reading."

She finished. *They survived, and in the mayhem of that giant hole you created, we all escaped to the far south. They wed, bought a farm, and when I last heard had ten children and were already up to twelve grandchildren. They fondly told tales of their adventures with their mysterious friends.*

I have lived a long and full life and thanks to you was able to get most of my order out of Laiandra. They have now scattered, including Gliandra, the woman who gave you this. She has the gift of long life, so hopefully it will get to your time. Thank you for saving us. And there is a rumor that the ghosts of the lost city have vanished—thank you for that as well.

Janus

P.S. If you were time travelers, you probably want to destroy this letter once you've both read it.

Lizeth swallowed and wiped away her tears and tucked the letter away. She would show it to Finnian, then they could burn it. She'd set a spell to release the ghosts a few days after they came back, but she never knew if it worked. Her spell singing wasn't as strong as it had been. Boan was certain it would come back at some point—which could mean years.

"What are we waiting for? Finnian's already tried to run once." Lizeth hadn't realized how much not knowing what happened to her friends meant, but the lightness that filled her now pointed that out. She started toward the door with Nevaine and Piallen scrambling to catch up with her train.

Flowers filled the corridors as they made their way to the ballroom. They got there as the last stragglers were being seated.

Piallen and Nevaine spread the train out behind her and then Nevaine came and pulled her veil down, but not before giving her a quick kiss on the cheek. "I am so happy for you both."

Then Lizeth waited for the bridal march to begin and two guards held open the doors.

The ballroom was magnificently decorated and filled with courtiers, nobles, foresters, and more, all dressed in their best. Her parents were off to the side on their thrones, and both were beaming.

The thing that stopped her, just for a moment, was Finnian standing at the end of the path. He was dressed in a magnificent tunic of grays and blues that accented the small stones in Lizeth's dress. He was tall, poised, and stunningly handsome. A far cry from the filthy woodsman she'd first come across. And he was hers.

A soft cough at her feet from Scruff, who'd taken his position as escort, reminded her to move again.

Finnian's smile grew larger as she came closer and it was all she could do to not run into his arms.

She finally stopped, equal with her parents' thrones.

Both stood up and turned. "The queen and I welcome Finnian into our family, by right of holding our daughter's hand."

Lizeth let out a breath and took the final steps.

The words shared by the priest were brief, and honestly not important. While working on their vows, she and Finnian had shared them to each other in a secret spot in the garden. Hearing them again was only for show.

Finnian held out a delicately carved band. And formally asked if she would be his wife.

"I will."

She was surprised that her hand shook as she held out his ring and asked if he would be her husband. His smile almost pushed her over as he said, "I will."

"By the power invested in me, by my order and the King and Queen of Astarious, I pronounce you husband and wife. You may kiss."

His last words were lost as Lizeth and Finnian were already kissing, and the quiet crowd became much louder.

And they lived happily ever after.

Dear Reader,

Thank you for joining me on a new adventure! I hope that you enjoyed this trip with Lizeth and will also enjoy Nevaine and Pi-allen's Challenges! As always, I appreciate you for coming along on the newest escapade.

If you want to keep up on the further adventures of any of my characters, make sure to visit my website and sign up for my mailing list. http://marieandreas.com/index.html

You can also sign up on Amazon to follow me and they will keep you updated. Marie Andreas Amazon[1]

If you enjoyed this book, please spread the word! Positive reviews are like emotional gold to any writer. And mean more than you know.

Thank you again—and keep reading!

Marie

---

1.   https://www.amazon.com/Marie-Andreas/e/B00SX81KIM/

About the Author

Marie is a multi-award-winning fantasy and science fiction author with a serious reading addiction. If she wasn't writing about all the people in her head, she'd be lurking about coffee shops annoying total strangers with her stories. So really, writing is a way of saving the masses. She lives in Southern California and is owned by two very faery-minded cats. She is also a member of SFWA (Science Fiction and Fantasy Writers of America).

When not saving the masses from coffee shop shenanigans, Marie likes to visit the UK and keeps hoping someone will give her a nice summer home in the Forest of Dean or Conwy, Wales.